Duality Protocol

Christopher B Lane

If you like my debut novel I'd love to hear from you

matlocklane70@gmail.com

Christopher B Lane

"Lane did a fantastic job of crafting the plot. The rapid reveals at the end were breathtaking. The themes were steadily sustained and developed."

    - Alice in Scotland, OnlineBookClub.org

"Not the usual Sci-Fi story, had me gripped from the beginning."

    - K J Pickett, Amazon reviewer

Copyright © 2021 Christopher B Lane

All rights reserved.

ISBN:

Cover design by Scott Gaunt

For my wife Bharti, who gave me the time to play, and for my friend Portia, who showed me how.

I felt a cleaving in my mind
    As if my brain had split;
I tried to match it, seam by seam,
    But could not make them fit.

— **Emily Dickinson**

Thou canst not touch the freedom of my mind

— **John Milton**

How do you decide who to allow to live?

You probably have your own views on this, but I made my choices, and now there are 2,165,335 fewer shits left to screw things up for the rest of us.

Time was running out, so this was the best I could do. Please don't judge me too harshly if it proves in the end not to have been enough.

- Millie

PROLOGUE
Millie's Citizenship

'HOW ARE YOU this morning, Mrs Adams, and how is little Millie?' asked the nurse. Despite being a redundant question, she still liked to maintain the civility of asking after a person's health; it was plain good manners and cost nothing. The readout of Mrs Adams' bio-stats showed she was in fine condition following her recent pregnancy, possibly not getting enough sleep, but that was only to be expected with a new child. The intermittent spikes in her beta wave patterns revealed an underlying level of anxiety that she knew was common for parents on their child's citizenship.

'Please call me Julie. We're both fine, thank you, but I do wish the rain would let up for a day or two. Derek has been slaving over his vegetable patch all year, but we've not got much to show for it.'

'Yes, I know my own little crop has suffered as well, but the forecast is looking better next week. Hopefully, we'll finally get some of that Mediterranean sunshine they've been threatening us with.' Julie's fingers tapped and swiped at the console as she spoke. 'Now, let me see, Millie is twelve weeks old, you and your husband Derek are full citizens, so everything is in order. I see, though, that you have not booked in for sterilisation yet. You know you both should really consider it. The government is quite right to remind parents that while it's still everyone's choice, we need to consider the future and don't forget all three of you will get priority at the clinics if you stick to having the one.'

'It's such a big decision. We're both from big families. I've got four sisters and Derek has four brothers. It doesn't seem fair on Millie not to have a brother or sister.' Noticing the frown appear on Nurse Forester's face, Julie quickly added, 'We're still thinking about it though, and Millie is so perfect maybe the government is right.'

Nurse Forester began setting up the couch. 'Anything you want to ask before I proceed with the affirmation?' she asked in a tone that Julie felt was distinctly less warm than a few moments ago.

'I hear it can cause problems later with teething, is that right? We're not getting much sleep right now, so would hate for anything to make the situation worse.'

'I can assure you, Julie, that's just some nonsense someone put out when their child got a minor ear infection following the procedure. I don't know how these rumours get past the net-filters, but you have my word there's no truth in it at all. Besides, it's so much easier at this age than when we had ours fitted. The skull has not hardened yet.'

'I thought as much, but I just wanted to check.'

'If that's all, Julie, could I get you to place your hand here, look at the red dot on the wall and read out the affirmation?'

Somewhat overwhelmed by the occasion, Julie wished her husband could have been there. Still, they had agreed he now needed to keep his job more than ever. And so she stood, placed her right hand on the gently pulsating pad, and spoke as clearly as her nerves would allow.

'I, Julie Adams, consent to my daughter Millie Adams taking up full citizenship of the United Kingdom with all the benefits and responsibilities that doing so entails. As her parent and guardian, I will endeavour to ensure Millie grows to be a model citizen, deserving of the privileges she now gains.'

'Wonderful, Julie, well done!'

Millie was sleeping peacefully in her carrier, her little

hands holding a brightly coloured comforter. Nurse Forester tapped at her console. The sterile clinic walls that had been displaying the date in big neon colours – 09:45, August 27, 2037 – morphed into a child's nursery with fluffy little unicorns and fairies dancing across a pastel blue backdrop, and a gentle lullaby echoed around the room.

'Julie, if you could get Millie onto the bed, I'll just set things up.'

Julie placed the still sleeping infant face up below where a strange-looking device was attached. It reminded her of the birdcage her parents had once had in the lounge of the house she grew up in. If she was a good girl her father would let the canary sit on her finger and feed it with a fresh millet spray, and all the while she would be hoping that the bird takes off and flies around the sitting room. Coaxing the bird back into its cage inevitably resulted in droppings over the furniture, which made Julie and her father laugh but made her mother angry. The memory of times lost helped Julie to slip momentarily into more of an alpha state.

Millie stirred as Nurse Forester gently applied the small arm and leg restraints and then adjusted the 'birdcage' cap to fit snugly around the little head of the now fully alert infant. Millie started to cry. Julie spoke calming words and put her finger into Millie's tiny palm. The baby's cries all but stopped as a look of bewilderment engulfed her face, and she instinctively gripped hard.

Nurse Forester did one last check on her console. 'Stand away from the bed please, Julie,' she instructed, while pressing the buttons to start the procedure.

The robot arm approached the top of the bed, holding the smallest of surgical drills. As the arm drew near Millie's head, the cage-like device lit up and a series of tiny electrical impulses sedated the restless infant. The drill tip slowly entered Millie's frontal fontanelle, what most people just call the 'soft spot'. After what seemed like an eternity for Julie but in reality was only twenty seconds later, the drill retracted and a brief pulse of laser light sealed the wound.

Nurse Forester checked the baby's skull and, following her own good-practice guidelines rather than a strict necessity, applied a small waterproof plaster. 'There you are, Julie, all done. The readout is looking good.'

Julie stood by the desk to see her daughter's EEG. She didn't understand what she was looking at, but the nurse seemed to be satisfied. Then a satellite map opened up showing the town and clinic with several blue dots. She saw her own name above one of the blue dots and Emily Forester above another and flashing in the centre '*Adams, Millie Jessica/mmi203793e-09f*'.

'There's she is!' exclaimed Nurse Forester, seemingly happy that everything was working as it should. 'Isn't our technology amazing?' Nurse Forester didn't really believe this at all. In fact, like most people these days, she thought technology was something to be wary of, but she kept smiling and stuck to the approved script.

'The records at the Board of Population Control will be automatically updated. Millie is now a registered citizen. That's her citizen ID number you can see. We'll be monitoring her stats remotely for a few days. It takes a while for the implant to settle down, but I don't expect there'll be any problems. You'll get notified when you need to bring her back for her inoculations.'

As she showed Julie and Millie to the door, Nurse Forester pressed home the government's message. 'Should you change your mind about sterilisation, we can fit you and your husband in at very short notice. It only takes ten minutes.'

2055

ONE

Bailey's Rude Awakening

HE AWOKE SLOWLY, allowing plenty of time for reorientation. Early morning sunlight, comfortably filtered, bathed the spacious bedroom.

Curiously, as his hearing regained clarity, what he took to be the sounds of a rainforest were reverberating throughout the apartment via the acoustic wall panels, mimicking a place and time that he knew now only existed in the archives. It was definitely not his choice to be woken by the replicated calls of extinct macaws, flowing water and the rumbles of distant thunder all set to a slow rhythmic electro beat and panpipes. Quinn must have tired of the regular piece he had programmed for their awakening.

Their music tastes were quite different, one of the few incompatibility areas with his wife of less than one year. She knew he detested the current fad for AI-generated *extinction retro*. The idea that an algorithm could create music for the human soul was anathema to him. He knew, of course, his prejudice was illogical, that music composed either from the result of personal creative inspiration or via predictive resampling software should be judged on its own merits. However, he chose not to be open-minded and deliberately restricted his personal library to late twentieth century progressive rock.

He smiled, listening to the dreadful dirge, thinking this must be his wife's way of telling him they needed to find something that they could both embrace for their new cycle awakening call.

Despite theirs being a young marriage and indeed a young relationship, their bond was rock solid. Music choices aside, disagreements were few and far between. The selection process mandated ninety-five per cent plus compatibility for couples since any relationship breakdown would be an unwelcome logistical challenge so soon into the project.

By nature, but also by years of training, he woke early. He was not one to linger in bed but would rise immediately to shower and get dressed. On the other hand, Quinn needed those extra minutes for snoozing until she absolutely had to get up. He found this slightly irritating since it always resulted in last-minute panics to find the correct outfit to wear, apply make-up and get her hair blow-dried. On balance, this was only a minor annoyance, and it did give him some quiet time to collect his thoughts for the day ahead.

It was, therefore, a surprise when his wife had woken before him and was emerging naked from the shower room, water droplets falling from her olive skin. Moving back to the bed, she crept under the covers and started to kiss him, slowly at first but with increasing vigour. He responded willingly to the movement of her body as she rose up to straddle him. Her long auburn hair resplendent and emitting a strong coconut fragrance was hanging in front, obscuring the full view of her breasts but still allowing her erect nipples to show through the wavy tresses. His arousal was complete, and their lovemaking became frantic and energetic.

That's the way to start a new cycle, he thought to himself afterwards. And as of today, the year of living just within the confines of The Village was over. They were free to explore beyond the perimeter fencing, and he relished the prospect of having two entire days together before he had to go back to work. Of all the things he had had to adjust to, the move from the front line to a desk-based role had been the hardest. Border security was not rocking his boat, and once they were given the all-clear he would see if he could return to his old unit in some limited capacity.

His exuberance crashed abruptly at the sound of her voice.

'Oh boy, Grey! Those counselling sessions have finally paid off. You certainly didn't exhibit body inhibitions just then. I'm so sorry, but I have to rush now, lover boy. Being late is not an option today. See you tonight.'

With that, she grabbed a random suit from the closet, dressed hastily and left the apartment, her hair not yet dry and without applying any make-up.

His heart, which had only just returned to a normal rhythm, started pounding once again as his stomach knotted up with the realisation that this was not his wife.

Where the hell was Quinn?

TWO

A New Shift at the Landfill

DEREK ENTERED THE Portakabin at precisely 08:25 and stared at the empty desk that overlooked the site. His counterpart from the night shift had apparently left early again. He was glad he didn't have to engage in small talk with her, but it meant that he would probably not see or talk to another soul for the next seven hours. This was the third time this month that Karen had not been here to hand over the supervision of the site. It was not as though there was ever much to hand over, things mostly took care of themselves, but that wasn't the point. If you were lucky enough to have a job, you should at least make the effort to be here for the entire shift and carry out your duties.

Karen was only a kid, fresh out of college, when she had started work at the landfill eighteen years ago. They had nothing in common, despite him being only ten years older than her. When he first tried to strike up a conversation about his impending fatherhood, she had looked at him disapprovingly.

'Really, Derek, I don't understand people like you.' As she spoke a look of disgust had consumed her face like she had unearthed some particularly rancid bag of waste. 'Here you are working in this shithole job with zero prospects of escape, and you want to inflict this on another human being. Unless it is lucky enough to be much smarter than you or somehow become very well connected, neither of which is likely given your status, what sort of life is it going to have? More likely, things will be much worse by the time it grows up. It's selfish if you ask me, Derek. I certainly won't be having any, I've already seen to that.'

She must have seen the pitying expression on his face because her voice became more strident. 'That's right, I got my tubes stitched up. How do you think I got this job in the first place? It's not because of my stunning looks, is it? Nope, I got it because I'm officially one of the "Truly Deserving". That's a laugh, isn't it?'

Derek knew there and then that he and Karen would not get on. He remembered the sense of guilt he was made to feel by Karen and others. Julie had told him to ignore the snide remarks, but maybe they were all right – he was selfish. But for fuck's sake, what was the point of it all if having children was no longer socially acceptable?

'Besides, Derek, it means I can get involved one hundred per cent in trying to fix this world that your selfish generation has screwed up.'

They had barely spoken since that day other than what was strictly essential for performing the site handover. The memory of her stinging rebuke still made him wince. *My generation,* he thought to himself, *doesn't she know it was 'my generation' that started the whole Extinction Rebellion movement while she was still in nappies?* He and Julie had been on their fair share of rallies demanding action. Of course, even back then, some so-called birth strikers had committed to not having children in response to the climate emergency, but for him and Julie that was a step too far. Now, later today, they will see their baby graduate. Where did the time go?

He checked the night shift logs: 'UGV serial no. LM998e malfunction responder code 54'. Damn it, she had left it for him to sort out. Although annoyed at Karen's failure to fix the problem, it did at least mean he would get to do something today. He hated quiet days.

Derek knew that technically an Unmanned Ground Vehicle was not a drone. For one thing it couldn't fly, but most people couldn't be bothered with the differentiation between one automaton and another. He had tried explaining to Julie the distinction between drones and bots, but she just gave him *that look*. After twenty-odd years of marriage, he knew when to quit and from then on, when with Julie or friends, he conformed to the societal convention of calling everything a drone unless it had a face or had a voice that sounded like it should have a face, then it was a bot. Only when filing reports or speaking with his supervisor did Derek ensure he used the correct terminology.

He had always worried about his daughter's future. They, or

to be more accurate, he, had tried to encourage her to become a nurse since it was one of the few professions that had so far bucked the AI trend. Statistics consistently confirmed a shorter recovery rate when a patient had a real person to look after them. Millie was more than bright enough to qualify as a doctor or surgeon, but he knew she would probably be unwise to embark on years of medical training in the hope of a lifetime career in either of those professions.

No, he was convinced that nursing was the way to go. Millie had shown a caring nature from an early age, always the first to provide a reassuring hug when a playmate was upset. When she was about seven years old they had been walking by the canal when they stumbled across nature with all its cruelty. A grass snake was coiled up on the ground with its head pointed to the sky, and from its jaws emerged the back legs of a frog gyrating wildly as if together they were performing some macabre modern dance.

'Daddy, Daddy, we must save that poor frog. Please do something.'

'But, Millie, the snake has to survive as well. It's best to leave nature to take care of itself.'

Millie pleaded for him to help the frog, so against his better judgement he used a stick to hit the back of the snake's head, which caused it to let the frog go and it slithered off into the water. The frog with blood streaming from puncture wounds no longer moved and died there and then, much to Millie's horror.

'I'm so sorry, Millie. I know you're upset, but that's why it's best to leave nature alone. Now the frog is dead and the snake goes hungry as well.'

Inconsolable, Millie screamed, 'I hate snakes! Why did God make snakes? Why doesn't he just make them extinct like he did with the dinosaurs and polar bears?'

From that day Millie became fascinated by wildlife and started reading as much as she could and asking the house assistant endless questions. On her bedroom wall above her homework desk, she made a mural decorated with images of tigers, sharks, eagles, domestic cats, crocodiles and many other predatory species, each labelled with the correct scientific name. Millie had emblazoned the entire wall with large lettering declaring:

ANIMALS GOD SHOULD MAKE EXTINCT.

It was shortly after Millie's fourteenth birthday while cleaning her bedroom that Julie discovered a picture behind her desk hidden from view. The image of a trophy hunter with a freshly killed giraffe was labelled *Homo Sapiens* and had a large hand drawn question mark underneath. They decided this was just a teenage phase she was going through and never mentioned anything to Millie. No point making a fuss over nothing and possibly inviting another psyche assessment.

THREE

Heather's Mood Swing

HEATHER MOVED QUICKLY down the five flights of stairs from their luxury apartment. Even though living in The Village guaranteed a working lift twenty-four hours a day, she now preferred to take the stairs. Of course, her old self had no choice but to live on the ground floor. Arthritis that started in her thirties had left her with very restricted mobility by her sixtieth birthday. Gene therapy had come too late to prevent the damage to her joints, and having had surgery early on, it was no longer a viable option.

My God, I do so love waking up with this body, a thought she had so far savoured on every awakening. She had had no qualms in using her position as Head of Duality Research to guarantee acceptance onto the program and with it a place at the front of the waiting list for a Host. 'What's the point of my putting all this effort in if I cannot be one of the first to benefit?' she had quite reasonably asked.

Still, some had expressed strong reservations about agreeing to her being part of the initial trial group to undergo the procedure. That's when she decided to leave them with no choice. 'Better to have my expertise for a full two weeks a month rather than to watch me decline to the point of uselessness. Besides, given my life will be at stake, you can be pretty sure I'll be committed to the success of the project.' It was a winning argument.

Two years on, it still raised her hackles that she had to fight twice as hard to get Grey accepted as a recognised Essential. His work had been pivotal on the project from the beginning, finding suitable matches. They'd be nowhere without her or him, and yet it still took months to get the approval of the Board of Population Control to get him on the list. Just because some members felt Grey's skills would soon be absorbed into the AI didn't change a thing as far as she was concerned. It was both of them or neither. Of course, those pen-pushing jobsworths caved in to her demands in the end.

Taking the steps two at a time, she found her new lease of life intoxicating. *Quinn, my dear, who'd have thought you and Bailey would show up when you did to volunteer as Hosts,* was another thought she had good reason to reflect upon. *The universe certainly works in strange ways.*

As she left the building a car drew up, the doors opened, and a man in his eighties emerged. He had the look of someone who had enjoyed a good life, bright and clear skin, brilliant white teeth, impeccably dressed. 'Good morning, Heather, ready for another battle with our glorious leaders?'

'Really, Robert, you didn't have to come to collect me. I am perfectly capable of finding my own way to the office.' Heather didn't try to hide the irritation she felt at the intrusion into her personal time. Her walks to and from The Facility had become an important ritual. They gave her space to think and, more importantly, a chance to use her new body.

'I'm sorry, but I do need to speak to you before our meeting. You see, Daniel Moccasin has flown over to attend in person.'

'Moccasin... Daniel Moccasin? But that's ridiculous. What on earth does he want, and whatever it is, why couldn't it be done on a VR call? The bloody Americans still haven't grasped it, have they? While the rest of us try to clean up the mess of their stupidity, they still think it's okay to fly at the drop of a hat.' Heather's earlier good mood had been quickly replaced by a wave of rising anger that was very visible in her ever-reddening face.

'For goodness sake, Heather, calm down. You know full well the new generation hydrogen jets are entirely eco-friendly. You need to get rid of that chip from your shoulder whenever I mention the Americans, and I believe I've apologised sufficiently for trusting Moccasin in the past, so please let it go. Look, something has come up that I only got wind of myself last week, about today's meeting. Please get in the car and we can discuss en route.'

Heather could see the worried look on Robert's face. Despite everything that was going on in this crazy world, he was still one of life's optimists. This quality that was so rare these days had endeared him to her. She bit her lip and got into the back of the vehicle.

'Parker, back to The Facility, please,' Robert asked the navigation system so very politely, that it momentarily resulted in a smile to replace the frown that had taken hold on Heather's face. It reminded her of the first time she had heard him speaking futilely to the ancient drinks dispenser in the lab's kitchen area. 'Tea with milk, please.'

FOUR

One Man's Rubbish...

HE LEFT THE Portakabin and got into a large-wheeled rover and headed across the debris-strewn wasteland. This landfill site had started its life back in the 1970s. Many millions of tonnes of 'rubbish' brought here had been compressed to form layer upon layer of no longer fashionable clothing, unloved furniture, toys, pots of unused paints, food waste, and every manner of stuff that was once someone's desire. All buried alongside the indestructible packaging they first came in.

However, amongst this refuse was something that in these times was considered precious. Discarded technology had kept him employed for many years. Not the hi-fi systems, games machines, computers or mobile handsets themselves but the metals used within their electronics. Gold, silver, platinum, copper and other more exotic elements that no one apart from the nerdy has heard of, yttrium, lanthanum, terbium, neodymium, gadolinium and praseodymium.

Mining the landfill for these was far cheaper and more profitable than extracting and processing ores directly from the earth. The geology of the UK did not include many of these metals and supplies from abroad were limited by both scarcity and the political situation. It also meant the site owners could claim green credentials and push out the sort of positive publicity that made the shareholders feel less guilty about their other investments.

As he looked across at the three hundred acre site, dozens of machines got on with their work. Locator drones drilled deep into the waste using sophisticated sensors to seek out the richest seams and then signalling back to operations the exact locations. A series of specialised mining machines then converged at the coordinates to tunnel into the waste and extract everything onto a conveyor that fed a sifting machine, which separated the genuine rubbish from the precious metal-bearing old tech.

When out with friends, Derek's favourite and oft repeated anecdote was that he was working with the same drones sent to Mars on the recent mining exploration mission. 'It's a good job that the Martians didn't leave behind loads of crap like we've got buried at the landfill, or NASA would have needed one of us to go along to dig out the drones five times a day.' He liked to exaggerate how much the site relied on him. 'I always fancied being an astronaut.'

'Astronaut! You get a nosebleed climbing the stairs,' was the usual response from his friends.

Waist deep in debris, he set about untangling the drill. He was a qualified mechanic, but even though he had been through a full apprenticeship and had years of practical experience, his skills were now outdated, and he could not afford to go on retraining courses. Even if he had kept up to date, the automated service centres could now repair or replace a unit far quicker and more cost-effectively than paying someone like him a decent salary. Derek also knew this site had seen its best days, with yields down year on year. It could only be a matter of time before he would be on the scrap heap too.

Two hours later he had cleared the tangled cables from around the drill and was about to restart the machine when the sound of sirens blared. 'Shit' was the only word he could utter as a large bulldozer followed by two skip lorries ripped through the security fencing on the south side of the site. He was too far away to make out who was at the wheel but he knew where they were going, the large skips containing the recovered electronic equipment.

Surveillance drones alerted by the security fence's breach took off and flew low, crisscrossing in a pattern guaranteed to cover the entire site. The four people wearing full-face helmets ignored the circling drones and hooked up a full skip to the winch on the back of each lorry and lifted them onto the back. The trucks with their bounty on board and the bulldozer raced back through the breached security fencing.

Derek had heard about similar raids at other landfill sites, assuming they traded the stolen electronics for their metals on the black market for a fraction of their actual value.

He watched for a while but felt no need or desire to play the hero. Ever since authorised security companies had been given access to the citizen's location database, culprits were captured within hours of committing a crime, making this raid a foolhardy venture. Video footage provided by the drones, along with location histories, was enough evidence for a conviction.

Like the majority he was in favour of the 2036 Law and Order act that had made citizen registration compulsory. Despite protests from the usual minority of extremists, it was hugely popular with voters who had seen nothing but constantly rising crime figures and illegal immigration.

When the Home Secretary herself was shown coming out of a clinic, being one of the first to get chipped, he and Julie were two of many fed up, disillusioned British that had gladly queued up at citizenship centres all over the country. Now everyone knew that only those entitled to live and work in the country could do so. Lower crime rates followed and far fewer police officers were now needed. Absenteeism from bogus sickness was a thing of the past, as bio-stats showed those who were faking it and those who were genuinely ill.

Derek went back to the Portakabin, and having notified head office he filed a crime report with the police. Content that he had done everything he could do he waited for Ed, the next shift supervisor, to arrive. The day had turned out to be far more exciting than he could have imagined at breakfast!

***

Two miles away, Millie watched as the burnt-out trucks lay smouldering on the dirt track, the illicit cargo having been sold on already.

Millie immediately sussed out Karen as being disaffected and angry when her father had shown her around the landfill four years ago as part of a high school environment assignment. She liked to think it was one of her unique skills to see through the layers of pretence that most people concealed themselves with.

Exchanging contact details so she could get insights from a 'Truly Deserving' did indeed help her get high marks for her essay, but her primary intention was always to find someone who could get her the item she desperately wanted. Of course, she did not know for sure if such things were real or not. Searching the net for implant blockers would have the police around in about five minutes flat. But if they were real, it would need electronics and expertise that you couldn't merely advertise for.

Despite their age gap, she had carefully cultivated a friendship with Karen, keeping it a secret from her parents. She knew Karen got a buzz from being a bad influence on her and that her father knew nothing about it. She pretended to be a rebellious teenager, eager to learn about the 'real world' for her part. Millie had joked with Karen about how wonderful it must have been years back when you could just disappear and no one could find you.

'You can still do it if you really want to,' Karen had said, confirming what she already knew, but now she could just play along.

'No, you can't, Karen, unless you're down a deep well, in which case you're not really having the sort of fun I was thinking of.'

'You may be bright, Millie, but you sure are stupid. Not everyone follows the rules like you and your dad do. I've got friends who know how to fool the implants.'

Feigning concern, Millie retorted with, 'Sure, but who wants to end up losing their citizenship and getting deported to the Falklands or some other dreary godforsaken colony?'

'I'm just saying, that's all. You don't have to bite my head off.'

'If it was so easy, why haven't you done it?'

'Who says I haven't?'

'When then?'

'Look, me and your dad aren't exactly good mates, you know. Why should I risk saying anything to Daddy's girl?'

Realising she needed a way into Karen's secret world, she knew she must offer a secret in return.

'Supposing I told you that I hacked my high school grades so that I could get into the uni I wanted to go to?'

'My God, you're a dark horse, Millie Adams. You look like butter wouldn't melt in your mouth. My nan told me they're the worst type. Did you really do that, hack your grades?'

Millie had learnt from an early age that lying was a vital life skill, but by using this skill sparingly you gained a reputation as someone who is totally trustworthy which heightened the effectiveness of any lie.

'Yes, but you've got to promise not to tell my dad as he'd go berserk if he knew, and he'd definitely report me to the education board. He's totally straight when it comes to the rules.'

'Yeah, I've noticed he likes to think of himself as an upright citizen. Uptight is more like it!'

Ignoring the insult to her father Millie pressed further.

'Tell me then, how do we do it? How do we go missing?'

From that point there was no turning back. It took another year for Karen to get the right people with the necessary connections to pull the raid off. The promise of easy pickings was enough of an incentive to those who do this sort of thing as a way of life, but having Millie come along on the day in one of the skip lorries to guarantee this wasn't some undercover police operation to flush them out was the icing on the cake.

Millie's reward was to keep the helmet she had worn containing the jammer and the mimic she had hidden in her bedroom. The mimic was currently broadcasting a recording of her signature bio-stats and location from the previous night when she was tucked up in bed. The date and time were changed to current so that no one would be any the wiser as to her actual whereabouts. But just as important as these treasures were the contacts she had established.

'Come on, Kaz, let's get home. I've got my graduation this afternoon.'

'You're hilarious. If only your dad could see you now, Mill.'

Millie bit her lip. She knew she was embarking on a dangerous path, but how else was she going to save the world?

FIVE

Bailey Seeks Answers

BAILEY SAT AT the kitchen table nursing a large Americano. Coffee was a rare treat these days and even being a Host could not guarantee access to a dwindling supply, but he felt in need of the natural caffeine hit the drink would provide.

Once again, the house assistant confirmed the date and time: '08:46, Friday, September 10, 2055.'

'Twenty-four hours early. How is that even possible?' he mouthed silently. Of course, everyone had been told of the possibility of implant rejection, but why would he now wake up out of sync after a full year of predictability?

Unlike most of his peers he had always been a bit of a technophobe. When all those around him had fitness chips implanted under their skin, he recoiled at the thought. There were the occasional moments when he was growing up, when he had wanted to join in and be part of the bio-stats revolution, like his school friends who shared their stats online to gain social approval.

Uncle Vince said they hadn't got a clue what secrets they were giving away and that their parents should know better. As in many other things, he was proved right and was always keen to say so. 'Goddammit, Bailey, didn't I tell you?' was his oft repeated catchphrase. Bailey heard it a lot when bio-stats disclosure became a requirement for gaining life insurance. From that day on Uncle Vince held no life policies. And although his uncle had been single for many years, he only gave up the search for a life partner when his favourite dating site began using bio-stats to match profiles.

'Goddammit, Bailey, didn't I tell you? We're all going to hell in a bio-stats shit-wagon. Just listen to this. "Finding True Love means sharing the right chemistry. Come share yours today." What happened to just needing good manners and a regular job? Looks like I'm going to be remaining single, son.'

When the Citizen Implant became mandatory in the UK,

Bailey's role in the army meant he was exempt. There is no chance of keeping a low profile in foreign parts if you've got a beacon in your head broadcasting your position to the nearest square metre. Yet here he was twenty-five years later, not only with an implant but also voluntarily sharing his body with someone who lived in a man-made brain inside his skull.

How times change, he thought.

Trying to remember the briefings he had attended, he recalled being told how his and other Duals' implants had been modified to monitor and record his body's functions and be his mind clock. This mind clock ensured that his consciousness was awakened alternate fortnights. He and Quinn were synched, as were Grey and Heather, their other selves who were wakened the other weeks. Well, that was until today.

'Peters, confirm my schedule for the day,' he requested.

'You have one scheduled meeting at 14:00 with the Duality Counselling Service,' came the reply in that annoyingly emotionless tone that was the default of these devices. One of the first things he had done after moving into the apartment was to give the house assistant a proper voice for when it spoke with him. He declined to use the synthetic speech of celebrities that others seemed to find amusing. Instead, he opted for the authoritative voice of his former army instructor, who had seemed only too happy to have his voice digitised. 'Excellent choice, Bailey, I'm glad you recognise greatness when you hear it,' he had replied only half-jokingly when Bailey had suggested it to him.

Despite the outward show of arrogance, he admired Major Peters and had a great deal to thank him for. Stationed together on Gibraltar as part of the Intelligence Corps, they had been on several North Africa tours during the early wave of migrations. It was Peters that had sanctioned Quinn's rescue and the Red Crescent volunteers held hostage in Algiers. *What a first date that was.*

He stood, took his coffee to the terrace that was accessed from the dining area to observe the people, all Duals, going about their daily routine. It had only been a year but everything already seemed so 'normal'.

Their two-bedroomed penthouse apartment was the finest in

Block A, Heather's influence no doubt. The same block was home to all two hundred couples on the program, and just like regular couples he and Quinn socialised with these, leaving the one thousand singles to do what singles always do.

A problem with body sharing is how you count people. The Board of Population talked about 'resourced persons' and 'legal entities' to differentiate. He still preferred to think there were fourteen hundred residents, even though there were only seven hundred living, breathing people.

On most evenings he and Quinn would sit out on the terrace gazing across to the other blocks, wondering what stories these other souls had to tell that led them to decide to be a part of this weird social experiment.

The accommodation blocks faced each other, with Block D being about one hundred metres directly opposite. What once must have been a large central lawn with flower borders had been given over almost entirely to food production, supplying fresh produce to the residents' supermarket. Four large hydroponic greenhouses ran the length of the courtyard with gravel paths in between for access. Solar panels on their roofs provided the electricity used to open and close ventilation windows to regulate the internal temperature depending on the crop being grown. Large water tanks buried under the greenhouses gathered rainwater, which was slowly pumped back onto the stacks of plants during the frequent dry spells. At one end of the courtyard covered in Bougainvillea, a wooden trellis was the only concession to ornamental horticulture, the colourful vines flourishing in the warming British climate.

The frown on Bailey's forehead deepened. It was one thing for his implant to malfunction, but how can the house assistant not recognise him? His spoken voice might be the same as Grey's, but his choice of words, the inflexion of his speech was as unique as his body's DNA, and his bio-stats should scream that he was awake and Grey was asleep, and yet it persisted in addressing him as Grey.

The only conclusion he could draw was that his premature awakening was not down to a fault in his implant but was somehow engineered, and Grey seemed the obvious suspect. How was this possible given all the safeguards in place? And why the hell would Grey do something that threatened his own existence? He needed more information to speculate any further, so he went back into the living room.

'Peters, play all my messages to Bailey Kennedy recorded in the last two weeks,' he ordered, hoping that Grey might have left something for him to make sense of things.

Although each lived their own lives there was often a need for Duals to let the other know what was going on. These 'notes to other self' were typically body related, like if they were in the middle of a viral infection that was being treated or to apologise for the hangover they had caused but wouldn't be suffering from.

There were certain unwritten rules that each Dual pair observed in the interests of harmony, an etiquette guide. Getting drunk before handover was considered bad form. Grey and Bailey had abided by this rule for the most part, but recognising they were still only human they had each transgressed a few times. The score was roughly equal and so they let it ride, each preferring to get payback in some other way. However, once, having woken with a full Bailey hangover, Grey got his revenge by penning a temporary tattoo the night before his handover. Quinn had laughed till she cried when she discovered **'Don't be a Knobhead'** along the underside of his manhood, and since that day he had always been fully sober on handover night.

'Message 1: 22:25, September 9, 2055.' As the house assistant spoke, Grey's head and shoulders appeared in the centre of the room.

'Hi, Bailey, nothing major to tell, but you may have some discomfort in your right shoulder. You might want to visit the physio at the gym. I was using weights again. Sorry, I know I have your physical strength, but my technique is still a long way off from yours. Maybe you could leave me some tips on your next handover. Oh, and regarding your request for our bio-stat history, I've left you a copy in your inbox. Look after us. Grey out.'

'End of messages.'

He was now used to watching his own image, talking to him about events his body had been part of, but his mind had not. In the early days he had felt he was missing out; *Why did his body get all the fun, but he only got half?* An irrational thought, he knew that, but one that he found hard to dismiss. 'Letting go' was perhaps a cliche, but it was the only strategy that had worked, and now after over thirty sleep cycles he was at peace with himself. Peace was something that had eluded him while he was serving on the frontline witnessing the desperation and terror of the emerging Central Zone exodus. As the image of his own body faded, Bailey finished the last of his coffee, so lost in his thoughts that the expensive bitter taste failed to register at all.

Grey's message was odd. He had no interest in bio-stats and certainly wouldn't have asked Grey to see theirs, leaving all that stuff to the quacks. He was proud of his physique that he still worked hard to maintain but did not require a printout to tell him if he was fit, so the idea of reviewing bio-stats history – *forget it!* The message had only been recorded last night, proving if there was any doubt that Grey knew Bailey would awaken early. *What was Grey up to?*

His instincts told him that his newfound peace of mind was at an end.

SIX

Thanks for the Memories

DURING THE SHORT ride to The Facility, Robert had briefed her on as much as he knew. Or at least as much as he was willing to reveal. He had told her the US was in deep shit, which she thought was something anyone who watched even the highly censored climate newscasts could have guessed, and so it told her nothing.

'I'm sure you can see, Heather, we really…' but Heather had stopped listening, her mind wandering back five years to when the mention of Daniel Moccasin had triggered an even more explosive reaction. She had led the research on enhancing memory for dementia sufferers using wetware neurocomputers, having developed them to compensate for the damaged parts of the brain. Moccasin's interference had a disastrous effect on one patient's life but had ironically provided the turning point that led to the Duality Project.

***

'How are you feeling this morning, Philip?' Heather stood at the foot of the patient's bed, studying his medical notes. Philip was a successful businessman who had built up a fashion clothing chain and had become very wealthy, but who had seemingly put all of his efforts into his work since his next of kin was recorded as 'None'. At the age of sixty-eight he had been diagnosed with dementia. He was now seventy-three. Before admission Philip struggled to cope with daily life. He had signed a power of attorney that instructed his money should be used for further medical research into his condition and that he would be willing to be a test case for any new treatments.

'I feel wonderful, Heather. It is Heather, isn't it?'

'Yes, it is, Philip. We met three weeks ago before your surgery. How much do you remember of that meeting?'

'You arrived at 12:23, a little early for our 12:30

appointment. It was a lovely summer's day, with the forecast predicting temperatures of twenty-six degrees. I could see children on the school grounds from my bed. Eighteen boys and fifteen girls split into various groups, playing as children do. They were supervised by just one teacher. Well, I presume she was a teacher. She was dressed rather casually I thought, not like my teacher at junior school, Miss O'Neil, who always wore a regulation tweed skirt, white blouse and sensible black leather shoes. You wore a well-worn grey suit, a green blouse and rather defiantly, in my opinion, a pair of bright red earrings. I recall the scent of coconut soap and that your hair was not brushed, which gave you an overall dishevelled look... Sorry, I didn't mean to be so personal.'

'No need to apologise, I've never been one for fashion and I'm at that age where I don't need to dress to impress, not that I ever did, impress that is, even when I tried,' said Heather smiling at some of the memories that came flooding back of her early career.

A long time back she had been desperate to get noticed at work, so taking her friends' advice that she needed to look 'professional' she set out to change her image by investing in top end suits, cosmetics, and regular hair appointments and so forth.

Despite some approving nods, she soon resented the time and effort this all required. Coupled with the sheer effort of it all, her new look had seemingly encouraged the unwelcome attentions of a particularly odious but influential colleague. She resolved from then on simply to make sure it was her work that got the attention and had barely bothered to renew her wardrobe since, preferring to employ an old-fashioned seamstress to patch her suits as and when necessary.

Ironically, this won her plaudits from the resurgent Make Do and Mend movement, whose chairperson had attended one of her augmented brain function lectures out of sheer curiosity. After the conference, she had caught up with Heather to say she admired her stance for, in her words, 'wearing something that had clearly seen better days'. Heather was not the least bit offended by this comment and was rather happy to have her image used wearing the battered suit on their promotional sites.

The following summer journal had the heading 'Heather Bernard – Neuroscientist – Proving smart people don't need smart clothes'.

'You were clearly in some pain, although trying not to show it,' Philip continued. 'You had sticks to help with your walking, yet I see you don't have them today?'

'They are in my office. I try to do without them. My husband tells me I'm just wearing out my arthritic joints quicker and should use a wheelchair and stop being so bloody minded.'

'You mean you can fix my failing memory, but you can't get your joints fixed?'

'I was diagnosed very early in my life with rheumatoid arthritis, I've had hip and knee replacements that have given me years of pain-free mobility, but the underlying condition is still there attacking my joints. There are always new treatments, but for me, the damage is done.

'Anyway, less about me, I came to assess your memory and general cognition. Your recollection of our last meeting is remarkable, the level of detail so far greater than what would be regarded as normal for most people. What about events before your surgery? Tell me about the day you were admitted to the hospital.'

'I don't really have any particular memory of that day. I remember feeling scared but not why. I'm sorry, it's very hazy. It's all a bit strange actually.'

'Why is that?'

'I can remember virtually every tiny detail after my surgery, things that I don't know why I still remember, like those children in the school. I could tell you exactly what each was wearing. I could recite the news reports for the past three weeks verbatim.'

'The memory prosthetics we implanted have an almost limitless capacity giving you a photographic memory. We have yet to perfect the brain's normal housekeeping regarding discarding what it perceives as irrelevant information. Can I ask do you find having this new ability to recall this level of detail worrying in any way? Until we resolve a way to tidy up the junk, you will have to live with ever more trivial memories.'

'I'm not concerned at all. The memories aren't flooding my thoughts, they are just there when I need them. I've found that I can skip the junk and pick out what I'm looking for quite easily. What about my past memories? The last couple of years seem a blank.'

'One of the prosthetics' functions is to stimulate the regions of your organic brain where long-term memories are stored. You may never have the same level of recall of your old memories before the surgery as you now have going forward. Still, as part of your rehabilitation, we will ask you to recall as much of your past as you are able, because these recollections will then be stored in the prosthetics.'

'So, the damage caused by my dementia will continue to affect my brain?'

'We have a better understanding now of the disease process and can slow things down, but we are still some way off having a full cure. Another function of the device we used is to help mitigate physical symptoms of dementia, such as problems with respiration.'

'I see,' whispered Philip.

Sensing his mood change, Heather sought to reassure him, 'Philip, you've got a good ten, maybe twenty, years ahead of you. Our understanding of the brain is increasing exponentially. I have assistants working with advanced AI systems that provide insights I never dreamed were possible only a few years back. We can isolate and map billions of neural pathways inside the brain. We'll soon beat dementia and other brain diseases, I'm certain of it. Right now, you have a new lease on life. If I were you, I'd grab it.'

'Thank you, Heather. I'm truly grateful. When can I leave here and get back home?'

'That's down to the medical team, but I can't see much reason for keeping you in. You'll need to come back for regular check-ups. I'll speak with the medics to give my assessment.'

'Excellent! Does that mean my daughter can visit now? I assume she was not allowed to see me before?'

Taken aback by his question Heather looked again at the file on Philip. *No next of kin.*

'Philip, we don't have a record of your daughter on your

file. I can't imagine how this could have been missed. What's your daughter's name?'

'Susan Long is her married name, she lives in Cardiff with her husband, David. They only got married last year.'

'She married late in life then?' quizzed Heather, trying not to show the growing alarm in her voice.

'I wouldn't say twenty-five is late. Unfortunately, Susan's mother was killed in a car accident. Her death really hit her hard.'

'Philip, how old were you when Susan got married?'

'Fifty-two,' he answered, thinking Heather was still assessing him and his capacity to recall specific events, but as soon as he uttered those last words a look of horror and panic came across Philip's face. 'I'm seventy-three, how could I have been fifty-two last year? But I'm absolutely sure I was. What's going on, Heather, I don't understand?'

***

As she entered his office, Robert looked up from his desk. 'I know that look, Heather, what's up?'

'Robert, we have a situation with Philip Jackson. He is either recalling false memories, which I seriously doubt because they are far too specific, or he recalls memories that aren't his, which should be impossible.'

'Oh.'

'Is that all you can say, Robert? You don't sound particularly shocked by what you must agree is a significant setback for us. Why is that? What do you know, Robert, that I don't?'

'You have to understand, Heather, that we have been lucky to maintain our funding levels. We've had to cut back in so many areas to keep you and your department operating.'

'Robert, I've always appreciated your support and I am aware you have had to let other departments close, but please don't tell me you've compromised our research.'

'I have to account for every penny that's spent and recycling the costly prototype memory prosthetics was something that we thought made sense. So, I authorised reusing the prosthetic from our first trial patient Ian Bonham.'

'You bloody fool, Robert, I didn't want to believe you had a hand in this, but it had to be you. Only you have the authority to bypass the protocols we all agreed on.'

'Please, Heather, I respect you and your work, but I will not have you talk to me like that. I am still your superior, even if you do think you are in charge. You are not the only neuroscientist in the world. I took advice from others who made it clear that provided we reset the neural pathways, they could be safely reused. I had a team in the lab perform the reset and prove it worked before certifying they were safe to use.'

'Ian Bonham died during surgery when the neural pathways in the prosthetic were still being synched with their organic counterparts, leaving many loose end memories. Whatever reset procedure you attempted clearly failed to remove these. Why did you keep this from me?'

'Because you would have kicked up a fuss, and I would have had to have made a choice between your work and other equally important research. I did not want to make that choice. As you are well aware, since last year this government has been hell-bent on total self-sufficiency for the UK, including the manufacture of clinical equipment. We are not allowed to import anything, and our own labs have been at full capacity producing the wretched Citizen Implants. The prosthetics we've been using until now came from the US with modifications made to meet your specification done here by our own technicians.'

'You do realise unless we remove the implants from Philip Jackson, his memories will be a jumble of confusion and inconsistencies that could easily see him slip into a state of psychosis. Just in case you don't remember, we don't yet have any experience of removing prosthetics safely from a living person. Even if we did, the poor man would certainly regress back to his former state of full dementia. My God, what have you done?'

'I made the call. It was my decision. I got it wrong. Can anything be done to erase the false memories?'

'No, you know full well that these devices are designed to be hack-proof once implanted, the right to privacy and metal integrity, remember? Who told you this reset procedure could be done safely?'

'Daniel Moccasin, head of neuroscience at Yale. He led the original design team for the wetware chips used in the implants.'

'You really know how to pick them, Robert. I met that jerk a few years back at a conference in Los Angeles. He gave a lecture on why cognitive liberty was a fine and noble ideal to strive for but, like all human rights, could and should be revoked for the greater good. He is a dangerous man, Robert. I can't believe you approached the Americans behind my back.'

'Heather, you may be brilliant at what you do, but you are naïve when it comes to the world. The US only let us have the implants in the first place because they wanted us to test them out. Their own trials failed and they were considering abandoning the project. I convinced Daniel that with your modifications, we would succeed where they failed.'

'Christ, Robert, so I've been played along by you and them just to help those world-wrecking climate-change-denying fuckwits?'

'That's exactly why I've had to keep this from you. Your political views and quick temper ruled you out of having sensible discussions.'

'Sensible. Is that what you thought they were? You've got the result I would have told you could happen if you had bothered to consult me. Why could we not get new implants from the Americans if they wanted us to succeed? Why get us to reuse ones we had?'

'That, my dear, is down to UK politics. We would need a special import license, which our new administration is not handing out. Like I said, self-sufficiency is the new mantra no matter what the cost.'

'I do watch the news; just plain stupidity.'

'Finally, something we agree on. Look, there are those in power who think our work is an extravagance. I've had ministers tell me we already spend too much as a nation on caring for old people without us finding new ways to prolong their lives. I tell you, Heather, the world's changing and not for the better.'

'You know you've left me no choice other than to resign, Robert, I can't and won't be part of this charade any longer. I trusted you. I'll pick my things up tomorrow.'

'Please, Heather…' Robert's words fell on deaf ears as she stormed out of his office.

***

The following afternoon, feeling deflated but totally resolved to leave, she made her way back to the clinic, fully intending to say a few farewells and retrieve her belongings. Robert was waiting inside her office with a short, and to Heather's mind, overly thin man who nevertheless had the demeanour of someone who knew his own importance. She knew her movements, like all UK citizens, could be traced via their implants, so them being there at the exact moment she arrived was no coincidence.

'Good morning, Heather, I'd like you to meet Doctor Spencer Child. We'd like a word with you if you don't mind.'

Child, well, that name certainly fits, she thought to herself without betraying her inward amusement. 'Good morning, Robert, I've really just come to pick my things up.'

'Ms Bernard, or may I call you Heather?'

'You may.'

'Thank you. I would prefer it if you just called me Child. Everyone else does. I don't mind, honestly. I used to mind, of course, when I was younger, but now I find being different an advantage, plus it serves to remind me why I dislike most people.' Without waiting for a response he continued. 'Heather, I've been following your work closely. You clearly have made great strides in advancing neuroscience. When Robert called last night to say you were quitting, I was, to say the least, very disappointed. Then, having explained the circumstances, it became imperative that I spoke with you. Do me the courtesy of thirty minutes of your time, and if you still want to leave I will not try to deter you.'

'I'm sorry, Doctor Child, I mean Child, but who exactly are you?'

'Before I answer, I have to let you know that whatever I tell you is unrepeatable to anyone. It would be denied if you did repeat it and most likely result in you being unable to work anywhere in the UK or anywhere else for that matter. However, I believe you may have stumbled onto something that could change the course of human history, and if you agree, you'll have all the funding you need.'

Heather knew her face must have been a picture. Never lost for words, she couldn't get her mouth to work for what seemed ages. How could this man she had never heard of make such extravagant claims and threats? And what could he possibly mean by 'changing the course of human history'? Her curiosity demanded only one response. 'Very well, Child, do explain what you mean. I am fully aware of the requirements for total confidentiality in my work.'

'I work as a special advisor to the Board of Population Control. My brief is to develop strategies for reducing the UK population to sustainable levels before the full impacts of the climate crisis hits.'

'My God, you certainly don't work for the government's PR department do you? I thought the self-sufficiency message was that if we all pulled together we would weather the climate storm?'

'I only deal with the facts and the truth as I see it. The reality is much grimmer, and I will go through the reasons with you, but only if you think my proposal is viable and agree to help us. You see, we had hoped to keep the people onside, but unfortunately the voluntary sterilisation program has not been the success we claim on the newscasts. The PM was just about to announce mandatory sterilisation for all long-term unemployed people over the age of twenty.'

'Christ, not exactly a vote winner, is it? But then we don't have elections anymore, do we?'

Still standing by the window, Robert seemed unmoved by his statement, leading Heather to speculate how much he really knew and was not at liberty to tell her.

'You said he was about to announce...?'

'Well, that is where I'm hoping you can help. You see, when Robert called explaining how the poor Mr Jackson recalled another person's memories, this bizarre thought came into my head. *If by pure accident, a person can end up with the memories of two people, why can't we by design have a single person with two separate personalities?'*

At this, Robert got up from behind her desk. 'You cannot possibly be serious. You must be mad to even think it.' Heather had never seen Robert so visibly shocked by anything before and certainly never heard him rebuke anyone with the authority Child claimed he had.

Child stood impassive, clearly prepared for this initial reaction. Heather, on the other hand, had been staring directly into his eyes and saw he was indeed serious, mad possibly, but serious nevertheless. Suspecting she already knew the answer, she had to ask anyway. 'Why would you want to do such a thing, Child?'

'I'd have thought it was obvious. With the right strategy we can guarantee the country's long-term security, preserve essential skills and solve the perennial question of what to do with our Undeserving. A win-win situation if ever there was one.'

SEVEN

Bailey Gets Counselling

OKAY, I'VE GOT an hour before Grey's appointment, Bailey thought to himself. *If the clinic scanners recognise me as Bailey, then there's nothing to worry about other than figuring what's gone wrong with the mind clock, but if they also recognise me as Grey, what the hell do I say?*

Reluctantly, he decided to take a look at the bio-stats logs that Grey had sent him. He wasn't sure what to expect, but he had assumed from his message there might be just his and Grey's stats. But somehow, he had got a hold of the logs for all Duals going back to day one.

There were millions of rows of data, ordered by the name of the Host, then date and time. The data clearly showed the current conscious personality, followed by over a hundred items of medical data. The timestamps indicated the stats were sent every single minute of the day.

He recognised some things, such as those related to the physical body, heart rate, blood pressure, and so on. But even the detailed breakdown of blood counts was way beyond his limited medical knowledge.

The rest of the data was even more alien to him. Even where he recognised the occasional term like Alpha and Beta Waves, the corresponding numbers were just gobbledegook. This was raw data before the AI had dumbed it down for the average human to read. He could have asked the house assistant to help but decided against doing so for now in case it raised a red flag somewhere. 'It's funny how quickly paranoia sets in,' he muttered under his breath.

He scrolled past the vast amounts of data to his own personal logs with no idea what he was looking for. What the hell did Grey expect him to find? He thought it seemed reasonable to check what was happening on either side of the fortnightly wake/sleep cycle. As he expected, when he scrolled through the months, the conscious personality switched between himself and Grey. Also recorded was both the time the personality switch was initiated and when it was complete.

Like all other Duals, Bailey had been briefed that each switch would take several minutes to complete and that it could only happen when the one currently *awake* was unconscious. This was unavoidable as reviving the organic brain or putting it back to sleep took time. It was also a practical measure to avoid the possibility of injury or accident that any sudden switch could result in.

He could see from the timestamps that the switch was initiated bang on midnight for the first six months, but then it started at 00:01. It seemed trivial and clearly went unnoticed by either himself or Grey. Filtering over the entire dataset, he found the same one-minute discrepancy had occurred on the same evening for two other Hosts: Mike Jervis and Stephanie Walsh. There was an even more significant discrepancy of ten minutes for himself and these others on two separate occasions.

Well, buddy, you've undoubtedly been busy, but why haven't you reported your findings? he mulled. *Who are you afraid of? Or are you just protecting someone?* Whatever the answer to his questions, Grey was clearly asking for his help.

Okay, buddy, since I don't really have any choice, I'll find out what's going on, but first I have to see your shrink and somehow do a damn good Grey impersonation or the game's over before it's begun.

***

In addition to the residential apartments, Block B contained an administration suite that included the counselling service, a nurse's office and the gym. As the lift opened to reveal an automated reception desk, Bailey tried rehearsing in his head what he was going to say to Grey's counsellor. No matter what story he came up with he was not Grey and so had no idea what personal issues had been discussed. Heather's remark earlier suggested Grey may have been experiencing body integrity dysmorphia, a condition that all Essentials had been warned about and prepared for before going through with the procedure. *I guess the theory is one thing but reality another*, he thought to himself. *I wonder how I'd cope with waking up in someone else's body?*

As he approached the appointments desk the clinic assistant's sickly sweet synthetic voice greeted him. 'Good afternoon, Grey. Doctor Kingsley is expecting you. Please go to Room B2.' By now, he was only mildly surprised that he was not being recognised by the Digi-Assistants, but the real test was about to come.

Bailey had met Doctor Kingsley briefly before, but ethics apparently dictated he and Grey had different counsellors. Bailey thought this was a stupid idea since someone, somewhere, must ultimately be comparing notes, and if it wasn't their counsellors then who was it? Still, right now that might work in his favour since Kingsley would not know him.

As Bailey entered Room B2, the silver-haired doctor had his back to the door and was gazing out across the central courtyard towards the greenhouses. Turning to face him, Bailey thought he caught a brief look of puzzlement from the doctor, but it may have been a trick of the light as a broad smile quickly broke out across his face.

'Hey, Grey, good to see you again, please take a seat.' With that, Kingsley sat opposite Bailey, not behind a desk but face to face, about two metres apart.

'Thank you, Doctor. Good to see you too.'

'What's with the formality, Grey? Everything okay? I thought we had agreed on first names.'

He was caught out with his first words. What now? Should he just brazen it out? Instead, he decided to play a game of bluff with the doctor. 'Actually, Doctor Kingsley, what if I told you you're talking to Bailey, not Grey?'

Kingsley didn't seem fazed at all by Bailey's admission, but simply took out an actual paper notepad from his pocket with what looked to be a real lead pencil. Bailey wondered if the anachronism of this simple writing tool reflected the doctor's own personality. Or was it just a shrink's prop to keep him guessing?

'Grey, the last time we met we discussed the feelings of guilt and loss of identity you had been experiencing, and which you put down to, and I'm using your exact words, "invading

Bailey's body." That must have been hard for you to share with me, Grey, but it means we are making real progress.'

'Doctor, you don't seem to understand. *I am* Bailey, not Grey. Don't ask me how this is possible, but I'm telling the truth. I had hoped you could diagnose the problem.'

'Come, come, Grey, what is this all about? I'm sure you know the receptionist will have verified your identity before admitting you. Had you been Bailey, as you claim, I and many others would have been alerted immediately. Let me show you.' He took the pencil he had just been taking notes with, and as he pressed the eraser a holographic image of a cranium appeared.

Bailey knew he was looking at himself, or rather the inner workings of his and Grey's minds. Surrounding his own brain was a micro-thin latticework of organic and synthetic material he knew to be the receptacle for Grey's personality and memories.

He had, of course, seen this image many times during and following the procedure. Lying in the clinical ward of The Facility, he had been able to observe the gradual envelopment of his brain. He had watched as it merged with his organic brain to gain access to the five senses, control over movement and other bodily functions.

At the top of his cranium was the Citizen Implant, the size of a rice grain, that now also acted as the master switch between the two minds using an atomic clock to mark their cycles.

As he watched the image in front of him a pulsating green light emanated from the Duality Band, a clear sign, he knew, that it was awake. Floating above the projection was a summary status report confirming what he saw:

Conscious: Essential Personality Grey Bernard
Unconscious: Host Personality Bailey Kennedy
Countdown to next cycle 9:45:31

'There's no fooling you, is there, Jim?'

'No, Grey, I've been a psych counsellor too long to be fooled, nor is there any fooling the scanners.'

Deciding to change tack, Bailey replied, 'Look, Jim, I'm really sorry for being such a pain, but sometimes I really feel like the real Grey has disappeared. I can't be the only Dual feeling like this. Am I?'

'Duality is still in its infancy. There are no references we can look up to say what is normal and what is not. It does take a period of adjustment and acceptance, and that varies from individual to individual. Grey, you may not believe me at this moment, but the very fact you just pulled that stunt tells me you are, in fact, coming to terms with who you now are. When you first came to see me you could not even mention Bailey's name.'

'I'm glad to hear that, Doc,' Bailey replied, giving what he felt was the required response.

'Now, since your next sleep cycle starts tonight, I suggest we end today's session and schedule another in two weeks just after you wake up again. Is that okay with you, Grey?'

'That's fine by me, Jim, as long as you think they are worth continuing.'

'Oh, definitely. I'm sure we are almost there.'

With that they got up from their chairs and shook hands. As Bailey left the room he was sure of only one thing. Doctor Kingsley knew precisely who he was, even if those damn scanners said otherwise.

***

Back in Room B2, Doctor Kingsley tore up the notes he had taken. Removing a PDA from his desk drawer and using the same pencil now as a stylus, he entered: *We have a problem. Need to meet ASAP. Room 3.19. Confirm time. K.*

EIGHT

Millie's Graduation

AS SHE TOOK her line in the queue, Millie could see the assembly hall filling with excited students and their equally excited parents. For the majority, this would be the first time they meet their cohorts in the flesh. She knew this explained the many 'Oh gosh, you are so much more *real* than your VR image' ice breaker conversations that could be heard between nervous young adults who, like herself, were somewhat overwhelmed by being in the physical presence of so many others.

As each student passed the authenticator scanner, they were allocated a seat number in the first fifteen rows closest to the stage, and their parents or other guests were given seats behind these.

'Millie Adams, please go to row C seat number six, Mr & Mrs Adams please go to row Q seats twelve and thirteen,' the steward smiled widely, seemingly enjoying the occasion as much as anyone attending.

As the remaining guests took to their seats, a procession of senior staff appeared from behind the curtains at the side of the stage. Millie and her peers stood while the robed professors sat on either side of the lectern to face the audience. The entrance complete, the room fell silent.

Millie recognised her own tutor, Professor Jenkins, head of Applied Science, to the group's left. In the centre was Professor Arkwright, the Vice-Chancellor. It was the latter who stood to address the gathering.

'Fellow students and guests, good afternoon and happy Graduation Day! Yes, I say *fellow students* because whereas graduation is a significant milestone in a person's life, it should never be regarded as the time when we stop learning but rather the beginning of a lifetime where we choose to learn something each and every day.

'I know many of you who have come here today to be

recognised for your achievements have already been assigned roles in industry and commerce vital to our country's goal of total self-sufficiency.

'A smaller number of you have been given grants to continue postgraduate research, and thus, you will have to put up with my and others distinguished VR heads and torsos taking up residence in your homes for a while longer.' Muted laughter came from some students and guests, but most sat expressionless unsure if this was an attempt at humour or not and whether it was polite to laugh or not. The Vice-Chancellor's own expression gave nothing away.

'Whatever the future holds for you individually, we wish you great success in these endeavours.

'Before we start the presentation ceremony, it has become a tradition for the Vice-Chancellor to address the graduands and guests in the hope that we can impart some final words of wisdom. I will let you be the judge of whether I succeed or not.'

Looking up and pointing to the university crest that decorated much of the ceiling, the Vice-Chancellor's voice boomed out, *'Nisi Sapientia Frustra.'* Without Knowledge, all is in Vain. This has been our motto for eighty-six years. Many things have changed over these years.

'It is only twenty years since students at this university and others in the United Kingdom started to graduate at age eighteen. As I'm sure you know, before this it was usual to only commence what was termed *higher education* at that age, the brightest often held back by the not so bright. Today our talented young profit immensely from the absolute knowledge that their bio-stats accurately reveal their individual potential right from infancy. Everyone in our society benefits from knowing what they can and cannot achieve at the earliest possible age. Valuable resources are, therefore, directed in line with those capabilities.

'It may seem paradoxical, but it is nevertheless true that advances in Artificial Intelligence have enabled such personalised tuition that a person's inherent Human Intelligence is maximised. You, our most gifted, are today graduating with masters degrees a full five years earlier than would have been possible in times past.

'Each of you is now armed with the collective knowledge of countless scholars. Many great people, dead or alive and now incorporated into the AI, have contributed to your achievements.'

As he spoke Millie absent-mindedly fiddled with the silver frog pendant she always wore around her neck and, keeping her eyes closed, entered the wakeful meditation she had practised for as long as she can remember. After the incident with the frog-eating snake, her anger at the injustice was picked up on her quarterly psyche assessment. Her assessor was sympathetic to her story but reminded her that uncontrolled anger would count against her, as future employers and life partners would prefer someone less volatile.

Millie had always disliked these assessments. It seemed unfair that someone got to see into her head when she could not. It was true that government regulated fitness monitors allowed everyone to check their bio-stats for physical wellbeing. But only authorised persons could acquire the sophisticated scanners used to interpret brain activity, so like everyone else she had at first no idea what was being recorded or when a dreaded psyche assessment was triggered.

Well, that was before enrolling on this degree course. Now Millie understood so much more. Psyche assessments were performed routinely by the AI. Abnormal brainwave patterns are quickly recognised, and in the case of children up to age sixteen a trained counsellor is assigned to prevent any descent into delinquency or self-harm. Adults could be sectioned simply on the evidence of their bio-stats.

Despite all the so-called evidence of a decrease in crime, anti-social behaviour, and suicide attributed to the Citizen Implant, Millie hated harbouring this spy within. Nevertheless, until that incident she had passed her assessments with flying colours. 'Exceptionally gifted child' was the usual comment. For this she was rewarded with her favourite treat of an authentic chocolate bar, not the fake stuff that masquerades as chocolate that's made in Britain, but the real thing. God only knows where her dad got it from.

On that occasion, however, she received her first cautionary notice: 'Exceptionally gifted but angry child. Recommend counselling'. Her parents had been distraught at this blemish on her record and that it was now likely to trigger a full assessment of themselves as well to see if they were the cause of Millie's anger.

The morning's events had raised her adrenaline levels, and for a while her heart had raced uncontrolled, but her training kicked in and now her body had resumed its 'normal' quiet state. She allowed her mind to resurface momentarily into the assembly hall to hear the Vice-Chancellor continue the same lecture he had given to first-year students three years ago.

'Would one of our guests care to remind us what happened in 1066?'

'Battle of Hastings, Norman Conquest,' someone shouted.

'That's correct, sir, and what else can anyone tell us of this momentous event?'

'King Harold was killed by an arrow in the eye,' shouted another.

'And how do you know that might I ask?' the Vice-Chancellor bellowed.

'It's shown on that tapestry. The whole battle with Harold grabbing the arrow that killed him,' replied yet another.

'Well done, everyone! Poor old Harold dying by an arrow to the eye, no less. This is an example of common historical knowledge ingrained in the British psyche. It is also, of course, in large part, a complete myth.' Spurred on by the murmurings amongst students and guests alike, he continued. 'There is evidence to suggest the Bayeux Tapestry was altered to add the arrow in question, possibly as part of restoration work centuries later. It is unclear whether the accounts of Harold being killed by an arrow to the eye came before or after this restoration. Some even doubt whether Harold actually died in the battle at all.

'Maybe changing the tapestry was an innocent act by over-eager French restorers who just wanted to liven it up a bit, a humorous depiction of "one in the eye for the English".' Pausing briefly for the hearty laughter that followed, he resumed his well-trodden monologue.

'Maybe it was done with the deliberate intention to reinforce the image of William the Conqueror rather than William the

Bastard, as he was also known. After all, we now know that it was only after the Battle of London that same year when William was crowned king.

'We are unlikely ever to know the real motive for this particular alteration to the history of the Battle of Hastings.

'This cannot be said, though, for the events of 2041. That year a student at this same university noticed what appeared to be an error on our database. Every query he made cited the date of the Battle of Hastings as 1086. When he investigated other sources, including the British Library digital archives, they all gave the same year of 1086.

'What we all know now, of course, is that there had been a sophisticated cyberattack on the Global Datasphere.

'Unlike previous state sponsored attacks where the motive was to steal secrets or to paralyse a country's infrastructure, this attack sought to alter every aspect of a nation's history by simply changing the dates when something actually happened.

'It was a highly sophisticated attack which changed dates subtly but consistently. For every reference the virus found for any event, the date would be changed. This included altering any images or film files to ensure anyone looking up some event from history was presented with a seemingly factually accurate account.

'What possible motives could the perpetrators have had to change history in this way? This only becomes apparent when you take an event like the Japanese surrender at the end of World War 2.

'The Japanese emperor announced their surrender on August 15, 1945, following the dropping of the atomic bombs on Hiroshima and Nagasaki on August 6 and August 9. But what if the emperor had announced the surrender on August 5 before the bombs being dropped? The Americans would have killed thousands of innocent civilians knowing they had already won the war, an act of unparalleled barbarity.

'As you can see, dates really do matter. They are the only way of understanding cause and effect.

'You might well ask, how did they think they would get away with such an audacious act of historical sabotage? The fact is that whoever did it was not concerned about being found out. The prime motivation was to create confusion and dissent amongst the international community.

'Even today, academics and historians around the world are endeavouring to fix the data using painstaking research into the remaining printed archives. Disputes between countries and between academics when so-called *correct* dates have been identified have destroyed any trust in the integrity of the Global Datasphere.

'That is why we in the UK, as part of the government's broader self-sufficiency policy, have built our own National Datasphere. This trusted source is now used by the AI and all digital assistants.

'In conclusion, "*Nisi Sapientia Frustra*" is as relevant today as when it was adopted all those years ago. We in the UK can be confident that our knowledge is based on facts and that our graduates are therefore better equipped to enter the world of commerce and politics.

'Thank you, Ladies and Gentlemen.'

Millie applauded politely alongside guests and fellow graduands and prepared herself for the short walk to receive her degree certificates.

'The graduation ceremony will now commence,' boomed the Vice-Chancellor triumphantly, clearly happy with the applause for his own performance today.

As the award recipients were called, different sections of the audience cheered and applauded as they held out hands to grasp the certificates they had worked so hard to achieve.

Finally, it was Millie's turn.

'Millie Adams, Masters Degree in Applied Biosciences with Distinction,' announced the Vice-Chancellor's congratulatory voice. As she took the award, her own tutor, Professor Jenkins, applauded as though his life depended on it. His smile beamed with genuine pride.

Taking her seat once more, she was uncertain what she was most relieved about, getting her degree, or that she would never have to sit through that tedious lecture ever again. The one thing she had taken from the talk was that it was not the gaining of knowledge that mattered at all, and likewise, those who say knowledge is power are equally wrong. It is the control of knowledge where the real power lies, and in this world that power was craved by predatory humans.

Annoyed that her thoughts had turned so downbeat on what was a day to celebrate, she decided to lighten her mood by playing a little game while waiting for the ceremonies to end. The game she settled on was 'What's my secret motto?' The only rule was it had to be in Latin as a mark of respect for the 'hallowed' institution she had graduated from.

Even though many scientific terms had their origins in Latin, the language was not one of Millie's strong points, which constrained her choices. As she struggled to come up with anything profound enough to adopt as her own motto, a phrase suddenly sprang to her mind. *Where the heck did that come from?* she thought to herself, inwardly smiling at how inappropriate it was for a budding neuroscientist but how totally appropriate for a budding saviour of the world.

'*Actio personalis moritur cum persona.*' Dead men do not sue.

NINE

A Desperate Plan

HEATHER ENTERED THE conference suite with a mix of apprehension and curiosity. She had always hated being unprepared for any meeting, let alone one with the Americans.

Daniel Moccasin was sitting alone at the head of a long table intended to seat up to twenty, a relic from pre-holographic technology. She knew as soon as Robert had said that Moccasin had flown over that this could only mean he was here for an extended visit, and not just for a one-off conference. Moccasin appeared freshly showered and shaved and wearing an expensive crease-free suit and open-neck shirt, clearly suggesting that unlike herself he was well prepared. She tried to ensure her irritation at being the last to know was not visible on her face.

The last time she had spoken with Moccasin was after the Jackson incident, when she had left him in doubt about what she thought of his interference. That didn't stop him from trying to hijack the Duality Project. Despite it being top secret the US somehow found out, and Moccasin had the nerve to try to get the whole program, including her research, transferred to the US. He claimed their state-of-the-art military labs and science staff would halve the time it would take for the UK to get the technology working using its 'outdated facilities and methods'. The misogynistic twat had even suggested she should be seconded as an advisor to the program.

For a time it was touch and go whether he would succeed. He had the US Defence Department's backing, and they had hinted at 'tactical withdrawals' from their commitments to protect the UK if we didn't play ball.

Although she avoided politics and politicians whenever possible, she was not naïve about how the world worked. This was especially true when it came to 'our friends' across the Atlantic. She knew the British people liked to believe there was a special relationship between the two countries. It suited politicians to foster this romantic notion of two nations with shared values standing together against the world. But she had long recognised that the reality was that Britain was always an unequal partner, and the Americans made sure we knew it. Any assistance they provided in times of crisis always came with a hefty price tag.

To his credit, Robert did his best to resist the pressure being brought to bear, but it was Child who recognised the strategic importance of keeping control of the emerging technology and had convinced the PM to keep Duality as a bargaining chip for when times got really bad. It looked like that time had finally arrived.

'Good morning Daniel, *what a lovely surprise* to see you again.' She barely tried to hide the sarcasm in her voice. 'Oh, sorry, silly me, you probably don't recognise me.'

Robert had followed her into the room and took a seat at the other end of the long table, making for an uncomfortably large gap between him and Moccasin. Heather decided to stand, further increasing the tension that rapidly filled the air.

'Oh my, I'd recognise that English sarcasm anywhere. You're sure looking well, Heather. There you are, standing tall, and forgive me for saying so, a damn sight prettier than I recall. I'd say you've done damn well for yourself.'

'Tell me, Daniel, are you still hoping to be a serious neuroscientist one day, because it's not for everyone you know?'

Not taking the bait, Moccasin continued, 'Heather, I'm hoping our past history is all water under the bridge. We've kept a watchful eye on your career and the amazing results you claim to have achieved and thought it time to pay the UK another visit.'

'*Claim to have achieved.* Aren't I convincing enough? I don't know why you're here, but I've got better things to do than *chew the baccy*, so get to the point. What are you after?'

'Well, at least I did try to be civil, but I guess I'll just have to make do with being as direct as yourself. I'm here...' But before he could finish what he was saying the door opened and the diminutive Spencer Child entered the room dressed in the distinctive dark green sweat top and khaki trousers uniform of the People's Council. He looked across, first at Moccasin, then to Robert, and finally to Heather. And despite his lack of stature, something in his gaze made her need to sit. Without introductions, he took out a PDA from his jacket pocket and pointed it at a large screen.

'I am authorised to speak on behalf of the Prime Minister. He needs you all to understand why you are here.' As he spoke, the holographic face and torso of the US Vice President, John McNeil, appeared above the centre of the table.

'Good morning, ladies and gentlemen. Thank you for your attendance. I will take questions shortly, but what I am about to read comes directly from the President.' With that, he proceeded to speak in a sombre tone.

'We are about to enter a new era. Despite worldwide efforts, we must now accept we have failed to curb the rise in global temperatures to sustainable levels. Current forecasts predict a continuing rise which will peak within the next twenty years at 4.1 degrees above pre-industrial levels, that is 2.1 degrees above where we are now. The process of atmospheric warming is accelerating. Gases that have been trapped for centuries by the permafrost are now being released at an uncontrollable rate. Our best scientists are still working on finding ways to recapture these gases, but we believe that whatever we might now do is too late and that the warming process cannot be halted.'

As he spoke, a map of the world appeared, filling a full half of the room. Two red lines, one labelled 45°N the other 35°S bisected west to east.

'Our simulations show that apart from some smaller coastal regions, those countries between the 45th Parallel North and 35th Parallel South will become almost entirely uninhabitable to humans. A combination of land lost due to rising sea levels and droughts that turn continents to deserts will leave only those countries within the marked green zones able to sustain any sizeable human population.'

As if to add unnecessary dramatic effect, the area between the two red lines turned a bright burning orange, either side of the red lines turned green, and a series of numbers glowed red:

- China 1.5 bn.

- India 1.7 bn.
- Southern Europe 1.7 bn.
- Africa 1.5 bn.
- USA 400 mm.
- South America 600 mm.

'As you can see from the numbers, approximately 7.5 billion out of a total world population of 9.5 billion currently live in the red zone.

'We predict that by 2074, the world you see before you will become a reality. So far, we have managed to avoid large scale panic in the US by convincing our people that the current dust bowls we are witnessing in our farming belts are temporary phenomena. Food shortages are not something US citizens have experienced since the 1930s, and the mood is turning very ugly. Radical groups such as Climate Pro-Life are attracting many supporters demanding the President comes clean on what is happening.

'Should our predictions become public knowledge, the current wave of northward migrations we see in Africa and South America would quickly turn to a full-scale Central Zone exodus.'

Unable to contain herself any longer, Heather stood to address the Vice President but was summarily cut short by Child, 'Please, Heather, not yet.'

McNeil paused while Heather resumed her seat, his hands shaking as he took a sip of water.

'Our scientists have calculated that by creating high-density self-sufficient megacities within both the northern and southern green zones, the Earth will be able to support a maximum population of five billion people. That's three billion in the North and two billion in the South.

'For the past four years, the heads of governments of the world's leading nations have been in secret talks. It is hoped that by mutual co-operation we can implement an emergency World Government that will oversee the building of these megacities and manage the exodus. Although still an enormous task, we have the technology and resources to achieve this.

'Unfortunately, so far, no agreement has been reached because those countries in the northern green zone are unwilling to commit to opening up their borders for such a massive influx of people and are insisting a maximum of two billion could be accommodated. This is clearly unacceptable to those governments representing citizens in the red zone.

'Without any such agreement the US believes it is likely that Russia, the largest single habitable country with a population of only 160 million, will seek to defend its borders at all costs. The Russians fear China may be considering releasing bio-weapons over its territory to kill its citizens, allowing the Chinese simply to annex their country. Intercepted intelligence confirms plans for a nuclear strike against China if any such bio-attack looks imminent. Should any such attack occur, the West would inevitably become involved in a global conflict that would directly or indirectly kill ninety per cent of the world's population.

'Alternatively, China may decide Australasia is a safer bet. Central and South Australia will be lost to the desert, but the rest could look very inviting to Beijing, who would be able to stroll in without much resistance if they chose to do so. Many believe that's the real reason for decades of building up their military presence in the South China Seas.

'We face stark choices if any of us are to come through this, which is why we are turning to the UK and why I am talking to you today.

'Your body sharing technology seems to have succeeded where others have failed. It offers us a glimmer of hope as to how we may get the climate refugee numbers down to a level acceptable to the governments of the northern green zone and how we avoid the scenarios I have described.

'I have asked Daniel to verify the results of the Duality Project, and if he confirms what I hear from Doctor Child, then I'm hopeful the critical political barrier to our northern green zone megacities will be resolved.

'If we can take in four billion refugees but only need to accommodate two billion extra bodies, I'm pretty sure we'll get that agreement.'

Looking up from the device he was reading from, McNeil addressed the room.

'I'll take questions now.'

TEN

Bailey's Mind Gym

HE WAS SURE Kingsley was lying, but why? He needed time to think. Uncle Vince had taught him that one of the best ways to work out the mind was to work out the body, and Grey's cryptic message had suggested he visit the physio, so he headed towards the gym which was conveniently located next to Kingsley's room.

***

His teenage years had not been easy. His mother died just after his thirteenth birthday. The Bollinger champagne his father had bought for their wedding anniversary was not as genuine as his supplier had promised but was contaminated with industrial alcohol. His mother reacted badly, losing her sight within hours, and her other vital organs gave up after two weeks in intensive care. His father did not have the same reaction to the poison, but knowing he caused her death destroyed him and he couldn't bear to look Bailey in the eye ever again.

Bailey was shipped off to live in the optimistically named Hope Valley, Derbyshire, with his uncle, a retired officer who had served as a soldier in the Intelligence Corps. Uncle Vince steered Bailey through his teenage years and engendered his passion for physical fitness, coupled with the self-discipline that gave him the foundations for a future career in the army.

'Let the pain and serotonin work its magic,' he drilled whenever Bailey's frustrations got the better of him. 'Come on, son, I'll beat you to the top of Mam Tor.'

To say that he initially hated his move to the countryside from London was an understatement. He thought he was being punished for his mother's death rather than his father, the real culprit. He longed to get back to the city and the VR cafes where he and his mates hung out battling alien warlords on some remote planet.

Instead of fire breathing dragons, he now only got to see sheep and more sheep and old people drinking tea and eating cakes, all just waiting to die. That summed up his feelings of country life, and he thought he would just sit back and join the queue to die like everyone else. But Uncle Vince was having none of that self-pitying nonsense.

'You need to build yourself up, Bailey. I've seen more life in a tramp's vest. We're going to have to do something about that.'

Despite being in his early sixties, Uncle Vince had lost only a little of the fitness he had gained in the army. From then on he decided he was going to give Bailey the benefit of his training. To his own surprise he actually enjoyed the gruelling workouts; jumping jacks, press-ups, crunches, and squats interspersed with weight training, all done outside in the fresh air, summer and winter.

The training sessions may have built his body, but it was the fell running that set his spirit free. The fifteen-kilometre circular route that Uncle Vince still ran most weeks was not the steepest in the Peaks but required stamina and sure footing to avoid twisting an ankle on the uneven ground. To evade the many tourists who flocked to the region, they always ran at daybreak before school. Starting nice and flat through pastureland, the trail gradually climbed across open moorland before rising sharply to Mam Tor's summit. Known as the 'Shivering Mountain' for the instability of its shale layers rather than any extreme temperature, it was nevertheless often very windy along the exposed ridges. They always carried a small rucksack with extra clothing, flasks of coffee, and bacon sandwiches.

***

Uncle Vince would not have been seen dead in a gym. He knew that for sure.

'Is my physio available?' Bailey asked the gym assistant.

'Good afternoon, Grey, nice to see you back again. Russell

Bains will be finished with his client in ten minutes. Would you like to wait?'

That name, Russell Bains, he'd seen it on one of the bio-stats logs. Russell's Host is Mike Jervis. They also had their mind clock hacked like himself. That must be why Grey wanted him to come here.

'I'll check out the running equipment. Please let Russell know where I am.'

'Of course. Grey, your kit has been laundered and is ready in the locker rooms.'

As he walked past a large glass viewing window on the way to the shower area, he stopped to observe those inside working up a sweat on the various pieces of equipment. Each person was a Dual like himself. What struck him as he watched was that it was impossible to know for sure who was a Host and who an Essential, who was *awake* and who *asleep,* despite all the assurances.

It felt strange wearing Grey's kit. Of course, everything fitted perfectly, but these were Grey's. Bailey felt being a Dual must be a bit like being an identical twin – wearing the same clothes might be cute for a while, but weird by the time you are in your thirties. He and Grey had very different tastes. The gaudy trainers he put on were a throwback to the 2020s, and frankly, he wouldn't be seen dead in them. *Thank God I'm asleep when you are walking about, Grey, that's all I can say.*

He stepped onto the running pad and put on the VR headset. There was a vast array of exotic locations he could have chosen from, but since the Peaks was not an option he selected fell running in the English Lake District. Intensity: Challenging.

It transported him to a rough trail that rose steeply to a ridge above Coniston Water. The running pad mimicked the uneven underfoot, forcing him to slow to a steady pace. It was an early morning autumn day and the mists hid the valley floor with just the higher crags peeking through. The weak sun bathed the bracken and heathers in amber light. His heart pounded with the effort and sweat streamed down into his eyes through a small gap in his visor.

For a moment or two he was captured, and maybe anyone else could have been forgiven for being fooled by the sumptuous settings the technology portrayed. But for Bailey it was a poor imitation. The breeze against his face was just a fan that lacked the subtle natural scents of the fells and did not bite through his layers of clothing like they should. The boggy ground never caused his feet to sink in that syrupy way he had experienced a thousand times. The peregrine falcon that flew above was far too willing to be spotted to be authentic.

A sense of loss overwhelmed him and he longed to run across the real fells once more, getting properly muddy and tired and cold and elated and awestruck at the pure beauty of his surroundings. He had denied himself this for the sake of the program and not wanting to risk injuring himself and, therefore, Grey. Being responsible for both of them had made him overly cautious, and he vowed there and then to go for a good run once he had sorted out the immediate problem.

He removed the headset to see Grey's physio, Russell, standing alongside. He knew Russell having had some treatments from him early on, but these days he preferred to do stretching on his own.

'Hey, how's the old rotator cuff? I hope you've been using those ice gel packs I gave you.'

'Errm, well actually, the shoulder's not too bad. I think a few more days' rest will do the trick.'

'I'll do a bit of loosening work on it if you like. It'll only take ten minutes.'

Bailey followed Russell to a small room at the side of the gym floor. Inside was a massage couch already prepared for the next client, and a glass display cabinet housed oils and various tools of the trade. On the walls hung posters depicting the human muscle groups. In the corner stood a full-size human skeleton. The room smelled strongly of lavender and peppermint and a mix of other heady scents that Bailey recognised but couldn't quite name.

'Remove your top and I'll take a look.'

Complying with Russell's instructions, Bailey went through a series of tests to identify any issues with his injured shoulder's range of movement.

It was over two years since he had his shoulder patched up at the naval base in Gibraltar and then flown back to the UK for surgery to save his arm. Weeks of intensive treatment followed, and now there was only the occasional twinge when he was doing press-ups. Grey, though, didn't have these memories, so he lacked awareness when working out, resulting in muscle tears more than once. Like all Essentials, Grey had to learn the Host body's capabilities and limitations and forget what his own brain thinks it knows.

Russell began some gentle stretching, coupled with some deep tissue massage, to loosen up the shoulder.

Although grateful for the treatment, he started to think his visit to the gym would not help him know what was going on. Until that was when Russell next spoke.

'I think that should help but apply some ice when you get back to your apartment. This isn't what you came here for though is it, Bailey? It is Bailey, isn't it?'

'Explain what exactly, and what makes you think I'm Bailey?' Bailey replied cautiously.

'Look, I don't need a scanner to work out you're not Grey. Your walking gait is more upright. Grey slouches. It's something we've been working on with him. You also know how to run, I was observing you on the pad. Grey still runs like the old man he was before becoming a Dual despite having your physique.'

'Impressive,' was Bailey's only response.

'Not really. Bodywork is what we do, and we are very good at what we do in our own ways. I'm pretty sure that's why we got on the program. What I do may not make me the Essential one in this partnership, but I'm sure Russell would bloody well miss me, the old fart.' At this he burst out laughing as he wiped the oils from his hands. His expression changed into a deep frown, and he lowered his voice to a whisper.

'Sorry, Bailey. I can see the confused look on your face. Surely you've worked it out by now. I'm Mike Jervis, Host to Russell Bains. This is fun, isn't it?'

Bailey knew that, given his own situation, he should not have been as surprised by this revelation as he was. *How many more,* he thought to himself. Right now he wasn't sure if having someone else in the same boat made him feel better or worse.

'And you both work here, in the gym?'

'Well, naturally. Russell is the real talent, although I would never tell him that to his face, if you know what I mean. He's already too much of a big head. Years of training and practice made him one of the top physios in the country. Worked for all the top sports teams at one time or another. Now he's the physio to all of us lovely Duals. You must know him?'

'It's been a while since I've had the need of a physio,' Bailey uttered, still processing this new information.

Mike continued talking at a fast pace. 'Me, I'm a sports massage therapist. Not quite in Russell's league, but I give a damn sight better massage than he does. That's how I got away with being Russell today, but I don't think I could carry it off for another week.'

'Have you spoken to anyone else about waking up early?'

'No. I wasn't sure what to do. You see, Grey sort of hinted this might happen.'

'He did? What else did Grey tell you?'

'He just told us both that if anything weird happens we should hang tight, don't raise it with anyone and wait for you to show up. We thought he was just kidding.'

'He told you both?'

'Yes. Ahh, I get it. You don't know. You see, we are on a different fortnightly cycle to you and Grey. That means I get to see Grey the first week of his cycle, and Russell gets to see him the second week.'

'But that means...' before he could finish, Mike completed his sentence for him.

'Yes, I've woken up slap in the middle of Russell's awake time.'

As the implications of this sank in for both of them, a tall and very irate woman entered the room.

'I'm guessing by the stupid looks on your faces I'm in the right place, so which one of you is going to tell me what the sweet Jesus is going on? Why am I still awake?'

ELEVEN

A Special Relationship

'AM I THE only one who thinks everyone else has gone mad?'

Heather struggled to know who to direct her question. Ignoring McNeil's floating head and torso, she turned to face those physically present in the room.

'Robert, Child, this has to be the worst joke ever, yes? I mean, it's totally ludicrous. You can see that, can't you? I really don't have to explain why this is such a dumb idea, do I? Was this your idea, Daniel? It's got to be because no one else would try to convince the US President that this was in any way feasible. My God, why do I get the feeling you're all taking this seriously?'

'That's enough, Heather,' came the response from Child. 'I appreciate that this has come as a bit of a shock, but I can assure you this is no joke.'

'But it has to be. We are barely into our second year of the project. We have just fourteen hundred people taking part with no idea of what the long-term outcomes will be.'

'And yet, Heather, here you are, living proof of what is possible,' chipped in Daniel Moccasin. 'Some might think you don't want to share this with the rest of the world. I wonder why that is. Are you hiding something from us?'

'Oh, for God's sake, you idiot, even you must see why this won't work. The numbers just don't stack up.' Heather's fingers tapped the table noisily as she spoke.

At the other end of the conference table, Robert cleared his throat to get everyone's attention.

'Child, how much has the government already shared with our American friends? Heather does have a valid point about the numbers being quoted.'

Heather was astonished at how Robert could be so calm in the face of this bullshit, but was nevertheless grateful that he was there to bring some sanity back into proceedings.

'Well, obviously, we have kept the US up to date with the program and of our longer-term intention to reduce the physical UK population to a more sustainable level. I may have suggested our goal is for a fifty per cent reduction over the next twenty years.'

'Just in time for the end of the world, apparently,' Heather suggested sarcastically.

At this Child turned to face her. 'Heather, you need to work with us on this. You knew from the outset where this was heading, so don't act now as if you didn't. If you think you are not the right person to be involved going forward, now is the time to say so.'

'You know we have our teams on standby, Doctor Child,' chirped Moccasin, a bit too enthusiastically.

Heather hoped that Child could see Moccasin's eagerness for what it was. Determined to remain composed and take back control of the situation, she countered, 'I am merely trying to sound a note of caution. The logistics are mind-boggling, but given we now have the US's assistance I'm confident I can scale up the technology to the next level. In fact, I've already started working on it.'

'I'm glad to see you're onboard, Heather, we will need you to lead on the global rollout.'

Taking his lead from her, Robert sought to assert the UK's leading role.

'I would think it best if Heather and myself explained more about the Duality Project to Daniel and how we go about finding suitable Hosts and Essentials.'

'I think that is a sensible idea. I would think it best if the Vice President and myself left you experts to it and ask you to report back to us.'

'Actually, Child, today is the last day of my wake cycle. I won't be around for another two weeks.'

'Sorry, Heather, I had forgotten. Then I suggest you make the most of the rest of today with Daniel. I'm sure Robert and Daniel will be able to brief us after the weekend.'

'Daniel has been cleared to stay in the UK until further notice,' said McNeil. 'To be clear, as I stated earlier, his brief is to confirm the validity of the results of the Duality Project. I'm sorry to be blunt, but if we are going to try to sell this idea to US citizens and the rest of the world, we've got to be darn sure that this is not a clever hoax. With all due respect to yourself, Doctor Bernard and other so-called Essentials, we need to know you are who you say you are and not some sophisticated copy and paste job.'

Child maintained the typical politician's poker face, ignoring the loaded comments from McNeil. 'Right then, I suggest Daniel gets settled in. Given Heather's absence, I need to brief her and Robert and report back to the PM.'

***

The guest quarters in The Facility were comfortably adequate, but nothing more. Daniel Moccasin was already missing the luxuries of his own home. *This place is like a homage to the 2030s,* he thought to himself as he studied the available environmental control options. Cosmic Bio-domes, rainforests, retro, and urban nights. *Well, that figures. Damn fine for the teenagers of twenty-five years ago.*

The room's walls, floor and ceiling, changed briefly as he hopped from one scene to another, contemptuous at how primitive the technology was; pre-full sensory; *definitely early '30s,* he concluded. He finally settled on what laughingly was described as New York Apartment Living. The walls turned into a full height glass and stainless-steel facade with a view over the old Central Park, when it existed as a natural park and not just a memory encoded into the AI.

As he looked out of the false windows at what was now a historical scene, he tried to remember the last time he actually set foot in the park. Being a born and bred New Yorker, Central Park played a huge role in his formative years. While watching ice hockey he met Dana and the park became their place to meet up without parental interventions and eventually fall in love.

Now, of course, anyone who could afford full sensory AR got to have the entire park in their home. He and his whole family had loved to share the boating lakes, picnic spots, ice rinks and running tracks without leaving their home. Not just some pixelated wall panels but a fully rendered augmented reality where they interacted with the other people who were visiting. He remembered how he and Dana savoured the alluring aroma of coffee and waffles dripping with maple syrup and the feel of the paths and grass underfoot as they explored in the comfort of their home. It was so very much safer in the AR park than the real thing ever was. Inevitably, when they and other middle-class families stopped visiting the real Central Park, it no longer made economic sense to spend millions of dollars on a facility just for the poor, so it reverted to the crime-ridden jungle of the twentieth century.

New times dictate new realities, and the giant aeroponic greenhouses that now covered all eight hundred acres of Central Park Farm contributed significantly to feeding the city, filling in for the falling yields transpiring in most traditional farms across the state.

Looking out at this ancient scene, he felt a pang of nostalgia and the taste of bitterness at the reminder of a place they visited daily. Ever since Dana had left him taking the kids, he could not face entering that fake fairy-tale world.

This arsewipe of a country is something else, he thought as he hung his suits into a cranky old wardrobe. Like the rest of the world, he'd seen the UK slowly turn into the basket case it was today. Ever since the '20s, it had pissed off every nation that could have helped them.

Everyone knew their trumpeted patriotic policy of self-sufficiency was forced on them, as they had few friends left when resources got tight. Now they had turned inwards and were left blaming their so-called 'Undeserving' for shortages of food and jobs.

What no one saw coming was how quietly they would give up their personal freedoms. Not even North Korea or China had dared to chip their entire populations, yet the nation that gave the world the Magna Carta didn't have to be forcibly dragged kicking and screaming into twenty-four hours of total surveillance. Even the Scots had fallen under the spell of the People's Council, deciding to rejoin the Union they had left only twelve years before.

No, amazingly, true to their stereotype, the world watched as the population queued up quietly at clinics.

If there was any dissent it was stamped out by publicly shaming individuals as unpatriotic. It seems the fear of being ostracised as a societal leper was enough to deter all, but the most determined, and those were efficiently dealt with.

Those early days are now long gone, and despite the UK's AI systems filtering all inbound and outbound network traffic, they had given him access to multiple intelligence reports which showed the country to be a tinder box waiting to explode. No one would have cared what happened to the UK had they not somehow pulled this incredible rabbit out of the hat.

How did she do it? That was what really grated on him. How did she beat him to the prize he had been working towards for years when he had all the resources and expertise of US Military Intelligence, and all they'd had was *this?*

The Village, with its more luxurious accommodation, would have been more to his liking, but he needed to be here at the heart of the Duality technology, and he was relishing the prospect of making the project his own. McNeil had promised him as much, and he intended to make sure that he delivered on his promise. The Brits had somehow stumbled onto something they couldn't possibly know the full value of. But he did, and so did McNeil and his friends. The refugee story was the perfect cover. Sure, they would save the world, or at least as much as they needed, but the bigger question was who they were saving it for. He smiled to himself at this thought.

What's a few weeks of roughing it when the ultimate prize is within reach?

***

Back in Robert's office, Heather's anger had turned to a cold wave of panic as Child made clear he expected herself, Robert and all staff and other Duals to convince the Americans that Duality was not a con.

'I'm sorry for calling you out just then, Heather, I hope you can see it was for show.'

'You were very convincing,' Heather replied curtly. 'You

realise Moccasin will attempt to take over the entire project?'

Ignoring her warnings, Child continued, 'Look, I don't like the situation any more than you do, but the reality is the US has threatened to withdraw all military support from the UK if we don't play ball. This would leave us seriously exposed to waves of uncontrolled migration and even the prospect of invasion. It isn't just the Americans who've realised the UK will be in the green zone. Everyone will soon see our island as some sort of Garden of Eden compared to most other places.'

'So not as self-sufficient as we claim,' Heather sneered.

'Our nuclear deterrent is useless in the present crisis, and our weaponised drones are vastly outnumbered by those of the European or Russian armies. As I've mentioned before, I deal with realities. If the US were to walk away, how long do you think it would be before we had Russian or even European warships coming up the Thames? Duality was to be the promise of sustainable good times for us in the UK, but if we are not careful we could end up either occupied or flooded with refugees, or both. The Americans have promised military support for the next fifty years. They will also ensure that we will be exempted from taking in climate evacuees, unlike other green zone countries. We will be free to pursue our own Duality program for our own citizens. This will be our reward for providing the technology and leading the rollout of Duality across the globe.'

'Are we not rushing into something which we cannot fully know the outcome of?' Heather recognised her pleadings were pointless; the decision had already been made.

'That's just it, Heather. We have ignored this problem for decades, hoping it will just go away. Well, the games up I'm afraid.'

'Okay, but at the risk of asking an obvious question, why would the US honour their promises once they have the technology?'

'I said we have to play ball, I wasn't suggesting we play fairly. Heather, I want you and Robert to ensure the Americans are convinced of your fantastic achievement and that without the UK's continuing expertise running the global rollout for the foreseeable future, there is no project. We need to make the UK seen to be completely indispensable. Otherwise, as you say, we will probably get screwed.'

Heather moved her attention to Robert who seemed lost in his own thoughts. 'Robert, you knew this was coming, didn't you?'

'Yes, but I don't have to like the mad rush any more than you do. What's that American expression? Oh yes, caught between a rock and a hard place. But if anyone could pull this off, then you can, and if we get this right here in the UK, then maybe there is a chance for everyone everywhere.'

'Thank you, Robert. I appreciate the vote of confidence. However, we still have the immediate problem I've already mentioned. I am at the end of my two-week cycle. Tomorrow Quinn will be awake. I won't be here to chaperone our US guest.'

'Well, what about using Quinn?' suggested Child. 'She is an excellent journalist, has a large domestic and international following and is ideally placed to be the Face of Duality. We can ask her to show Moccasin around enough of The Facility to convince him that what we have is real without revealing all of our secrets. I propose we have some of our very bright but less capable technicians giving him the grand tour, with Quinn keeping a watchful eye. This will serve to illustrate your unique importance, Heather.'

Heather knew when she was being soft-soaped. 'What do you mean by the Face of Duality?' She also had a good idea now where this was going already, so she was unsurprised by the response.

'Just that, Heather. We will need a full-on PR campaign to persuade our population to get ready for accepting Duality as a fact of life. It's one thing getting 1,400 volunteers who each have been through a rigorous selection process and offered massive incentives to sign up, but I suspect it will take a lot more when we make it government policy and a legal requirement to sign up.'

When Robert offered no challenge to Child's plan Heather yielded to the inevitable. 'Okay, okay, I know when I'm beaten. I will brief Quinn fully on what we have discussed. I'm sure given her reasons for volunteering to be my Host and her passionate reporting of the refugee migrations, she won't take much convincing.'

'That's settled then,' said Child, very obviously pleased with himself. 'I will update the PM. One last thing, Heather. You and Quinn are the most valuable people in the country right now, no offence, Robert. I'll make sure security is stepped up for yourself and for all Duals, but you'll need to be vigilant and make sure Quinn understands this as well. We wouldn't want you being smuggled out of the country, would we?'

As they left the room, Heather realised this whole day had been meticulously planned by Child and that she and Quinn were just pawns in a transatlantic game where the stakes couldn't be higher.

TWELVE

A Worry Shared

'I PREFER STEPH or even Stephie, but definitely not Stephanie which sounds just too much "rich girl", if you know what I mean? Which I'm not, by the way, rich that is. Obviously, I'm doing a lot better now that I'm a Dual, but I've never had a silver spoon or would even know what to do with one if I had one. Sorry, I'm blathering I know, but this is stressing me out. Everything was going so well.'

'That's okay, Steph,' Bailey said. 'It's come as a shock to all of us. We just need to figure out why it's happened to us and what to do next.'

It was apparent none of them had the faintest idea why they would be awake, out of sync. Steph explained she had received a VR call from Grey a week ago, asking for her help in the matching algorithm he was working on for the Duality IT team. He claimed her background as a statistician would be immensely useful.

'It was an odd call,' Steph started. 'I didn't know Grey or the work he was involved in, but he seemed to know a lot about me. I guess that's because he helped match all of us Hosts with Essentials. He must know a lot about everyone involved. When he explained he needed someone to verify his latest work, I was taken aback. My skills had been incorporated into the AI years ago, so I thought what the heck would he need my help for? What could I possibly do that he couldn't get some bot to do in seconds? I was intrigued, and I thought it would be fun to use my brain for a change. I can't tell you how dull checking out dates on the Datasphere can be.'

'I certainly wouldn't be happy with doing something I didn't feel passionate about,' Mike interjected. 'You tell them you want something more stimulating, hun, that's why you became a Host, right?'

'Oh, I don't have to do it, I know, but it suits me right now while me and Lucinda get to know each other. Besides, my supervisor is a cutie, so it does have an upside.'

Irritated by the conversation getting sidetracked, Bailey jumped in.

'Come on, guys, let's focus on the matter at hand. Tell us what happened with Grey.'

'He sent me the data he was working with and the algorithm he was using to match potential Essentials and Hosts. From what I can tell the methodology looks sound, but you'd need to be a rocket scientist to understand the data.'

'Or a brain surgeon, perhaps?' Bailey suggested.

'Yeah, maybe. Anyway, I called Grey to explain and he said to hold on to things and someone would be in touch who could help out. That was two days ago and I've heard nothing since.'

'Is Lucinda your Essential?' Bailey asked.

'Yeah, she's a lovely lady. We mostly get on well.'

'What is Lucinda's qualification for being an Essential?'

'She is, or more correctly was, one of the country's leading lawyers specialising in human rights. From what she's told me, she was not expecting to be chosen as an Essential for the project as she had been a fierce critic of the Citizen Implant, often representing clients who refused to be chipped. But somehow, she was asked to take part in drafting the Duality Protocol and impressed everyone involved. To cut a long story short, she suffered a bad stroke before completing her work and ended up inside my head.'

'You still haven't explained why you're here today. I've never seen you or Lucinda in the gym before,' Mike inquired.

'Lucinda left me a message saying she was concerned about our declining fitness levels and said she wanted me to check out the gym today. I was a bit annoyed at first. I may not use the gym, but any decline in fitness was not down to me. But then I thought she must have got mixed up on the dates as I was due to go into sleep cycle today. When I woke up again this morning, I knew something was very wrong. The house assistant called me Lucinda and reminded me of Lucinda's appointment here at the gym. I had to come to check it out.'

'To be honest, guys, despite Grey's warning, when the house assistant called me Russell it freaked me out,' Mike said. 'I thought I might end up back in the lab with my skull open and those guys in those dreadful white boiler suits poking around looking for a loose wire.'

Whether he meant to be funny or not, both Bailey and Steph laughed out loud at Mike's confession. At first Mike looked perplexed by their reaction, but seeing the funny side joined in with the laughter.

The tension that had been building in the room had found a temporary release. Bailey was the first to bring the mood down again. 'It seems to me both Grey and Lucinda are working together on this charade,' Bailey declared. 'I'm not sure if Russell is also complicit, but best to assume all three are involved.'

'Involved in what?', 'Involved in what?' Mike and Steph asked in unison.

'I cannot be certain, but the facts seem to point to our Essentials orchestrating our meeting up today as they need our help.'

'Why didn't they just leave us a message?' Mike quizzed.

'Because, Mike, I suspect they have somehow unearthed a plot to control the one thing that was guaranteed to be beyond anyone's ability to hack, namely our mind clocks. If you can make Hosts and Essentials wake and sleep at will, maybe you could choose not to wake someone up at all.'

'Sweet Jesus, fucking body snatchers,' Steph's fearful whisper escaped her lips as the blood visibly drained from her face.

THIRTEEN

Death and Rebirth

FLASHES OF COLOUR emerge from nothingness. Electric greens, blues and reds explode across her visual cortex. Slowly and painfully, without her consent, the world starts to reassemble, and as it does the tranquillity of nothingness recedes into the distance.

The young girl, carrying the family's water, trips, spilling precious drops onto bone dry ground. Like she always does.

The earth no longer has any use for this gift but takes it anyway, sucking it into the sun-baked sand. As she stumbles their eyes meet fleetingly, a lingering second at most, but enough for her to feel the fear held within. The next water station is still three-days march away.

A woman... herself, helps the girl up from the ground. She rearranges the makeshift sling hanging loosely by the child's side, securing the aluminium urn as best she can. Like she always does.

Wait, there is something wrong with this procession. Not the exhausted men, women, and children. Something is missing. Where are the elderly, the sick? What has happened to them?

And still they come. Like they always do.

Must stay objective. Must keep focused. She knows that she is here to witness, to report, to make the world see. But the world has seen already. Too much, maybe. They know all of this already. What is she doing here?

A minute, a day, a week passes by. Time has no hold here.

So close now. The smell of the sea. She feels the anticipation rising within those who have made it this far. It is almost dusk; the light is starting to fade, but they begin to walk faster, forcing their reluctant bodies to take those extra steps, and families gather close together to avoid getting separated. Some try to gain an advantage by moving up the line. Then, up ahead, a commotion.

It starts again. Like it always does.

Angry, unintelligible screaming. Then gunfire. Then screaming. People running in all directions as the men on the large open-sided truck open fire with automatic weapons. They look the same, those who kill and those who are being killed. Only a yellow neckerchief worn by each of those with a rifle in their hands marks them apart.

She wants to help. She needs to help, but her legs won't respond. She screams silently, helplessly. Bodies are falling around her. They see her and they see the drone above her head filming, recording, bearing witness. They stop firing and run at her. She is surrounded. Still, her body refuses to move. Her feet are stuck in the morasses of her nightmare.

'Hey, friends, look, we have an English spy,' spits the man with the cap. 'What do you think you're doing bringing them here? There is no place for them. Take them back, or we will shoot each and every one of them.' The tip of the barrel of his weapon pushes into her stomach.

'*No soy inglegsa, no soy inglegsa*,' she shouts again and again, but this is not a day for polite misunderstandings. His eyes are fixed on the logo of the *Gibraltar Chronicle* stitched onto her jacket.

'What do you think you are doing in my country if not spying for your colonial masters, the treacherous English?'

'I am just a reporter,' she shouts, 'the world needs to see what is happening in Algeria and the rest of Africa so that they wake up and do something about it.'

'I am already doing something about it,' he shouts back into her face, his finger on the trigger of his rifle.

'They are just people like you,' she pleads. 'You are murdering innocent women and children.'

'No one is innocent in this world. They come and steal our food and water. Do you think we have such an abundance we can tolerate this? No, we too are hungry and thirsty.'

'I am Spanish, you can see that. I have no love for the English.'

'Maybe, maybe not. It does not matter to me. Spanish, English, you are all the same. They close their borders and turn away everyone from entering their continent. But still, they like to watch us in our misery on their big screens and pretend they are shocked. Okay, if that's what you want then we give everyone a big show, you and me. I will make us both famous.'

They grab her, bind her hands and throw her in the back of the truck. One of the gunmen takes the drone controls from her jacket, guiding the hovering camera into his hands. He looks into the lens, smiles and raises his arms in triumph.

A rifle butt hits her face and she passes out. Like she always does.

The taste of blood in her mouth greets her as she wakes. She is in a large tent, her hands still tied. To her left, right and behind her are other captives, bound and gagged. They are wearing the jackets of Red Crescent workers. Facing them are the walkers guarded by men and women with rifles. They are all kneeling, hands behind their heads. In the front row is the young girl who spilt the water. The urn is gone and strangely so is the look of fear from her face. It is replaced instead by a sadness, a resignation to her fate.

The man with the cap shakes me. 'Hey, English Spanish lady, is your filming live?'

She hesitates, terrified of the madness she sees in his eyes. He slaps her around the face, bringing fresh blood to accompany the dried remnants from before.

'Please, lady, don't fuck with me. Is your filming live?'

'Yes, everything is streamed back to the office in Gibraltar. But they choose whether to broadcast or not. It's not down to me.'

'My men tell me they have seen nothing on the newscasts. Only the usual shit, begging wealthy English and American bastards to send money to us poor people in Africa. So sad! I think maybe you also give money to Africa's poor children. Is that true? Are you a Spanish saint? Should we bow down?'

'I am trying to help, that's all. Please let these people go. They don't mean you any harm.'

'But they are doing us harm and I intend stopping it today. You say you want to help, well you will help by showing what happens if any more walkers come to my country. And you will help by showing what will happen to any spies like you or these Red Crescent workers that come here illegally.'

The gunman who took the drone stands up, and the drone lifts above the kneeling refugees, the red flashing light indicating filming in progress. He navigates the small device to hover in front of the face of their leader.

'Hey, world, glad you can join me. My name is Basem, and I've been wanting to talk to you for some time. The people of Algeria are no longer prepared to deal with the problems you have created. These walkers you see behind me believe they will cross the sea to Europe to escape the desert. They think you will welcome them with open arms. But your robot boats are too quick for their dinghies, and you force them back onto our shore. No, you do not shoot them, do you? You are far too civilised for such barbarity. So now thousands line our beaches and we have no choice but to defend ourselves and our families. We can no longer let them steal our food and water while we suffer hunger and thirst.'

The drone turns and hovers over the front row of the kneeling refugees. Two men with rifles take aim. Two other armed men at the back prevent anyone from fleeing.

She screams as the rapid hammer sound of bullets tears into the flesh of the men, women and children in the front row. The girl looks at her as the bullet enters her chest and she spills the last of her life. Like she always does.

'Stop. Stop. Please, dear God, stop.'

'Hey, world, I guess you know now this is real, that I am not bluffing. But I'm not so sure that you care if I shoot all the walkers. I wonder if you feel the same about the others we have here. In one hour, we will kill the Red Crescent workers and so on until you have the guts to show this on your live newscast. If you do this, those who are still alive will be freed to go back to their own country. But first, just to show you we do not discriminate, we have a special show.'

As he speaks the drone turns to face her, gliding within a few feet.

'You send spies to help the walkers. We will show you what happens when we catch them.'

No, please, God no. She knows she has only seconds to live. Her heart races, her breathing is rapid and shallow. She tries to free her hands to no effect, and even if she could, there is nowhere to run or hide.

He takes his rifle, and as the drone circles above him she yields to her fate.

'*Querida Jesús ayúdame,*' Quinn whimpers as she is reborn once more.

FOURTEEN

Millie's Dream Job

DESPITE HER FATHER'S ongoing appeals, becoming a nurse was not an option as far as she was concerned. Not if she was going to make a real difference. It was almost as if she had known from an infant what she needed to do. Getting a first-class degree was an important step, but it would amount to nothing unless she could get inside The Facility.

Before the announcement took place she was still not sure what to study or where. Her father had wanted her to take a nursing degree, so said she should concentrate her efforts on biology and technology. Although excelling in both of these subjects, Millie felt pressured by her father and resisted his suggestions. But then came the announcement which changed everything. On the evening of Thursday, August 1, 2052, the Prime Minister addressed the nation, and from then on she knew precisely what she needed to study and how to keep her father sweet at the same time.

***

'Fellow UK citizens. As your Prime Minister I am here before you with a unique and compelling invitation to each of you to help us complete the task you set us to make our great nation self-sufficient.

'We embarked on this grand voyage twenty years ago, a project that no one thought in the international community that this country would have the guts to undertake. But we are brave and have proved all doubters wrong.

'If we continue to commit fully to the logic of our mission, we will ensure continuing prosperity and that it will be we UK citizens, that hold sovereignty over our nation's resources. History has taught us that we cannot be held hostage to fortune or to the whims of foreign powers that do not have our best interests at heart.

'By your sustained efforts, we have dramatically increased our manufacturing capability so that now we produce ninety per cent of everything we need, from medicines to communications networks, from hydrogen-powered vehicles to the best designer clothing. Your enthusiasm for, and acceptance of, automation has achieved all of this. We are world leaders in Artificial Intelligence, and you should rightly be proud of this. Because of this success, I am confident the final ten per cent is within our grasp, making us the first totally self-sufficient nation on the planet.

'Not only this, but Britain is still the destination of choice for the tourists of the world, and we welcome them with open arms to our glorious country. Yet, with the fantastic success of the Citizen Implant program, we can be confident that no one outstays their welcome.

'I recognise becoming self-sufficient in food has meant foregoing certain pleasures, but in true British spirit many of you have risen to the challenge. With our excellent improving climate, many things previously impossible to grow now thrive in the UK. On my way to Westminster, I see outstanding examples of city farms demonstrating our inherent ingenuity and resilience when we have a shared purpose, a shared vision.

'However, our success has brought new challenges, which is where I need to be honest with you. As we get closer to our shared goal to automate our economy, more and more citizens lack the skills to offer anything useful back to society. Yes, we are committed to retraining anyone who loses their job due to AI, and there are many success stories, but it is sadly becoming more often the case that retraining is futile and a life living off the state beckons.

'Unfortunately, this undermines the efforts of those who have embraced new roles in support of the AI economy.

'We are a small island, and going forward it will be impossible to sustain a population of eighty million where one in two adults of working age is unemployed. It is patently an unfair burden on those who keep the country going to support those who cannot shoulder their fair share.

'But what if there were only forty million mouths to feed instead of eighty million? With an automated economy, ample food production and rewarding jobs for all who wanted one, these forty million would surely live like kings.

'How could we achieve this, I hear you say? Many of you have taken up our generous offer of sterilisation for the sake of future generations, and we rightly call you "Truly Deserving" and reward you accordingly. No, I am not proposing mandatory sterilisation, nor am I suggesting resettlement of large numbers to the southern colonies.

'We can achieve this by genuinely sharing our lives. The truth is our exceptional scientists have made a breakthrough that will change the course of human history forever, and I am now asking for courageous individuals to come forward to be pioneers in this revolution. These individuals and their families will immediately be recognised as "Truly Deserving" and will enjoy exceptional benefits.

'Tonight, I am announcing the start of the Duality Body Sharing Project.'

The speech went on some more as the Prime Minister attempted to explain the outrageously bizarre project. He handed over to Doctor Child, who had so far been sitting silently throughout the proceedings. Specially briefed journalists asked prepared questions that sought to reassure people that the UK's leader had not gone insane and that this was not a hoax.

'As the Prime Minister has indicated, we are looking for volunteers to be Hosts to the leading minds who are essential to our country's ongoing success. It will be vital we do not lose critical human expertise as we incorporate all knowledge into the AI. We will determine who these essential minds are and find compatible Hosts. Together they will form a unique bond, a lifelong symbiotic relationship, and as the Prime Minister has just outlined will be rewarded for their selfless act.' From then on Child always used the terms 'Host' and 'Essential' when describing the individuals who took part in the project.

***

The following evening at the dinner table, Millie made her own announcement.

'Mum, Dad, I've been thinking about what you've both said and I've decided to do what you suggest. I'm going to concentrate on science and tech subjects next year. It looks like they'll be needing all sorts of people with the right qualifications if this Duality Project takes off.'

'That's great to hear, Millie. I'm sure they will need nurses more than ever for anyone crazy enough to take up the PM's offer.'

Her father, now suitably placated, Millie began devouring everything there was to read on neuroscience. One person's work stood out as being head and shoulders above the crowds in its scope and vision, with numerous research papers, lectures and books on the subjects of cellular and molecular biology and neuroanatomy: Doctor Heather Bernard, current Head of Neuroscience at the Sheffield Research Facility.

Millie's work placement assignment two years ago as part of her degree course in the prosthetic memory labs at The Facility was so tantalisingly close to her goal of working for Doctor Bernard on the Duality Project. It was a disappointment for her that she didn't get to meet her secret mentor at that time. Still, she impressed those she worked with sufficiently to receive a conditional offer of a job based on her getting the appropriate degree and passing security vetting.

Now, the day after graduation, in her inbox, she had received a personal message from Doctor Bernard. The time log indicated that it was sent late last night. It remained unopened. Logic dictated that it must be confirmation of the job offer. Why else would she take the time to correspond with her? But maybe, despite her first-class degree, they had changed their minds and were only being professional in sending a personalised communication. It was stupid speculating like this when all she had to do was play the message, but this was the most pivotal moment in her life. If it were bad news she had no plan B and she would not be able to save the planet.

Thinking these thoughts, she recognised the inherent arrogance of her conviction that she alone could save the world, but she had played it out a thousand times in her head and knew if she got the chance it would change everything.

'Play message from Doctor Bernard.'

She was taken aback by the image that confronted her. A stunningly good-looking woman in her thirties, with an olive complexion, looked out from the VR viewer in her bedroom.

'Good day, Millie, I am Doctor Heather Bernard, head of neurosciences at the Sheffield Research Centre. Apologies that I cannot yet meet with you in person, but I will explain why in just a moment.

'Firstly, many congratulations on gaining your degree. It is a genuinely exceptional achievement at any age, but at eighteen, I can only imagine the hard work you put in. However, despite what our parents tell us, hard work only gets us so far. I'm sure you know this already. Clearly, you must also know you are a very gifted and unique individual.

'I can imagine you may be somewhat confused by my appearance if you've seen any of my old lectures. I've had confirmation of your security vetting clearance, so I can disclose to you that not only do I lead the neuroscience department, I am both the lead researcher and one of the first Essential volunteers on the government's Duality Project.'

Doctor Bernard paused in her message at this moment, as if she knew this news would require time to process. Millie's reaction was to laugh out loud and shout, 'I knew it, I bloody well, fucking well knew it.' *Thank God this isn't a real-time call*, she thought as she laughed uncontrollably.

'Millie, what's going on up there?' her mother shouted from the lounge.

'Sorry, Mum, just watching an old movie. I'll keep the noise down.'

Doctor Bernard continued with her message.

'Millie, you are now officially employed to work on the Duality Project. I'm sure this is what you must want, but you need to know that you would have been seconded to this project with your qualifications in any case. As such, you are bound by the strictest of confidentiality laws and will be subject to enhanced monitoring accordingly.

'Your talents will be vital in the coming months, and I look forward to catching up with you in person in two weeks when I am next awake. Meanwhile, Robert Collins, our Senior Director of Operations, will contact you about when and where to report for work.'

Millie played the message back four more times, pausing the playback each time to study the face of a genius. What other words could you use to describe her achievement? And to have the balls to volunteer to be part of the experiment that you had created. Literally mind-blowing. Millie's admiration for Doctor Bernard jumped several notches.

As she settled on the suit that she would wear for her first day at work, one prevailing thought occupied Millie's mind.

Doctor Bernard, I really hope I don't end up killing you.

FIFTEEN

Tears and Fears

HE WATCHED OVER her as she relived the nightmare yet again. It was five cycles ago that she last awoke into the hell of her captivity to rewitness the death of the young girl and other climate refugees.

He knew not to wake her while her brain and body were getting reacquainted. He had done this only once. Quinn's screams of anguish and confusion at being forcibly woken before her rescue frightened the life out of him. 'I'm dead, I'm dead,' she wailed repeatedly. Her bio-stats must have been off the scale since medics were at their apartment door within minutes.

At that time, he was so thankful that they monitored all Duals twenty-four by seven. Handover day was the 'big event' for the scientists who watched and recorded their progress. For the first six months they underwent complete diagnostic checks for every reawakening at the on-site clinic.

Looking back, it was remarkable how few problems there had been for either him or Grey. Meeting up with other Duals in the social room, it seemed that everyone was adapting fine. Of course, there may have been issues that only the docs knew about, but the technology worked perfectly as far as he was concerned.

It was only what he called his own sensory reorientation that had taken time for him to adjust to. His surgeon had asked him to explain what he meant by sensory reorientation, so he had tried to describe how awakening after being asleep for two weeks was entirely different from the normal waking up everyone experienced every day.

'First off,' he had started, 'there is the weight of your body. From being in zero gravity one moment, to the full force of 3G the next. Like a rollercoaster ride, it makes your stomach feel like it's about to come out of your mouth.

'Second, you notice the taste of your own tongue, not the

taste of the meal the other one had had the night before, but the actual *taste* of your own tongue. It's like when you've got someone else's tongue in your mouth but nowhere near as much fun.

'Third is the noise of my own breath. It sounds like I'm in some horror movie with an asthmatic ghost floating over the bed.

'Finally, the hard-on, and not just the usual morning thing but something to be proud of but also quite painful.'

This last revelation had amused the docs, but coupled with the other sensations it made for an unwelcome cocktail.

'How long would you say these sensations last?' the doc had queried.

'It's hard to say for sure. Everything is a bit of a muddle, just like normal waking, but I would say thirty minutes or so. Is this normal?'

'These symptoms pretty much align with what we would expect from anyone waking from a medically induced coma, which is essentially what you are in for fourteen days. We expect over time they will lessen, but it may just be something Hosts have to live with.'

He'd now become accustomed to the weirdness of awakening, but Quinn seemed to find it much more difficult. Her repeating nightmare had started before the procedure, and it was touch and go whether she would pass the medical evaluation that they subjected all Hosts to.

His unit had been in Algiers for a couple of months as part of a European task force to assess the growing unrest, work which still required boots on the ground as they built the trust of the local Algerian People's Armed Forces.

Their goal was to disrupt the activities of the people traffickers and close down refugee routes into Spain and Gibraltar. It soon became apparent to him and his boss, Major Peters, that whatever measures they took would only delay an exodus that was gaining momentum.

They received word of a particularly nasty Algerian militia group targeting refugees near the coast a couple of miles from the capital. Orders arrived to assist the local forces with intelligence gathering but not to engage, leaving that delight for the Algerian forces.

While they were en route, they received word of the capture of up to thirty Red Crescent workers close to their position. The recon drones were sent out, and it didn't take long to spot the tent compound four miles north, near a secluded beach where the hostages had been taken. Six gunmen held the captives, four were patrolling the tent's perimeter, and two were inside with the hostages.

The data was relayed to the Algerian command, and that was going to be that for his unit. But then onboard sensors detected automatic weapon fire coming from a large area of scrub to their left. They pulled up off the road to assess the situation. The journalist's footage of the killings and her capture was routed through to them. The video's coordinates pinpointed the location to be less than two miles away.

'Well, everyone, it looks like we will be late for supper,' Major Peters exclaimed. 'You'll be delighted to learn the journalist is a Gibraltarian and therefore her safety comes under the remit of our standing orders. Time to utilise some of this so-called smart tech we've brought along with us. Sanchez, get Robocop ready, and Harris, send the recon drones out again. We need to confirm if this Basem character is part of the same group holding the Red Crescent workers.'

Robocop was actually another drone but fitted with two fully automated machine guns that targeted anyone carrying a non-registered weapon. Unlike the old movie, this Robocop, once activated, gave no warning and could, in theory, take out forty enemy combatants in under five seconds. However, theory was not reality and deploying the drone anywhere near the hostages would, just like the movie, most likely result in unwanted casualties. Besides, the model they were carrying could not identify other weapons such as knives and grenades, so human eyes were still needed for now.

'Sir,' Harris called out as he watched live images from the recon drones, 'we have five more armed assailants with a group of twenty-five prisoners. Heading to the tent compound. They'll arrive in seven minutes. I can't identify the journalist.'

'Shit. Okay, thank you, Harris. Let's go dark and get there ASAP. Find somewhere close, but we need this to be a surprise.'

'I've found the perfect spot one fifty metres from the perimeter. ETA eleven minutes.'

With the navigation system put into stealth mode they continued across the scrub, both unseen and unheard.

It was agreed Robocop would be deployed against those on patrol outside the tent with Sanchez as backup. Harris would stay with the vehicle in the event they needed its full firepower. That meant he and Major Peters would have to neutralise the threat inside the tent.

Then as they approached their destination, live footage from inside the tent was played on their monitors, and they were forced to watch helplessly as the hostages were mown down.

There was no time to finesse their plan, no time to worry if they would get to eat supper that night at all. Leaving the vehicle, he and Peters used their night visors to get within spitting distance of the tent, while Sanchez sent the armed drone high above the compound.

Having routed the live footage to their headsets, they could see Basem getting ready to shoot the journalist.

'Go, Sanchez, go!' ordered Peters.

As the six patrolling gunmen were efficiently taken out, Bailey and Peters stormed the tent. Basem turned in time to see Peters kill the two guards at the back. That left just Basem and two others at the front. The hostages panicked, fleeing the tent and causing Peters to lose sight of the remaining gunmen.

Meanwhile, he still had eyes on Basem, who was training his rifle on the journalist. She was kneeling, transfixed, as though she were about to receive communion instead of a bullet.

In one motion he raised and fired, finding his target's head. Then a volley of bullets hit him hard in the shoulder, the force of the impact taking him off his feet. The two other gunmen were bearing down on him, and had either of them shot there and then he would have been finished, but the sight of the dead leader caused them to hesitate just long enough for Peters to fire. They fell next to Basem.

Fifteen minutes later, a squad of Algerian troops arrived. They and several million others had watched the entire drama live. Quinn's drone still hovered ten feet above their heads.

Bailey understood that for whatever reason, it wasn't his time to meet his maker that day. He also understood God would be exacting a heavy price to pay for his reprieve.

They were flown back to Gibraltar where Bailey had emergency surgery to save his arm. Quinn's physical injuries were minor, but she was deeply traumatised. The medics felt that both should be taken to the UK for specialist care.

The rescue's video footage had gone viral, catapulting Bailey, Quinn and Peters into instant worldwide fame, which the UK government had yet to work out how best to exploit. Despite Gibraltar's citizens not currently being required to have the Citizen Implant, Quinn's Gibraltar passport still entitled her to enter the UK. The following day they flew into Heathrow and from there to St George's Hospital in London via air ambulance.

Quinn opened her tear-filled eyes to feel Bailey lying next to her, his muscular arms holding her tight.

'I gotcha,' he whispered.

'It was so real, Bailey. More real than when I was there on that day. Why do I have the same nightmare time and time again? Why do I never get to see you shoot Basem?'

'By my reckoning it has been five cycles since you last awakened into that place. That's the longest gap yet. The docs are sure they will stop. We just have to have faith.'

'I wish I could believe them. I just don't understand why it is only on the first night.'

'Do you remember before the procedure? You were having the nightmare most nights.'

'I know, but somehow it has become more vivid, even more cruel. I think one day you will not be there to rescue me, and if I die there I will die here. Besides, my body does not really need me anymore.'

'That won't happen, darling, I swear. And for your information, I need you.'

As they lay together in silence, Bailey had his own demons to contend with. He knew he had to tell Quinn about waking a day early and about the others. But how could he explain what had happened with Heather? What did Quinn just say about her body not needing her anymore? If he confessed to his 'accidental' lovemaking with Heather, that would prove her point.

The piano line began right on cue at 08:00, followed by the organ and glockenspiel. Bailey, already awake, was angry with himself for thinking Quinn would have changed their wake-up song for some poor imitation of a rainforest. Despite her general dislike of the genre, Quinn agreed that the near six-minute introduction piece to 'Tubular Bells' was the perfect antidote to being asleep for two weeks. Much later, when he had explained the role of the music in a movie about demonic possession, she laughed and teased him mercilessly.

'See where your love of rock music has got you, Bailey? You invited the devil in, and now we too are possessed.'

He now wondered if that light-hearted remark was prescient given Steph's cry of 'body-snatchers'.

'I need to go for a walk, Bailey. Somewhere I can clear my head and not just around The Village. Why don't you show me where you were brought up? It's near to here, right?'

'Great minds think alike. I didn't realise how much I'd missed the Peaks until…'

'Until what, Bailey?'

He had stopped himself just in time from saying 'yesterday', wanting the right moment to explain what was going on.

'…until this morning, lying awake and thinking about Uncle Vince. It's a brilliant idea, we've been cooped up in this apartment for too long. We'll need to inform security, they'll get us a vehicle.'

Quinn's sombre mood instantly lifted. 'I'll pack a picnic and some nice wine. Well, English wine anyway,' she laughed.

'Didn't you know Derbyshire is the new Rioja!' countered Bailey.

'*Jamás*, no matter how warm it gets here, we Spanish have centuries of expertise and tradition. But I agree English wine has improved a lot,' she said in a half-serious tone, 'it's so good for brushing your teeth with.'

Their faces both lit up at the repartee, a reminder that one of the reasons they fell so much in love was their shared sense of humour.

They had had plenty of time to discover each other while convalescing in separate wards in St George's. Apart from the obvious physical attraction, they both used humour to make sense of an ever more crazy world. They knew that neither could return to the lives they had just been saved from, but equally could never have anticipated just how much they would be willing to sacrifice in the hope of making the world a little less insane.

'Bailey, are you going to check Grey's handover message? I know I should check Heather's, but I just want today to be for us.'

'We can do it together this evening. Today we just bunk off,' Bailey replied, grateful for the suggestion. 'Peters, connect me with security.'

'Security, how can I help?'

'Good morning. We are going out of The Village today and need a vehicle.'

'Is the vehicle for just you, Mr Kennedy?'

'No, it's for myself and Ms Diaz.'

'Sorry, Mr Kennedy, but I have a note to say Ms Diaz must be accompanied by an armed guard if leaving the perimeter of the compound. I need to check who's available. What time are you thinking of going out?'

'What are you talking about? Who said Quinn needed an armed guard? What's going on?' Bailey tried not to sound too alarmed but feared this must have some connection with his situation. He couldn't imagine what that could be, but it could not be a coincidence.

Emerging from the kitchen, Quinn's previously smiling face was replaced by one of fear. 'Bailey, what did he just say about an armed guard?'

'Sorry, Ms Diaz, but we need to get someone to accompany you if you're going out. The order came in yesterday. Apparently, Ms Bernard should have explained the situation to you.'

'I want to go out on my own. Ms Bernard does not get to

interfere. It's my time now. Do you understand?' Quinn, clearly upset, looked at Bailey for backup.

'Please, Ms Diaz, I'm just following orders–'

'Who gave the order?' Bailey interrupted.

'It came from the Board of Population's office, Doctor Child. I guess that's just about as high up as you can get these days.'

'Peters, disconnect the call.' Quinn commanded.

As the face disappeared, Quinn regained some of her composure. 'Bailey, I'm scared, but I'm also furious. This goes against everything they promised. It goes directly against the agreement we made and the Protocol itself.'

Feeling as though events were overtaking him, Bailey knew he had to act. Facing Quinn, he moved in close. 'I'm so sorry about all this darling…' and before she had time to react he opened his arms and wrapped them around her as if to comfort her, but as he did he whispered directly into her ear, 'I was awake yesterday. I think we are both in danger.' Then pulling away, he resumed '…there'll be another chance to go for a picnic. It looks like right now you need to play Heather's messages to see what the hell is going on.'

Quinn studied Bailey's face. He hoped she could see he had gone back to his training and was in survival mode. Were they being watched or listened to? He couldn't be sure, but better to assume so for now.

'It's just that I was really looking forward to spending the day with only you and me. But you're right, there'll be plenty of other days.' She pressed his hand, and he knew she understood that now was not the time to lose it.

'Peters, play my messages from Ms Bernard,' Quinn commanded, a steely resolve transforming her face.

SIXTEEN

Away From Prying AI

THE CAVE WAS quite unlike the more famous tourist attracting caverns of the region that she had visited with her parents. For a start, there was no magnificent amphitheatre, no giant stalagmites or stalactites to make people gape in amazement. Maybe in a few more hundred thousand years, the slow drip-drip of water through the rocks will transform this place too. But right now, it was just a largish, uninspiring hole in the side of the hill.

Millie had reluctantly partnered with Karen, who refused to accept her plea of 'I'm not feeling well' as a good enough reason for her to miss what promised to be a significant event.

'Mill, if you want to be part of what's coming, you need to be there. I can't go alone because everyone has to have another person with them to vouch for the fact they've had their jammer on from when they've left home. It's too late for me to find anyone else. Please, Mill, don't let me down after everything I've done for you.'

'Who is he anyway, this mystery man you are willing to risk our necks for?' Millie had probed while still trying not to sound too interested. Having literally just been told she was now subject to 'enhanced monitoring', she realised it must be a particular sort of stupid to attend the meeting given what was at stake.

Like most people her parents watched the regular government's newscasts where the so-called faces of the 'Undeserving' were paraded.

'Undeserving of the resources that had been spent on them amid unprecedented challenges that face our nation,' was the usual line spewed out by the government spokesperson. 'Undeserving of being a UK citizen.'

If you were to believe the news most of the population agreed with the government and thought keeping any Undeserving in the luxury of prison far too good for them. Shipping them off to the South Atlantic Islands to fend for themselves was felt to be the appropriate punishment.

Millie knew if she were caught attending any meeting where there was talk of revolt, that could be her fate. On the other hand, she would kick herself if she missed something that could get in the way of her own plans.

'Look, all I know is what I've been told,' replied Karen. 'We're all to get there by midday when there is a big announcement about that facility place where they are making those freaks with two brains.'

The mention of The Facility had settled it for her. The real question then was whether she could trust her jammer and mimic to fool whatever new monitoring tech they had put on her.

What made this cave so special was that it was deep enough to provide complete screening from the implant tracking system. Everyone could safely remove the full-face helmets that housed their jammers without fear of detection. But what if they used just good old-fashioned human surveillance? She had wanted to ask Robert Collins more about what Heather Bernard had meant about enhanced monitoring when he had called, but she knew it would only raise questions about her suitability for such a sensitive position. 'Why would anyone with nothing to hide be concerned about a bit of extra scrutiny?' she imagined him asking.

In the end, she hoped that since her confirmed start date was Monday, they had not yet had time to set in place anything. It was a calculated risk but one she felt obliged to take.

She had not told Karen or indeed anyone yet about getting the job at The Facility. She was planning on telling her parents that evening, so she had a good excuse for not mentioning it just yet. However, come Monday, she knew her father would be bragging about it to everyone he knew and probably to anyone else who would listen. Keeping it a secret from Karen was going to be impossible. And then what?

One problem at a time, she thought to herself as they sat on a rocky ledge deep inside the cave. *Karen is tomorrow's problem.*

'It's got to be something important to get everyone here like this,' Karen exclaimed excitedly.

Millie sat impassively. Even though she had no particular reason to dislike Karen, she just did. It was probably because she talked too much without actually saying anything. Millie knew that that was a feeble reason to dislike a person, but she was happy to make an exception in Karen's case. However, just like learning how and when to tell a good lie, Millie understood the need to keep Karen on her side. 'Do you really think they're going to try and blow that place up?'

'Maybe, I hope so. I'm up for it. It's time we showed the fucking People's Council what we really think.'

Now looking around at the expectant faces, Millie felt exposed and had wished she could have kept her helmet on, but two mean-looking men at the cave entrance had insisted they were removed 'for security reasons'. *Whose security?* she wondered. At first, she thought there was no one here other than Karen that she knew, but then she spotted the face of Professor Jenkins. His wide eyes hinted at surprise or shock at seeing her here and maybe a little fear, but then a broad smile erupted over his face. She was compelled to respond in the identical restrained way when really she wanted to go over and hug him. Who would have thought the sweet but rather ordinary Professor Jenkins was secretly up for a bit of sedition?

'Friends, thank you for the courage you show in coming here today.'

The voice came from deep inside an unlit part of the cave. Only the outline of a figure was discernible and did not appear to be wearing any sort of jammer helmet. Karen had insisted they arrived early and, as a result, got a place at the front. How did the speaker get past her without her noticing?

'We are living in perilous times. Ever since the People's Council imposed a state of emergency, they have sought to control every aspect of our lives. We allowed them to make us think they were doing it for the greater good. They told us that only through accepting and embracing AI could we guarantee a future for everyone.

'We allowed them to convince us that only through newer and better technology could we be prepared for the inevitable consequences of climate change.

'We allowed them to turn us away from the rest of the world in the name of self-sufficiency, when what they really want is to isolate us to control us.

'And what are the realities of their lunacy? Now thanks to the Citizen Implant, we literally cannot take a leak without our bio-stats registering where and when we did it. There is not one aspect of our lives that they do not control.

'And who benefits from all of this? The usual mafia of the rich and the powerful. Their greed knows no limits.

'I know you know all this, and I haven't asked you to be lectured at. It's time we fought back.'

At this, a round of applause echoed inside the chamber, followed by loud cheering. Those that had come were already up for the fight and needed little encouragement. Karen got to her feet to 'whoop whoop' at the top of her voice.

Millie felt increasingly anxious but wanting to blend in she whistled and cheered with the best of them. She tried to make out the speaking man's features but he had chosen his spot well, making it impossible to discern anything more than a general impression of a tall male. There was nothing notable about his voice, no accent, neither low nor high pitched, just bland. She reasoned he was most likely anonymising it with a vocal synthesiser. *Why do that*, she thought? Of course, he could just be being careful, but it might indicate his voice is well known. *Intriguing.*

'Told you, Mill, I knew this was going to be the big one.'

A steward at the front gestured for quiet, and they fell silent immediately.

'When they announced this so-called body sharing project, we all thought they were crazy. We pitied anyone who volunteered, thinking that would be the last anyone saw or heard of them. But as we now know, the mad scientists have actually gone and done it, and just twenty miles from here in their own high-security village in Sheffield, there are living breathing Duals as the People's Council like to call them. Essential and Host, surely the most heinous crime against humanity ever committed.

'How long will it be before they force us to share our bodies, just like they forced us to have these chips in our heads?

If we don't act now it will be too late.'

Someone shouted, 'They've gone too far this time. Let's kill the bastards.'

'What about these Duals? What do we do about them living like bloody kings laughing at us?'

'Kill them as well, they're just as guilty as the government.'

'Blow up the fucking labs that are creating these monsters.'

Millie noted with increasing concern that this last suggestion definitely got the approval of most who were present.

The same person gestured for silence again.

'Yes, friends, we will go after their labs and processing centres, halting all work on the production of the synthetic brains and the Citizen Implant. But we must leave these Duals alone. We must remember that they are victims as well.'

The gathering did not seem entirely convinced by his last command, but the speaker continued regardless.

'We will need lots of diversionary events to distract the police and army. This is where we need your help while our experts work on the primary target, The Facility. Go home, follow your everyday lives, and you will get instructions very soon.'

Leaving the cave, they began the forty-minute walk down to the road. Millie stopped just outside the entrance to adjust the chin strap on her helmet. There was no need to do this, but she wanted to count the number of those who exited. Inside the cave she had counted thirty-three, not including herself, Karen or the mysterious speaker.

'Hurry up, Mill, I'm famished.'

Thirty-three helmeted persons came out.

'I bet ya glad you came now, aren't you, Mill? One day we're liberating ancient cell phones, the next, we're blowing up super freaky tech. You've gotta admit we're at the cutting edge.'

Karen's exuberance was in stark contrast to the subdued mood of Millie.

'Kaz, how do we know this guy's legit? He could be a government spook looking to round us all up in one go.'

'Coz, if that were the case we'd already be in cells by now, wouldn't we?'

Millie knew it was hard to argue with that logic. If the police had any inkling of today's meeting, they would have rounded them all up before they had any chance to cause disruption.

Still, something was not right about that speaker. Something was nagging at the back of her mind, but what was it? When did he leave, or is he still inside waiting for them all to go before emerging?

The heavy full-face helmets that housed the jammer made conversation difficult, but at least the crude electronics did allow for the sense of freedom others in the past must have taken for granted.

Millie had often wondered who the genius was making these devices from the scraps of decades-old components. Amongst the many provisions of the 2036 Law and Order Act, the possession of unauthorised technology was prohibited. Government-issued PDAs replaced imported devices, and all homes were linked to the UK Datasphere through the 5g network. This provided just about anything anyone would need. That is unless, of course, you wanted to disappear from prying AI eyes.

Whoever it was making the jammers would undoubtedly be jailed or deported or both if caught. Millie had put him or her at number two on her silent heroes list. This was currently a very short list as up to now Millie had only one other entry, and that was the person or persons who had hacked the Global Datasphere and changed all the dates years back. Professor Jenkins was now a contender for the number three slot.

Karen's bike was where they left it. Proudly displaying the Triumph insignia, an icon of British design and engineering excellence, the company had been invigorated by the policy of self-sufficiency. Supported by the People's Council, Triumph was promoted as the patriotic choice.

'It's a fantastic machine, Mill. Just because the bastards have hijacked it for their propaganda doesn't make it any less brilliant.' Riding the bike or being a pillion gave the perfect cover for wearing their helmets as they took the short journey back into the city.

***

After they had eaten their evening meal, Millie told her parents about her job at The Facility but decided to be economical with the truth.

'I'll be working in the clinical department. I'll find out more on Monday.'

'Oh, that's lovely news, Millie,' her mother effused. 'Does that mean you will be looking after these patients with two brains?'

'It will be a while before they let me loose on my own, Mum. They said I'll be on a three-month trial period, so Dad, please don't tell anyone yet just in case. Promise me, Dad.'

'Millie, I'm really proud of you. I don't know what you're worried about. I'm sure they'll keep you on, but I guess we can keep it just between the three of us for now. But after that we're going to have one helluva party.'

Alone in her bedroom, she went over the day's events, one part wishing she had not got so involved with Karen and her dodgy mates, the other part glad that she knew about their plans because they needed to be stopped.

How do they expect to get into The Facility? Have they got someone on the inside? That seems highly unlikely given the vetting process and enhanced monitoring Heather Bernard mentioned.

What is it about that mysterious speaker?

Finding no answers to her questions, she went into the quiet place in her mind, letting herself just 'be', ignoring the itching nose that always manifested itself at the start of her meditations until there was only her breath.

When she finally opened her eyes, that which she already knew but which had been unable to make itself heard was in centre stage.

She had been right about the vocal synthesiser, but he wasn't using it because he was well known. No, he needed it to disguise his accent. But there was no disguising his choice of words, 'mafia', 'leak', 'diversionary'.

He was an American, and what's more, he was never really there at all.

SEVENTEEN

Karma

THEY WATCHED IN silence while eating some freshly baked croissants as Heather went over in great detail the meeting she'd had with Doctor Child and Daniel Moccasin.

Even now, Quinn had not got used to seeing Heather work her body. It unnerved her that it seemed to fit her like a glove. Unlike herself, Heather did not make any effort to embellish her appearance with make-up or do anything but simply comb her hair. Quinn knew she was more than moderately attractive but had always felt the need to present a better version of herself to the world. Heather, on the other hand, seemed totally at ease inside her own skin, even if it wasn't her own skin.

Occasionally she looked across fleetingly at Bailey. He looked uncomfortable watching Heather. Quinn was desperate to know exactly what he had meant when he said he was awake yesterday. He was not prone to lying or exaggeration, but could he be mistaken? Did he experience some sort of semi-consciousness ahead of waking today? Heather had been speaking for over thirty minutes now and had not spoken one word about Bailey being awake. Surely, she would have known that Grey was not there?

'...so, you see, my dear, I really had no say in the decision, but at the same time this does present a perfect opportunity for you to resume the work you felt so strongly about without exposing yourself to the same dangers as before. Spencer Child is a smart guy, very shrewd, but I'm not happy either about having a full-time bodyguard. Once we get rid of that idiot Moccasin, I think things will become more relaxed. Don't be fooled by Moccasin, he's a snake. Good luck!'

Quinn stood and went to the balcony. Looking across the courtyard, she saw other Duals out on their balconies. Some of these would also be getting used to being fully alive once more and enjoying the privileges they earned from their status.

'There is always a price to pay,' she said quietly to herself and then, turning to face her husband, her friend, her salvation, she spoke with an assuredness that seemed beyond her only hours ago. 'Bailey, I should have known that there's nowhere to hide in this crazy world. I think my karma has just found me and reminded me that this body needs me after all.'

Not giving Bailey a chance to respond, she continued, 'Peters, ask security to provide me with transport to The Facility in one hour.'

'We do need to discuss some things; maybe you can sort that out while I get over to The Facility and check on our guest, Mr Moccasin. I will just introduce myself to him today. I have no intention of spoiling our entire weekend, so he'll have to wait until Monday for the grand tour.'

With that, she went to her dressing room and styled her hair, applied her favourite make-up and dressed in the smart trouser suit she used when giving live newscasts.

Applying some classic French perfume, she walked back into the kitchen where Bailey was finishing his breakfast. 'I know I've said this many times before, but I do hate the smell of that cheap coconut oil Heather uses. It takes ages to get rid of the stink from my skin. But I do love this perfume you got me for my birthday, darling.'

Peters announced her car's arrival, and moving over to Bailey she kissed him slowly on his lips and whispered, 'I love you.'

***

As he entered the gym for the second time in as many days, he couldn't help but wonder if he was off the hook with Quinn. Her coconut oil jibe served only to remind him that Quinn and Heather were like chalk and cheese.

As they watched Heather's message, he could see that it was having a significant impact on Quinn. Although Heather was the actual target of any potential threat, Quinn was a hostage to the situation. The irony would not have escaped her, and he sensed that at that moment, she had no choice but to resolve to face 'her karma', as she called it. He would do everything in his power to protect her, but they were both going to need Grey's and Heather's help this time.

Bailey was confident that Grey was the key to unlocking the puzzle. But why does Heather not seem to know what he is involved in? By all appearances, Grey was working independently of Heather. Was this because he wanted to protect her, or because he did not trust her?

Bailey needed to make sense of all the seemingly unrelated events that had happened in the last twenty-four hours. It didn't need someone with two brains to work out that they were all connected but, *who* and *why* were still the same questions he needed to answer.

The intervention of the US had undoubtedly broadened the scope of suspects and motives. Their green zone's plan seemed utterly unfeasible, but he and Quinn knew only too well the reality of the ever-growing numbers of climate refugees. It could, though, provide the perfect cover for something darker, more sinister. Given their situation, it seemed sensible to meet with the others again today to see if they were all still awake.

Entering the massage room, Bailey could see Steph sitting at the desk with her back to the door. She turned and smiled warmly at him and, unlike the Steph he had met the day before, spoke with a soft but confident voice. 'Good morning, Bailey, I'm Lucinda, so glad to meet you finally. Grey speaks highly of you. Apologies for all the cloak and dagger, but it was the only way we could think of to keep us all safe and get you guys up to speed with the situation.'

'Hold on, slow down,' insisted Bailey, gesturing with his hands as he spoke. 'You may know what the situation is but I certainly don't. Should we wait until Mike is here, or is Russell awake now as well?'

'I'm sorry, of course you're right. It's still rather strange to us all, I imagine. Well, it is for me trying to remember who is who and what we have discussed already.'

'Yes, and I'm now thinking those in charge of the program have been less than honest with us.'

Right on cue, the door opened. 'Good morning, Russell checking in. Sorry I'm a bit late, but this is all a bit disorientating.'

Once all three had sat down, Lucinda, seated between Bailey and Russell, began. 'I will start at the beginning, and you stop me if you need to ask anything. We are quite free to talk in here, there are no assistants.'

'Good, but I assume conversations elsewhere on the campus could be compromised?'

'If you mean are we being listened to, then of course we are. The bloody People's Council is terrified of any dissent or unpatriotic behaviour, as they like to call it. I've defended no end of clients who have had their rations downgraded automatically by the AI just for having a rant in their own homes about the food shortages, so you can imagine what would happen to anyone talking about protesting. But as for us Duals, I doubt they have anyone actually sitting there all day actively listening to all our conversations, and Grey didn't think they had updated the AI to listen for new keywords, so my betting is that us talking about mind clocks won't be triggering any alarms. Nevertheless, given our present situation, it's better to be safe than sorry as they say.'

'Understood. Please continue.'

'As I'm sure you know, Grey's work on the Duality program came about from his analysis of UK citizens' bio-stat data. His team were looking for ways to match potential Essentials with suitable Hosts for the pilot project. Grey's partner Heather said getting a good psyche match would improve the chances of successfully bonding the two personalities. If I'm honest it makes little sense to me, but I'm no scientist. Anyway, after becoming an Essential himself, Grey continued on the project but now only analysing bio-stats of the pilot group.'

'And he spots the anomaly of our wake-up times,' interrupted Bailey.

'That's right.'

'Then why not tell Heather?'

'I'll come to that. You see, it should not be possible to alter the mind clocks. The Protocol that I helped to draft expressly forbids it, and like myself I'm sure you were all told it couldn't happen, safeguards in place and so on. Well, it turns out that there was a way to do exactly that in some of the prototype

Duality Bands, a way to alter the clock.'

'What do you mean by prototype? I thought we were the first to get one of these fitted?' asked Russell.

'Oh, we are,' continued Lucinda, 'but according to Grey they had to do what he called "stress testing" on the Duality Bands themselves to ensure they would last a lifetime. To do this, they repeatedly woke up and shut down the prototype units by resetting the clock.'

Looking more and more concerned, Russell continued. 'But who were they waking up and shutting down? I knew we were all freaks, but this sounds positively ghoulish.'

'According to Grey, it was one of Heather's old patients who had memory implant surgery that subsequently failed. As you know, under law organ donation is mandatory, so he became the first person to have his personality transferred to a Duality Band but not to a Host. They used him in the lab to perfect the process.'

'Look,' started Bailey, 'I wasn't totally naïve when I volunteered for this. They would have had to have done this before embarking on a full pilot. I doubt there was just one organ donation involved. What I had not thought about is how they would go about testing the technology.'

'I was not aware of this phase of the program either, Bailey. I should have asked more questions. When I spoke to Grey he was adamant that this clock reset facility was meant to be just for the lab prototypes.'

Aware that he was clenching and unclenching his fists, Bailey stood up to regain some composure. 'It appears we have to assume that this is what has happened to us. Does Grey know how it is done and by whom?'

'He thinks it would need to be done by someone in close physical proximity.'

'Like a doctor.'

'Yes, exactly, probably by using an adapted scanner.'

'What about the Digi-Assistants not recognising me? I saw Grey's Duality Band pulsating in Kingsley's office.'

'Grey ran some diagnostics on the AI systems. His job gives him virtually unlimited access to the Datasphere. He came across some recent modifications to the personality recognition subroutines. Bailey, Grey was scared by what he found and knew his probing of the AI would leave a digital footprint. He said he was going to force their hand, whoever "they" are. He must have found a way to reset our mind clocks directly via the AI.'

'At least we know the score. Although Kingsley is mixed up in whatever this is, he does not strike me as any sort of mastermind. One final question, who signed off the design specification for the Duality Bands we have fitted?'

'According to Grey, there is only one person on the program with the right level of authority and expertise. His wife, Doctor Heather Bernard.'

***

The bodyguard was older than she had imagined for someone in his line of work but assumed that meant he must be good at his job. Not much of a talker, but polite enough when asked a question. He had a gun holster strapped over his shoulders with the pistol grip showing in front. The sight of the weapon sent a chill through Quinn's body.

'My orders are only to escort you to and from The Facility. Once inside, I will wait for you in the basement security room until you are ready to leave. Please do not go outside without me.'

'Thank you. I don't expect to be more than two hours. If I'm going to be longer, I'll let you know.'

At under a mile from The Village and within the same secured perimeter zone, they reached The Facility in less than five minutes. As the vehicle made its way up to the security gates, one of the three guards in the gatehouse came out. The guard scanned both her and her new 'friend' before signalling to the others to open the gates.

As they entered the underground car park, Quinn looked up at the four-storey building's smoked-glass frontage. It was just over a year since she and Bailey had both come here to donate their bodies. Was it the right choice? She had so many more doubts today than she had back then. The year away from the madness had given her too much time to reflect. The luxuries that came with being a Dual had given her fears too much time and she had become self-absorbed. But now the fates were moving once more, and she had a role in shaping them.

Leaving her bodyguard behind, she took the lift from the car park up to the fourth floor. In the twenty-two seconds it took to reach the top floor, she brushed out the creases from her trousers and checked that her make-up and hair still held the image she wanted to project and that being she was definitely not Heather. That is what he had come to ascertain after all.

As she entered the client lounge area where they had arranged to meet, Moccasin stood up from the comfortable looking leather armchair. The look on his face told Quinn she had succeeded in her first objective.

'Mr Moccasin, so pleased to meet you. I am Quinn Diaz.'

Moccasin seemed to be caught off-guard by her friendly greeting but then held out his hand.

'Ms Diaz, thank you for interrupting your weekend to meet with me.'

'Please, call me Quinn. I'm sorry that this has to be a short meeting today, as you can appreciate this was quite sudden and I need to make specific arrangements for the tour of The Facility. I do hope you don't mind too much waiting until Monday?'

Offering Quinn a seat and pouring out coffee for both, Moccasin continued. 'Quinn, that suits me just fine, and please call me Daniel. It will allow me to read up on the research and clinical notes I have been given access to. Sorry, I should have asked first if you wanted tea or coffee, we don't really care too much for tea back home.'

'Coffee is fine, thank you. I would be of no help to you with anything technical, I'm afraid. I am at a total loss as to how Heather and other Essentials manage to exist in their little Duality Bands. But what I can offer you and what I hope you are here to observe is my experience of living as a Host.'

'That is precisely why I am here. To be blunt, Quinn, I need you to convince me that you and other so-called Duals are what you claim to be. For all that we know, you could not only be a journalist, but a fine actor put up to impersonating Heather Bernard by your government. There is too much at stake. I hope you understand this.'

'Of course. Likewise, I hope you understand, Daniel, that what is at stake is why I volunteered to share my body with Heather. As a journalist reporting from the front line, I felt powerless. I was not saying anything that everyone did not know already. Like me, I believe most people also feel helpless to change anything. I intend to show them they are wrong, which is why I absolutely have to convince you of Heather's existence. Where do we start?'

'You sound like you will be a powerful advocate for what you guys are calling Duality, and I genuinely respect your commitment to your cause. You will understand then that whatever I ask you and the other Duals will be asked by everyone in the US and the rest of the world. I can guarantee you we will meet with the stiffest of opposition from an array of different groups. We will need to be ready for this and have a compelling story if we are to succeed in getting this off the ground.'

'I understand. I'm a journalist, not a politician and certainly not a scientist, but this is so much more important than any of those things. Trying is no longer good enough. The world needs us to succeed.'

'I tell you what, Quinn, if you guys can prove to us beyond any doubt that what you have done can save us all, then we are going to need people like you in the US so that the folks there can see you're for real. We are going to need someone with your passion and unique experience. What do you say?'

Taken aback by Moccasin's sudden offer, she remembered Heather's warnings. 'As you can appreciate, Daniel, that would not just be my decision to make.'

'Ahha, I'm not trying to catch you. Oh, I know, but Heather's ego would not let her turn down the opportunity of leading the worldwide rollout of this technology, and realistically that can only be done from the US. We will need to square things with your government, but I cannot see any alternative.'

'You've clearly thought about this a lot, Daniel. Have I convinced you already of Heather's achievement and that she lives inside me?'

Hesitating just long enough for Quinn to see a brief look of irritation flash across his face, Moccasin countered, 'No, not yet, Quinn. Look, I absolutely know what you guys claim is possible. My own research in the US is well advanced so we may not even need to bother you guys.'

'Really, you already have your own Duality program? I didn't realise.'

'We don't refer to it as Duality, but the principle is the same. Our Mindshare program is highly classified. Only a fellow neuroscientist working in the same research field would understand the detail, which is why I will be expecting Heather to analyse our research and make recommendations. Then and only then will I be convinced.'

Quinn's years of interviewing experts in their particular field had honed her ability to sense when she was being sold, what the Americans like to call 'horseshit'. Knowing not to show she didn't believe him, she simply smiled. 'I'm sure she will not disappoint you, Daniel, it sounds like you two will have much to discuss. Unless there is anything else I can help you with today, I would like to get back and plan for the fortnight ahead.'

'Sure thing. Just one other request. I'm hoping to interview some of the other Duals you have on the program. Once I can convince Robert to give me a list of all Duals' names, will you accompany me?'

What a strange request, she thought. *Why would he want me tagging along?* 'Of course, Daniel, I would only be too happy. Now, if that's all, I shall see you Monday.'

Making her way back to the basement car park, Quinn decided Heather was quite right in her assessment of Moccasin. He was a reptile. Best to keep him in plain sight.

***

Finishing the last of his coffee, Moccasin took out the PDA Robert had given him and watched a meeting held by the UK Board of Population Control, discussing how to identify which Dual personality was awake. Fingerprints, retina scans, breath analysis and even DNA were no longer sufficient techniques, they concluded. The meeting had elicited strong views from the attendees, although the more ridiculous suggestions were quickly shot down in flames.

'People have a right to know that who they're talking to is who they think they are talking to.'

'What do you suggest, we get them to wear name badges? That's not going to work, is it?'

'I was thinking more of an "H" or "E" showing on their palm, for example. It could be quite discreet.'

'Oh, thank God. For one second I thought you were going to suggest having it emblazoned on their foreheads. You've obviously been watching reruns of *Red Dwarf* again, haven't you?'

'We could have all Essentials awake for two weeks, then all Hosts for two weeks. We could publish the diary so everyone would know who is awake when.'

'Brilliant idea, that means everyone who knows anything about anything is asleep at the same time.'

Finally, the chairperson stepped in.

'Robert Collins, the program director, has recommended upgrading citizen scanners to recognise which personality is awake. All AI systems would similarly be upgraded. Apparently, our IT guys have said this is straightforward. It sounds sensible to me since anything else could be worked around by a rogue Dual if they were determined enough.'

'Finally, a decent idea! Given how much we already have invested in the Citizen Program, this would seem to make perfect sense.'

Looking up from the device, Moccasin felt a surge of excitement. Checking the time, he got up and made his way to the elevator. Stopping on the third floor, he walked unhurriedly to a small room at the end of a long corridor. 3.19 was a simple storeroom and had escaped the fitting of the all-pervading Digi-Assistant. He opened the unlocked door to be greeted by a very nervous looking Doctor Kingsley.

'Something's gone wrong. They were not supposed to wake up at all, but one of them came for a counselling session and claimed he was awake.'

'Slow down, Kingsley, what the heck are you talking about?'

'Grey Bernard, Heather Bernard's partner, came for his regular appointment but then claimed he was Bailey Kennedy, his Host. All the scanners showed it was Grey. Don't you see?'

'No, I don't *see*, Kingsley. I told you only to prove it could work, I did not tell you to *make* it work.'

'But it wasn't me. I did exactly what we agreed, just a few minutes when no one could notice, and that was weeks ago.'

'Are you absolutely sure it was Bailey?'

'Why else would he claim to be him, and besides, he just seemed different somehow, not like the Grey I've been counselling for the past twelve months.'

'But your scanners didn't think he was Bailey. You must be wrong, you're just panicking, you idiot.'

'What if Grey found out about our little experiments? I told you it was foolish picking him… just because of your issues with Heather beating you to the prize.'

'Be very careful what you say next, Kingsley, that is if you still want the pick of the Hosts when this is over.'

Kingsley stayed silent. The already claustrophobic room seemed to shrink even more as he stared intensely at the cleaning supplies that filled the metal storage racks, as if he were seeking some solution that was just outside of his grasp.

'What about the others?'

'I don't know,' came the sullen reply.

'Okay, we keep an eye on all three of them, or to be precise, *you* keep an eye on them, but we do nothing just yet. We carry on with the plan, but you arrange for Bailey and the others to be here at the gates when it goes off.'

'You mean–'

'Yes, I do mean precisely that. It could actually work in our favour in getting the project relocated back to the US. The British government will be seen as incompetent and incapable of running one of your proverbial tea shops, let alone a project of such importance.' Seeing Kingsley's concerned expression, Moccasin continued, 'If you have qualms about killing these three, or is it six individuals, Kingsley, then you aren't going to be much use to us later, are you?'

Staring Moccasin straight in his eyes, Kingsley replied, 'You don't have to worry about me. You forget it was Heather that vetoed my application to be an Essential but then convinced the board to give her dysmorphicly challenged husband that status. I should have got Bailey, not him. So no, I have no qualms, and besides, you know what they say? "*Actio personalis moritur cum persona*".'

'Spare me the Shakespeare, Kingsley.'

'Not Shakespeare exactly, but I think he might have approved. "Dead men do not sue".'

Moccasin smiled as he saw the hatred in Kingsley's face. 'Seems like we both have issues with that woman.'

'Our charade at the cave worked beautifully. The rabble-rousers are ready for action. You really got them fired up.'

'Yes, I made quite an impression, didn't I?' Moccasin laughed.

'That portable AR kit is so far ahead of what we have here, even I couldn't tell you were standing exactly where you are now. We've become a joke. I can't wait to move to the US.'

'Just be patient, Kingsley, we are nearly there.'

'Patience is overrated,' came the reply.

'We'll need to set up another meeting soon, so keep the AR transmitter safe until then. You mustn't get caught with it.'

'I'm not a fool, it's safely stowed away in my clinic room. There's so much equipment in there no one will notice another piece.'

'Good thinking!'

'Like I said, I'm not stupid, but the longer we leave it the riskier it gets. I suggest we go for the Saturday when Heather wakes for maximum impact. I'll get the word out to our cave dweller friends to prepare for the big day.'

'Agreed. That will give me time to work on Quinn. She has no idea about Heather, has she?'

'No, none at all.'

'Excellent! We'll keep that piece of information for the appropriate moment. As they say, *what goes around comes around*.'

***

The short hike from where they had left their vehicle across the moors to Stanage Edge would, in normal times, be enough to lift Bailey's spirits. The early morning autumn mist hung loosely below them, the tops of native pine trees beginning to emerge as all three stood on the escarpment. The blue sky was crystal clear allowing the sun's rays to slowly warm the air and dissolve the fairy-tale scene.

Keeping a tactful distance, Quinn's bodyguard seemed indifferent to the majesty that surrounded him. He was focusing instead on looking for potential threats, escape routes, and places to take cover. It had taken Quinn threatening to boycott any further meetings with Moccasin to get permission to leave The Village for the morning.

Bailey pointed to a spot about fifty metres below where they stood to show Quinn an early rising pair of white mountain hares leaping defiantly across the moor. He was glad to see these hares unique to these hills were somehow still clinging on despite the warming climate. As the British temperatures continued to rise, he wondered how much longer they could defy the odds.

What he was sure of was that he needed this place and all the others like it. Without them life would be soulless. He struggled to fight off the creeping doubts that his and Quinn's decision to pave the way for everyone to survive the coming world was about to be hijacked by those who care little about anything but their own survival.

'What is that English expression? Yes, I remember, *a penny for your thoughts,* Bailey.' Quinn always knew when he was struggling with an internal conflict, and she also knew how long to give him before stepping in to offer her help.

'I'm sorry, Quinn. I was lost in my own private world for a moment.'

'Not a problem, my darling, but remember to let me in now and then. You know they say two heads are better than one, and in our case four brains should be even better. Am I not right?' Her face dropped when he failed to smile at her joke.

Finding a large rock to sit on, he took Quinn's hand, then checking to make sure the bodyguard was still out of earshot recounted his meetings of the past two days and watched as at each turn of events Quinn's eyes betrayed her inner anguish.

'My God, Bailey, do you realise what you're saying. You are saying Heather could be planning to steal our bodies – my body. I don't believe it. I won't believe it.'
'Nothing else adds up.'
'Bailey, this may not make any sense to you, but I just know Heather could not harm me. I cannot explain it logically, but I am sure of it. I have always felt safe having her in my head. I've never said it to you before because you would just say I'm crazy, well, even crazier than you already think. Heather arranges for my clothes to be laundered for when I wake, and that's from someone who seemingly has no interest in looking smart. So no, Bailey, I think you're mistaken.'
'I wish I could agree with you, Quinn.'
'Listen to me, Bailey. This American I have to babysit, there is something I do not like about him. Remember, Heather warned us about him.'
'Maybe he knows her better than we do.'
'You know I trust you with my life, Bailey, and yes, you are the one who worked for Military Intelligence, but please do something for us both before taking any action we may regret. Please check out this Moccasin guy. Let us find out who is friend and who is foe.'

EIGHTEEN

Thrown in at the Deep End

'MS ADAMS, YOU really have joined us at the most critical time in our history. When you get to know Heather better, that is Ms Bernard, you will begin to understand how highly she regards your achievement in earning your master's degree at such a young age.'

'Thank you, Mr Collins. Would it be unprofessional of me if I requested to be called by my first name?'

'Not at all, Millie, and please call me Robert. I may be a dinosaur, but between you and me, I find being called Mr Collins makes me feel positively ancient. Mind you, there will be times when it will be necessary for me to refer to you as Ms Adams, such as when we are in a meeting with government ministers. Is that acceptable to you?'

'Oh, totally.' Millie knew instinctively that Robert had a kind heart and warmed to his sympathetic personality. He had managed to put her at complete ease within seconds of her entering his office. *Should I confide in him? Too soon* came her own immediate reply.

'I see you had a work placement in one of the labs, but how much do you know about what we do at The Facility?'

'I've tried to acquaint myself as much as possible with the history of The Facility. The work you do here has always been at the leading edge of our knowledge of the human brain's workings. But if I'm honest, much of what you do is clouded in secrecy, so people make stuff up. You know, urban myths.'

'Please tell me more, Millie. I don't get out much these days to hear these things.'

'Apparently, you have already downloaded everyone's personality using our Citizen Implants and are using them to create an army of bots and that the Duality Project is just a smokescreen for killing off all the Undeserving and replacing them with uncomplaining synthetic versions.'

'Amazing, why on earth didn't we think of that? It would be

so much easier than getting people to share a body, wouldn't it?'

Millie burst out laughing, followed immediately by Robert.

'I have to say, Millie, I think we will get on just fine. Now to the serious stuff. You are going to be made to work hard like you've never been before. You will need to read all of Heather's research and thoroughly familiarise yourself with the process of personality transfer, not just the theory but the actual clinical method. You will need to become an expert in the technical design and production of the Duality Bands and how the personality is not really transferred at all but sort of grown.'

Her mind reeled at the sudden change from the light-hearted banter to full-on expectations of her capabilities.

'I'm not scaring you am I, Millie?'

'Not yet, Robert, but if you checked my bio-stats right now you'd detect a sudden increase in adrenaline and beta activity. Once I have become this expert in Duality science what is it you want me to do?'

'This is where your security clearance kicks in proper, Millie. It looks highly likely we are going to be asked to roll out Duality across the globe. Think very big numbers, billions, in fact. Using our present methods it takes two months to harvest a personality and one month after surgery to integrate with the Host brain. If we are to achieve anything in time, we need this entire process brought in to a few days at most, preferably hours.'

'Now, I am scared, Robert.'

'Good, that makes two of us. Let's not waste any time then. Let me take you to the labs where you'll be spending most of your days. I need to introduce you to the team. Heather is obviously in charge there and has been for many years, but given her unavoidable absences the hope is you will be able to cover for her.' Seeing Millie's startled reaction to this suggestion, he continued, 'Oh, don't look so surprised, Millie. We do have some excellent people, but no one comes close to Heather. She is one of the few real geniuses I have ever met. I would never tell her this to her face because she also happens to be one of the most arrogant people I've ever met. You should know this from the outset because she can be challenging to work with.'

'But, Robert, why would you even think I could cover for her. I can be quite big-headed myself, but even I realise I need to put in many years in the real world just to become competent.'

'We both read your thesis, *The Continuing Evolution of Predatory Instincts in Humans*. I'm not going to deny that most of it went over my head, it's been many years since I was a true scientist rather than the pen pusher I am now. Nevertheless, even I could see it was the work of someone with a rare insight and gift. As for Heather, well, she came into my office and demanded we hired you. Her words were along the lines, "Robert, this young woman reminds me of myself, but my God, I was thirty before I would have been able to comprehend what she has just written at seventeen. If you don't hire her the Americans will find out about her and steal her from us."'

Millie felt her cheeks burning at what she felt was unwarranted praise and was unsure how to reply.

'Apologies, Millie, I can see I have embarrassed you, but there is no place for false modesty here. You will find we all have a pretty high opinion of ourselves, even myself, in my own regard for my brilliance at keeping everyone happy.' Robert laughed again at this confession.

'Robert, can I ask you a personal question?'

'As they say, Millie, you can ask but I may not respond if it is too personal.'

'Why haven't you taken the opportunity to become a Dual yourself?'

Robert suddenly became quiet and Millie sensed her question had struck a nerve, 'I'm sorry, Robert, very presumptuous of me when we've only just met.'

Robert looked up from the floor. 'A singer once sang "Who wants to live forever". I've had a long and useful life and I'm hoping for a few more years, but let's just say I would hesitate at saying I was essential to the survival of mankind, and as you can see, I don't have the body to be a Host.'

'Now then, let us go meet the team.'

***

Trying not to feel completely overwhelmed by the scale of the task ahead, Millie sat at her allocated desk just outside of Heather's office and attempted to quieten her brain. Fifteen minutes was usually enough to calm the raging torrent of random thoughts that constantly vied for attention. But today was not like other days. Feelings of inadequacy were at the forefront, closely followed by a multitude of fears; fear of being caught by the police and losing her job, fear of acting too late to stop the bomb, fear of being utterly wrong about everything.

She had been aware for some years that the problem with having what others called 'an exceptional brain' was the tendency of her mind to over analyse, to focus on the worst-case scenario. Knowing this still did not stop her from thinking this way. It was how her mind worked, after all.

Fortunately, she had learnt to take the rough with the smooth when it came to problem solving. Often when she tried to calm her mind, she would face the same recurring images of dissection day at school. Having just turned eleven, this was to be her first and last few weeks of attending a regular school. Being smart did not win you many friends, as she soon found out. It wasn't as though she was bullied, but her classmates were uncomfortable around someone who made them feel bad about themselves, so they just tended to avoid her. Most of the time this didn't bother her because, quite frankly, it was hard work trying to dumb down just to fit in.

She had earned a placement at an academy for gifted children that used VR tutoring and was looking forward to the solitude it would bring. But for the moment she had to grin and bear it, and on this one day in science class the students were asked to get into teams of three. In her white lab coat the teacher called for everyone's attention, and looking very serious declared, 'Today we are going to dissect a frog.' Gasps echoed all around the room. 'Yes, you heard correctly. The school governors have been asked by the Board of Education to reinstate dissection into the biology curriculum. Your parents have been informed that pupils wishing to be considered for any science degree will be required to participate fully.'

A wave of nauseous panic overcame Millie as the teacher passed from group to group, handing out to each a glass jar with a dead frog. As she approached their bench, Millie protested. 'But, Miss, this is not fair. What can we possibly learn from this barbaric practice that we cannot from the excellent anatomical studies already documented? And besides, amphibians are already threatened with extinction, what moral right do we have to kill these specimens?'

Her tutor continued to smile, but not in a way anyone would consider friendly. 'Miss Adams, we are all aware of the high esteem in which you hold yourself, but us mere mortals like to follow the guidance of those who have spent a lifetime refining the educational needs of all students. In science all theory has to be backed up with rigorous experimentation and empirical evidence. I would have thought you would know this. These particular species are still in abundance. Of course, you may leave the room, but it will count as a Fail on your grades, and yes, before you ask, these grades will be rolled forward to your new academy.'

Her fellow students remained silent but a boy in her group nudged her and winked. He opened the jar and turned out the frog onto the bench, and after poking it cried out, 'It's not real, Miss.'

The class and teacher erupted into laughter. 'Of course it's not real, Fred. It's a perfect synthetic replica, anatomically correct in every way.'

The humiliation of that day had continued to haunt her. For a long time *stupid bitch* became the only mantra in her head and one she applied equally to herself as to her former tutor.

After an hour had passed in the outside world, from somewhere deep her true self surfaced and reminded her that this same mind had earned this job, had dared to believe in herself and a better world and that her brilliance meant she could be the catalyst.

This was no time for being a scaredy frog!

NINETEEN

Quinn Plays the Good Host

'GOOD MORNING, DANIEL, I trust you had a valuable weekend familiarising yourself with Heather's research papers?' Quinn knew that until Bailey could prove a link between Kingsley and Moccasin, she had to play her part as the gracious Host. It was possible her instincts about Moccasin were wrong, but there was something about him that made her want to get back to the apartment and take another shower.

'Good morning, Quinn. Oh yes, a productive weekend indeed, although it does seem that some notes are missing.'

'Really? Would you like me to look into that for you, Daniel? If you tell me what you think is missing, I will see what I can do.'

'Oh, please don't you concern yourself with it. I will speak with Robert Collins directly, it's probably just an oversight.'

'Very well. I have arranged for you to visit the labs where the Duality Bands are manufactured and tested. The technicians should be able to answer any questions you have.'

'And will I get to speak to other Duals? I must get to speak to as many as possible so that I can make my assessment?'

'Of course, Daniel. I thought you could come to The Village later this week and see our community first-hand. I'm sure we can get some of the other residents to speak with you.'

'Excellent, the Vice President will be expecting an update. Who knows, we might just be able to wrap this up this week.'

'Won't you need to speak with Heather before concluding your assessment?'

'Ah yes, maybe I'm getting a little ahead of myself. But many of the gaps have already been filled in, and I hope the rest will follow this week. Besides, talking with you is pretty convincing. I somehow don't see how you could have pulled off such a good impression of Heather last week. That lady has a sharp tongue, and you, if you don't mind me saying so, have a sweet one.'

Forcing herself not to show her true feelings for this American 'charmer', Quinn was even more convinced that her instincts about him were correct. The next two weeks were just a play-act for Moccasin. But for what purpose, and what was the real motive for him being there?

'You're so kind, Daniel, although I have to warn you us, Duals stick together. Heather and I may not be natural soul mates, but as you can see, I trust her with my life.'

'That's told me for sure,' Moccasin started. 'I guess I still have a lot to learn about how you guys choose each other.'

'In our case it's not a big secret. Heather approached Bailey and me once we had decided to volunteer ourselves. It seems we were a perfect match.'

'You don't say,' Moccasin replied, grinning.

***

The laboratories occupied the entire second floor of The Facility. Dozens of white-coated technicians, seemingly oblivious to both herself and Moccasin, quietly carried out whatever investigations and experiments they were engaged in.

Quinn had realised she would not be able to offer any helpful commentary for Moccasin and so had arranged for one of Heather's own staff to accompany them. It was very tempting to suggest to Moccasin that she would leave him in the capable hands of the assistant. The less time in his company the better. Still, while Bailey was hopefully checking Moccasin out, she needed to keep a watchful eye on him. And if that meant just tagging along and flashing the occasional smile, then so be it.

'Yes, Dr Moccasin, that's correct. All Duality Bands are manufactured within these labs. Each lab has responsibility for producing one of the seven components used to create a single Duality Band.'

'I'm surprised at how few components there are,' Moccasin interjected. 'Surely that cannot be right?'

'I take it you have studied Ms Bernard's specifications?' asked the assistant, looking somewhat confused by the question. 'I understood you had spent the weekend getting up to speed.'

'Not yet. I need to see Robert Collins about getting access to them.' Quinn saw that Moccasin looked visibly irritated and wondered why Robert had held these back from him.

'Very well, in that case maybe it would be more sensible if I skipped the manufacturing labs and took you straight to the assembly lab. It will give you a good idea of what we have achieved here and a context for when you get to study the blueprints.'

'Daniel, I believe we will need to pass Robert's office on our way. Can I suggest we pay him a short visit and ask about the blueprints and the list of names you wanted?'

'Sure, let's do that. Strike while the iron is hot as you guys say over here, is that right?'

'Yes, but we also have the same expression in Spanish: *al hierro caliente batir de repente.*'

'I understand you are from Gibraltar, Quinn. You must miss living there?'

You have been busy checking me out, haven't you, Daniel? Quinn thought before replying, 'That's right, Daniel, although I'm actually Spanish. I've lived and worked in Gibraltar all my life with my father. Yes, I do miss it and the people, but that's the reason for my agreeing to become a Host.'

'We need to find a way to save them or as many as we can. We both know that the climate refugees we see today from central Africa is the future for us in southern Europe and even the great USA. Nothing can stop that now. Why else would anyone willingly share their body?'

'Why else indeed, Quinn? Such a powerful argument. That job I mentioned, it's still yours for the asking.'

As she was left yet again contemplating Moccasin's motives, they approached Robert Collins's office. Moccasin entered without knocking, but Quinn stayed in the doorway.

'Hi, Robert, glad we caught you. There's a bunch of stuff I haven't been sent yet, including the technical blueprints for the Duality Bands. Your man here is going to take me through the assembly process today, but I really need to see those master blueprints. Oh, and that list of names, Quinn has agreed to show me The Village, I'd like to speak to a few of the folk there.'

Without acknowledging Moccasin's demands, Robert beckoned her into the room. 'Quinn, please come in and take a seat.'

Given his status on the project the office was quite stark, just a desk where Robert had docked his PDA, some guest chairs and a cabinet, no ornaments, pictures, or executive toys. In Quinn's eyes this frugality made him more rather than less impressive.

'So sorry, Daniel, but my hands are tied. You will need to take this up with Child. Until I get his clearance you will have to make do with the tour of The Facility.'

'Look, Robert, we had an agreement. What are you guys playing at?'

'Above my pay grade I'm afraid, but I'm guessing the PM wants some cast-iron guarantees before handing over the crown jewels, so to speak. My apologies, Quinn. I should have let you know before so you could organise accordingly. I will endeavour to keep you better informed from now on.'

'I would appreciate that, Robert,' Quinn replied, but as she spoke Robert got to his feet and, opening the door to the office, called across to a young woman.

'Ah, Millie, please come in. Let me introduce you to Quinn Diaz and Daniel Moccasin. Millie here works with Heather, just started today but don't let her youthful appearance fool you. We have very high hopes for her.'

Quinn had noticed her earlier sitting outside Heather's office, staring at her. *Poor girl, looks like she's seen a ghost, or should that be a Host?*

'Pleased to meet you, Millie. I think maybe you have not yet got used to working with Duals.'

'You're the first actual Dual I've met, Quinn. I've only met new Heather by VR. We met briefly on my work placement when she was...' the young woman paused as if she were struggling with finding the correct word, '...well, when she was old Heather.'

'You ain't missing much, young lady,' chirped in Moccasin. 'Believe me, Heather could learn a lot about common civility from Quinn here.'

'You'll have to excuse Daniel here, Millie, he and Heather

don't always see eye to eye,' said Quinn light-heartedly, not wanting to get drawn into comparisons between herself and Heather.

'You're American, Mr Moccasin, how fascinating and such an…interesting surname. That's my first real Dual and my first real American and on my first day.'

'Quinn, would you mind if Millie tagged along, she has a lot to catch up on before Heather awakes, and the assembly lab is an ideal place for her to start?'

'Of course, Robert, if we are all going to be working together it makes sense to get to know each other.' Despite Robert's words, Quinn could not help but feel Millie looked far too young to be anything other than a junior lab technician. However, she knew the dangers of underestimating anyone based on their age or physical appearance. Behind those green eyes and youthful freckles, she sensed that Millie was weighing her up just as much as she was Millie.

***

Before entering the assembly lab, they had to change into a biohazard suit with a pumped oxygen supply. The technician led them through a large twin airlock door that was just about big enough for the four of them. As the inner door opened the visor immediately darkened as a brilliant green light hit them.

Once inside Quinn glanced around wondering if the others were as surprised as herself at the absence of anything that resembled an assembly line. There were no conveyor belts or robots in sight. In fact, there was a distinct lack of any visible machinery or movement. Instead, a series of interconnected liquid-filled tanks hummed gently.

Millie turned to the technician without waiting for an explanation. 'You're not actually assembling anything here, are you? You are growing something. These are culture tanks.'

'They are indeed culture tanks, but I think you'll agree it is pure semantics whether we are growing something or simply allowing nature to do the assembly work for us from the cocktail of components developed in the other labs.'

'Now I see what all the hush-hush is about.' Moccasin's

whisper was picked up and magnified by the audio sets in their headgear.

'Yes, sir,' the technician replied. 'This is where Ms Bernard had her breakthrough. What you see here represents years of trial and error to get the correct combination of organic and non-organic compounds to bind together to create a self-sustaining neural network. The first tank is seeded with an inert graphene mesh containing trillions of links. As this mesh passes from tank to tank, new brain cells are assembled or grown if you prefer, creating quadrillions of connections. The final piece of assembly is performed unseen by a small AI-controlled device that wraps the mesh into what is commonly referred to as a Duality Band. Thousands of living interface filaments extrude from the band, at which point it is ready to be used to harvest the personality.'

'What gives with the green light?' Moccasin asked.

'One of the components is a friendly photosensitive virus that programs each cell to make it respond to stimulation by light. In this way we can...' He paused just long enough for Millie to jump in and finish his sentence.

'...switch them on and off. That's how you do it, isn't it?'

'That is a very simplistic description, but in essence you are correct. Without a light source the neural networks in the mesh hibernate as it were.'

'And the casing, the Duality Band provides that light source?'

'Correct again. We are not talking about office lighting here. Much less than one lux is all that is needed to fire up the neurons. A modified Citizen Implant regulates the power going to the Duality Band, and hey presto.'

Quinn began to realise why she, Bailey and presumably all other Duals had never been shown this process before. Those in charge of briefing the volunteers had used words like a 'technological breakthrough', 'synthetic materials', 'new generation', 'wetware chips', and of course 'assembly'. Looking back it is obvious they had wanted to give an overriding impression that Duality Bands were a natural progression from the everyday organic computers everyone had in their homes. Just another upgrade. When they showed her and Bailey the final product it was not immersed in a tank, but presented in a glass cabinet on a small stand, shimmering like some extravagant gaming headband worn by all the kids these days in the VR cafes. But now, seeing them up close in these tanks, they more resembled floating jellyfish. This so-called assembly lab has all the hallmarks of something created by an obsessed Frankenstein trying to play God, but instead of robbing graves for brains they were growing them. Quinn shuddered involuntarily, knowing that one of these was now an intrinsic part of her.

As if reading her thoughts Millie tapped her on the shoulder.

'Isn't it beautiful, Quinn? You know, humans have been performing brain surgery since at least 7000 B.C. I'm personally glad I wasn't around then because it doesn't look like they had any anaesthetics, and their surgical instruments were as crude as flint chisels. Still, there are plenty of old skulls suggesting they were successful in whatever they were doing. We've come a long way since then, and once we accepted memory implants this had to be the next logical step.'

'The young lady is correct, Quinn,' Moccasin added, 'and it won't stop here. It won't stop until we achieve immortality.'

The technician signalled for them to make their way back out. Quinn was grateful for the silence they had fallen into as they walked back to the airlock.

Is that what you are here for, Daniel, immortality?

TWENTY

Bailey Goes to Work

PASSING THE WELL-stocked residents only supermarket that occupied the ground floor of Block C, Bailey headed instead towards the entrance to Block D.

One of the project's critical success factors was that where practical, both Essentials and Hosts would pick up their lives from where they left off. It was, of course, entirely possible for many to work from their apartments, but Duals were encouraged to make use of the community work hubs located in Block D. Apart from having the benefit of VR conference facilities, the breakout rooms enabled residents to meet up with others and share experiences and tips for sharing a body. Digital noticeboards located throughout Block D had the latest anonymous words of wisdom scrolling non-stop. Bailey stopped briefly to read a page titled *Etiquette for Duals*.

> *'Sharing is caring but don't expect me to eat your leftovers'*
> *'Waking up to fresh linen makes me want to hug us both'*
> *'We may be sharing a body, but keep your hands off my chocolates.'*
> *'To save embarrassment, just ask my name. I might not be me.'*
> *'I think we can afford a toothbrush each, right?'*

Bailey ignored the elevator that serviced the work hubs and instead made his way to the stairs that lead down to the lower ground floors. Although he had to resign his commission, his knowledge of the people smugglers' tactics and routes used through Europe made him a natural for the position of Advisor to Border Security.

The underground rooms housed a thirty-strong army detachment assigned to protect residents and keep looters away from the supermarket. As yet there had been no recourse to make use of their training, but ongoing food shortages were causing rising tensions at home and abroad. Given his work's classified nature, it made sense to share the highly secure military AI hub located here.

Reality soon dispelled any illusion that this new role meant he could escape from the human misery he had witnessed on the front line. One function of the team he was advising was to monitor the dozens of drone patrol boats and planes that 'dissuaded' would-be migrants. Anyone attempting to cross by water faced generators that created fifteen-metre-high waves to push back any unauthorised vessel entering British waters. Should any boat make it past these it was targeted with ultrasonic blasts that incapacitated all on board, allowing the patrol boat to tow the vessel back to sea. Airborne defence drones forced light aircraft or anyone in flying suits to turn around.

They were using non-lethal force until now, but it seemed inevitable that this would change as the crisis deepened. He knew Duality offered the only chance of preventing massive loss of life and was determined not to let his and Quinn's sacrifice be in vain.

Despite Quinn's pleas for him to check out Moccasin, he had to assume MI5 had done their job in vetting him before allowing him access to The Facility. Even if he still had access to Military Intelligence databases, he knew he would probably find nothing.

Kingsley, on the other hand, was a different matter. Was he working with Heather or Moccasin or some other party yet to be identified? His links with Heather via the Duality program were there for all to see, but what about possible links to Moccasin?

The Border Security database contained all records of those leaving or entering the UK for the past twenty years or more. International travel was far less common for the average UK citizen than it was even a few short years ago, and was virtually impossible except for those directly involved in humanitarian work or climate-related conservation efforts.

Bailey found no record of Moccasin having entered the UK at that time. However, Dr James Kingsley travelled to the US in August 2047 and the stated reason for travel was 'attending conference'. The dates coincided with a trip by Heather Bernard, who also stated 'attending neuroscience conference'. Even more significant was that Kingsley stayed for a whole week longer than Heather, giving him plenty of time to establish contact with Moccasin.

Well, Quinn, it looks like you were right, but what the hell do we do now?

TWENTY-ONE

A Visit from CID

SIPPING HIS FIRST mug of tea of the afternoon, Derek watched as a car with blacked-out windows stopped outside the security gate. One of the passengers opened his window and looked into the camera, waving an ID card.

'Open the gates please, CID.'

Derek was surprised that the police had come out. No one was hurt in the raid, and the brazen but ultimately stupid culprits would soon be captured.

Detective Sergeant Brent Young stood by the Portakabin door tapping into a PDA, while Detective Inspector Kerry Simmons sat on a chair in front of Derek's desk scrolling through the site logs and, seemingly satisfied, looked up at Derek.

'Mr Adams, in your report you said the surveillance drones flew over the culprits. How close do you think they got to the raiders?'

Puzzled by the question, he nevertheless answered, 'I was some distance away but I'd guess between five and ten metres above their heads. The drone's own footage will confirm this.'

'The thing is, Mr Adams, there is no footage to check. All that we got from the drone's cameras was static like they were flying through a snowstorm.'

'What? All of them?'

'Yes, three drones, all seemingly malfunctioning at the same time. Bit of a coincidence, wouldn't you say?'

'That's not possible, we check them at least once a week. You got their IDs, though?'

'Actually, now you mention it, no, we didn't. From what we can tell from central location records, there was no one other than yourself here at the time. You understand why we're here now?'

Derek didn't like the way this conversation was heading. 'They must have been using some sort of jammer to interfere with the drones?'

'That could explain why there was no video, but even if that were the case it doesn't explain why we cannot ID the culprits.'

'Must be non-chipped illegals.'

'Yes, you're probably right. You didn't record anything of the incident yourself?'

'No, didn't think I'd need to. Besides, like I said, I was quite a distance away. What about the lorries and bulldozer? You must have found them, they're not exactly inconspicuous.'

'They were abandoned a couple of miles from here, the skips were empty, and the vehicles torched, so it's unlikely we'll get any useful forensics.'

'Crikey, they've gone to a lot of trouble for a few thousand pounds of scrap metals. Doesn't make sense to me.'

'According to our records, there are just three of you supervising this site, yourself, Karen Summers and Ed Wildegoose. Now there's a name you don't see often. Friends of yours?'

'No, not really. We each run a shift. The only time we get to see each other is when we handover, and that only takes five minutes. I finished early on Friday because I was going to my daughter's graduation. Look, I've never had any trouble here before. If my boss thinks one of us was involved in this somehow, he'd have no hesitation in firing all three of us just to make sure he got the right one. Is that what you think, one of us had something to do with it?'

'To be frank with you, Derek, may I call you Derek? It doesn't look good for you at the moment. These things are usually inside jobs. It is just possible that none of you are involved, but we need to start with the most likely culprits. You do understand, don't you?'

'We've all worked here for years. If it was one of us, why now?'

'Well, Derek, that's our job to find out. In the meantime, if you think of anything else I'd appreciate a call.'

***

Outside in their car DS Young finally spoke. 'What do you

think, Ma'am, he doesn't look to have the wit to be involved in this?'

'I think you're probably right, his family's records show they are model citizens. It's not widely known that some geeks have built implant jammers from old junk. It's best to let everyone believe they are after the scrap value of the metals. Otherwise, there would a very long queue of disgruntled taxpayers wanting their own piece of freedom.'

Tapping on his PDA, the male officer smiled. 'Yup, Sherlock here confirms his bio-stats indicate ninety-seven per cent probability he was telling the truth.'

'Sherlock used his brain, don't ever forget that. That thing you're holding is nothing but a glorified fitness monitor. God help us if we ever let it do our job for us.'

'Understood, Ma'am. Where to next?'

'Karen Summers has earned herself a Truly Deserving accolade. We should probably leave her until last. Let's pay Mr Wildegoose a visit and hope his name isn't an omen.'

***

'Of course, Wildegoose goes back hundreds of years. In fact, there are records of a Wildefuel during the Crusades, but in those days, *fuel* was how they spelt *fowl*, so it was really Wildfowl.'

Ed Wildegoose clearly loved his name. It took only seconds for DI Simmons to work this out, and she pitied any fool stupid enough to ask him about it. He even had his family tree lovingly hand-painted onto the whitewashed walls of the lounge in his small cottage.

'Somewhere along the way it got changed to Wildgoose and then someone added the extra "e", and that's how I come to be a Wildegoose.'

'Thank you, Ed, most fascinating. I can call you Ed, can't I?' she asked, doing a remarkable job, she thought, of feigning interest. Still, anyone who knew her well enough would know she would rather have her teeth pulled out than listen to Wildegoose prattle on about his ancestors' ridiculous name.

'The thing is, Ed, like I explained to Derek, until we get the culprits locked up you and your colleagues are the prime suspects. Nothing personal you understand, it's just common sense really.'

Ed Wildegoose completely ignored what she had just said and carried on talking. 'You see, duck, the name Wildegoose has always been held in high regard. Wildegooses have always been honest and trustworthy people. Did you notice I said Wildegooses and not Wildegeese? It's a common mistake people make.'

Losing patience and the will to live, Simmons shouted, 'For fuck's sake, Ed, do you know, or do you not know anything about the raid at the landfill?'

Taken aback by the sudden change in her tone, Ed Wildegoose, looking deflated, replied with a single word.

'No.'

DS Young had difficulty keeping the serious 'you are in a lot of trouble, mate' look on his face, checked his PDA, and looked across at his boss and shook his head.

'Good, I think we can safely rule you out of our investigations. I believe we've finished here. Good day, Ed.'

With that they made a hasty retreat to their vehicle.

'That stupid fool could bore for England! Did he call me "duck"? He did, didn't he?'

'They call everyone "duck" around here, Ma'am. It's a term of endearment.'

'Don't you bloody well start giving me history lessons on local dialects! I take it by your head shaking he's not our man?'

'No, Ma'am. Ninety-seven per cent certain.'

'Now there's a surprise. Old Sherlock never says a hundred per cent, does it? Just enough doubt to exonerate the AI developers if he turns out to be the villain. Not that Wildegoose could possibly be involved in any gang, they'd shoot him within an hour of him joining.'

'That just leaves Karen Summers to interview, Ma'am.'

'She'll keep until tomorrow. Do you fancy a drink?'

***

'For God's sake, Millie, what's so urgent we had to meet up

with our jammers on? You know we should only use them when we really have to.'

Her first day at The Facility had been a revelation for Millie. Working with some of the most brilliant people she had yet encountered was such a buzz. Then going home, the cold reality of her actions came back to haunt her.

'Kaz, my dad had a visit from the police, the CID. They're investigating the raid at the landfill. They want to know who tampered with the security drones and why it looks like Dad was the only person on the site. They told him they think it's most likely an inside job, so they are going to question you and the other guy who works there. Dad says one of them has got a scanner to see if you're lying.'

Even looking through the visor on her helmet, Millie could see the confused expression on Karen's face quickly giving way to one of fear. She had got her message across.

'Shit, shit, shit! Well, that's me fuckin' screwed. It looks like I'll be losing my Truly Deserving status. I'll be lucky if they let me stay in the country.'

'Kaz, you can't let them catch you. They'll get you to name everyone involved.'

'Thinking about yourself, are you Mill? I'm not a snitch. I swear I won't say anything. If I grass on you or the others you'll get picked up and you'd end up telling them about the meeting and the plans to blow up The Facility. Fuck! Fuck! Fuck!

'I knew the risks, Kaz, but I simply can't get arrested. My dad could end up losing his job because of me. He doesn't deserve that.' *And I cannot lose my job, not now when I'm so close,* she thought to herself.

'It looks like I've got no choice then, does it? I need to disappear for a while.'

'No, Kaz. If you did a runner now you'd get picked up in no time and we'd all go down.'

'What then, Millie, tell me what choice I have got? You're the one with the fuckin' science degree. Think of something.'

'I have thought about it. Look, I'm not an electronics geek, but what if we use the mimic when you're being questioned? We could hide it in the room somewhere.'

'That's a crazy idea. There'd be two signals of me at the same time. I've only ever used it when I've got my jammer on. I can hardly wear my helmet now, can I?'

'I don't know if it will work, but the handheld scanner they use might just pick up the strongest signal.'

'You know what, Mill, you may be smart but I'm the fucking genius in this partnership. I know exactly how to do this. First off, I'm going to have to get myself a dose of something nasty, and you're going to help.'

Hopeful that Karen had come up with the same idea and plan that she had already thought most likely to succeed, she followed Karen back to her apartment. It was going to be a long night!

***

At 8.15 am the following day, Detective Inspector Kerry Simmons and Detective Sergeant Brent Young were sitting on the settee in the lounge of Karen Summers's first-floor flat. She sat opposite on a large reclining easy chair with her feet up and wearing a white dressing gown with a large pink towel covering her hair. Karen's forehead glistened with sweat droplets from the fever that had developed the previous night. A bowl sat next to her emitting a strong smell of vomit and discarded tissues littered the carpet.

'Look, I don't want to be rude or anything, but I've just had a shower. I feel like shit and just want to get back to bed. Like I said, I have no idea who might have been involved, and I'm not happy with your suggestion that it was one of us. I don't particularly like Derek but he's as straight as they come. As for Ed, well, you've met him, so you know he isn't capable of some sophisticated robbery.'

'Ms Summers,' started DI Simmons, 'after we went to the landfill this morning and having been informed you had called in sick we checked your bio-stats. This illness has come on pretty quick, wouldn't you say? Your stats show you are a very healthy adult. The last time you took time off work was over ten years ago.'

'Yeah, well, I'm not usually one for staying in bed for any

little sniffle. If you're a Truly Deserving like myself we get to work no matter how we feel.'

'Yes, we saw that on your file. You were sterilised at the age of sixteen as part of the government drive to cut down on excessive births amongst the less well off. Is that how you can afford that Triumph bike sitting outside?'

'How else...' Karen started. 'Oh, I see, you think maybe I've been going out robbing. Well, your files must tell you I don't pay tax, that was part of the deal when I got done. That bike is my reward for years of working at that shitty job.'

'If you must know, last night I heated up a piece of leftover chicken pie. Don't give me that look, eating real chickens isn't illegal yet. Bloody stupid thing to do. It was in the fridge for a week, but I couldn't be bothered cooking anything and I'm paying for it now.' With that Karen erupted into the already half-full bowl.

Looking decidedly queasy, both officers got up and headed for the door.

'We'll leave you alone to recover, Ms Summers, but if you do think of anything please give us a call. Thank you for your time.'

***

As the door closed Karen smirked and gave the finger to the departed officers. As she unwound the towel from around her head the jammer fell onto the settee. Karen deactivated both it and the mimic that she had hidden in the box of tissues.

Her smile faded abruptly as she heaved once more into the bowl.

***

Back at their HQ, DI Simmons listened as Detective Chief Inspector Macey used the opportunity to vent months of her pent-up anger and frustration on her and DS Young.

'I don't give a rat's arse as to why you *think* you have failed to get a single solid lead in this investigation. The facts seem to confirm that what everyone else is saying is true. Do you want to hear what they're saying, DI Simmons, DS Young?'

DI Simmons knew this was not a question she should answer. On the other hand, DS Young seemed to be under the illusion his opinion actually mattered, and she watched as he took out his PDA scanner and jump in with his size ten feet.

'The thing is, Ma'am, it all points to an inside job, but they came up clear when questioned. Ninety-seven per cent clear to be precise.'

'DS Young, don't you bloody well interrupt me while I'm bollocking you,' screamed Macey. 'What *they* are saying, and what I'm beginning to believe with *you* pair, is that you couldn't find a tart in a brothel without a scanner in your hands pointing the way.'

DI Simmons gauged this was now the moment to speak. 'Ma'am, we are hamstrung by the courts as we all know. Scanner bio-stats evidence wins every time. That doesn't mean I have to accept what the scanners are telling me.'

'Really? Well, tell me more before I decide to put you both on patrol at one of the regional food distribution warehouses. I can guarantee you will not enjoy that one little bit.'

'My instincts tell me Karen Summers is not the Truly Deserving model citizen she wants to portray. The scanner says she's as pure as the driven snow, but my gut says she is a damn sight more clever than her lack of educational achievements suggests. We know that this gang has fooled our so-called infallible technology on more than one occasion. I think she was taking the piss when we visited her, and like you, Ma'am, I don't like someone thinking we're mugs.'

'Then how are you going to prove it?'

'I want the tech geniuses to explain to me why their state-of-the-art scanners say all three suspects are ninety-seven per cent likely to be telling the truth. What does that even mean?'

'Good, about time we got those IT nerds to do something more useful than using the system to check up on who their partners are screwing behind their backs.'

'I'll need you to get me into The Facility, Ma'am, so I can take our scanner for tests and to talk to their IT guys eyeball to eyeball.'

'That's not going to be easy. Security has been ramped up

ever since the Duality program started.'

'Ma'am, if this gang can bypass our location tracking capability to nick some old tech, who knows what else they're capable of doing?'

'Good angle, Simmons. I'll make a few calls and get back to you. In the meantime, keep an eye on Ms Summers. Oh, and DS Young, I suggest you stick close to DI Simmons. You never know, you may even learn how to engage your own brain instead of just playing with that thing you're holding in your hands.'

TWENTY-TWO

Meet the Duals

WHAT QUINN HAD thought was going to be a short meet-and-greet had suddenly become an international event.

'I've spoken with the US Vice President. He tells me Daniel has been impressed with what he has seen so far, and in particular he is impressed by you, Quinn. They aren't quite ready to acknowledge our work publicly yet, but I believe the visit to The Village will seal it.'

'And you don't think this is a little strange how quickly Daniel has become convinced? Heather does not trust him, and to be honest neither do I.'

'I hear you, Quinn, but McNeil has agreed that the UK will lead the worldwide rollout.'

It surprised her and Bailey when Child had suggested an in-person meeting at their apartment, when a VR call could have sufficed. But she had come to recognise Child as a master of the art of politics and therefore knew a face-to-face meeting lent greater importance not only to his words but to her own status. It was designed to flatter her, and yet despite her knowing this she was still nevertheless flattered. That he had anticipated her reaction bothered her more. Was she really so easy to manipulate?

'The US visit is a perfect opportunity for us to show the British public the rewards of living life as a Dual,' Child continued, 'it has only been fitting that until now our volunteers' identities and results of the project have been kept secret. But, if we are to reduce our population in time, we have to prepare our citizens now. I have arranged for three unattached Duals to give their stories, life before, life after, etc. We will use the footage taken of these six volunteers prior to the procedure and then do a Q&A session with these three Duals, which I will personally lead.'

'Where do I fit into this?' Quinn asked.

'I would like you and Bailey to be the Dual couple we talk

to. Guys, your story is the most powerful. Quinn, your newscast followers already know your stance on the climate emergency, they've seen you both face death and believe in your integrity and passion. Quinn, you have the power to persuade millions of people to follow your lead. I would also say that now that we have the technology, your role is even more important than that of Heather's.'

Yet more flattery, Doctor Child, but now you have overdone it. The spell is broken.

'You are placing a great deal of faith in us, Child, but also a significant responsibility on our shoulders.'

'Believe me, Bailey, I am fully aware of what the country is asking of all of you. I promise you will get anything you need to guarantee our success.'

Quinn was glad of Bailey's interruption to give her a moment to think. The fact that they had decided not to disclose his early awakening with Child only served as a reminder that they still trusted no one. Even so, she knew Child was right, and this was perhaps her last chance to make people sit up and pay attention to the change that was coming their way, whether they liked it or not.

'Don't worry, darling. We can handle this. When are you planning this event for Child?'

'This coming Friday. We will add some government messages after and broadcast on Sunday. There's no further need for you to chaperone Daniel until then, so I suggest you take the rest of the week to prepare.'

'And Daniel will be just an observer?' Quinn asked.

'Actually, I will introduce him as the Chief US Scientific Advisor to the project. The Americans have their own domestic audience to bring on board, they need to make their citizens believe the US was an equal partner all along.'

'I should imagine Heather would have an opinion about referring to Daniel Moccasin as the "Chief" anything when it comes to the project,' Quinn said, feeling the need not only to stand up for Heather in her absence, but was taken aback by how Moccasin had somehow managed to get himself elevated into a role he had no right to claim.

'Let me handle Heather. She has to realise this is too big

even for her ego. How about you guys, is there anything you need from me?'

'Not that I can think of right now,' Bailey answered before she had a chance to speak, 'but if we do think of anything can we contact you directly rather than going through your office?'

'I don't see why not. I rarely hand out my details for obvious reasons, but since we are now one team I think it's appropriate. I'll ping you later.'

***

'Peters, play a selection of smooth Spanish music from my library. Come dance with me, Bailey. It's been ages since we went out and had some fun, and I don't see us being able to go anywhere on our own any time soon. So here will have to do.'

Holding him close, she allowed him to lead her slowly around the living room as the sound of acoustic guitars filled the space around and between them.

Choosing to savour the moment, they said nothing for a full ten minutes. Finally kissing him tenderly on the lips, she leant into his body and whispered, 'You know we will need to talk to someone soon, Bailey.'

'I know, and Child may well be that person, but we can't rule out him being involved either. Apart from proving Kingsley may have met Moccasin at a science conference we don't have anything substantial. Where's the motive? Moccasin seems to have got what he wants already.'

Pausing briefly as one track ended and another started, Bailey whispered, 'The two people who could probably shed some light on things are in our heads oblivious to everything.'

'If Grey could wake you early, can't you wake him?'

'I wouldn't know where to begin. I'm no IT expert, and even if I were his access to the AI would be disabled while he is asleep.'

'Sorry, a dumb idea.'

'I don't have any brighter ones. We may have to wait until Kingsley or Moccasin, or whoever else is involved, makes a move.'

'What sort of move, Bailey?'

'I don't know, but someone must be panicking somewhere about us three Hosts knowing what we know. Given the level of security in The Village and The Facility, I can't see how they could make a move against us.'

'Yes, maybe, but we both know a desperate person will risk anything.'

As the music continued its slow seductive rhythms they fell silent once more, locked in a slow dance embrace. Bailey led her to the bedroom.

'I've disconnected the assistant in here. Peters won't hear a thing.'

'Then why are we whisper... my, my you are a crafty one, Bailey. *Un diablo astuto.*'

***

Her first week had been utterly exhilarating. She had thought uni was mentally stimulating but reading Heather Bernard's research papers took her to a different level. It would be impossible to explain to anyone the sheer rush she got from comprehending not just the written words, charts, data and diagrams but also, more importantly, the mind of the author.

The leaps of reasoning that had ultimately led Heather to develop the world's first artificial but fully organic brain revealed a massive, ruthless intellect. She had ignored all conventional wisdom that suggested the only way to preserve a personality was by downloading it onto advanced semi-organic chips for subsequent transfer to some cloned body. This, of course, would at best just create a copy of a personality. Not that anyone, as far as she knew, had even succeeded at doing that. But no, from the minutes of meetings held at the formation of the Duality Project, it was clear Heather Bernard had crushed all the intellectual minnows that had stood in her way.

Millie had wondered from time to time when and if she would ever feel an emotional connection with another person. Oh, she liked boys well enough, had even dated a few that her parents knew nothing about. She was definitely attracted to the male physique but had yet to find one with a mind that appealed to her in the same way.

Heather Bernard's mind, on the other hand, was something else.

'Millie, are you coming down here to watch the broadcast? It's about to start.'

Millie's parents always watched government broadcasts. Her father had been a member of Extinction Rebellion long before it got hijacked by nationalists who turned it into the UK's People's Council. Of course, that is not precisely what the records show, and her father would admonish her if she ever suggested it, but she knew it was a closer version of the truth than his. He was probably their most ardent supporter still. *Well, Dad, I wonder what you'll make of their latest plans?*

'Coming, Mum,' she shouted through her bedroom door.

The VR viewer sprang into life, and the broadcast began with the usual anthem.

'All the world is listening to us now
Every citizen takes pride
To share what we have today for the people of tomorrow
As we forge ahead unswerving
All the world is watching us now
In our mission to be Truly Deserving.'

Doctor Child stood in the centre of their living room and in millions more around this country and world.

'Good evening, fellow citizens, and welcome to all our international friends watching. Today our anthem is more relevant than ever. "To share what we have today for the people of tomorrow". Such powerful words.

'As you know, it was just three short years ago that we embarked on the Duality Project. We have tried to keep you informed as best we could of our progress, but we have kept secret the identities of those involved for reasons of national security.

'The time is now right for us to share with you the stories of eight courageous individuals who exemplify the philosophy of our anthem and of our great nation.

'No more talking from me. Let the heroes introduce

themselves.'

As Child's image faded, three men sitting on high stools now faced them. Two of the men seemed identical apart from the clothes they were wearing. The third, a much older man, looked unsteady on the stool.

The man on the left spoke first.

'Hi, my name is Robin, and I'm a Dual. To be precise, I'm one half of a Dual. I am the body Host to Jonathan.'

'Hi, everyone, Jonathan here, and I am the other half of the Dual. I am the Essential personality sharing Robin's body. Actually, this is a recording taken when I was awake, but I'm told some creative editing will place me side by side with Robin. I can promise you we are not identical twins, nor am I Robin doing a double act. To my left is my former self before I became a Dual.'

Millie was as mesmerised by what she saw as her parents. No one spoke. She saw her mother's expression change during the course of the broadcast from bafflement to wonder to fear. Meanwhile, her father maintained the expressionless face he often adopted when he couldn't process what he saw.

Robin and Jonathan answered Doctor Child's prepared questions that were clearly designed to normalise these Dual people's abnormal lives.

'Would you say you were missing out on life by only being awake for two weeks out of every four?'

'Not at all,' replied Robin. 'In fact, my two weeks seem more intense, more real than when I had twice as many days. I would go so far as to say I'm actually one hundred per cent conscious now, whereas before only fifty per cent at best. I wasted so much of my time before.'

'I'm so grateful for the new lease of life I have been given,' effused Jonathan. 'I am now able to continue my important work advising the government on conservation and self-sufficiency.'

And so it continued.

Bella and Angeline introduced themselves as fun-loving girls who had known each other for years. Inseparable best friends they volunteered immediately, knowing it was the right thing to do 'for the sake of the planet'. Unlike many Duals there was no age difference, both being twenty-three when they underwent the procedure.

Millie noted that the VR editing was perfect for these girls, as they seemed to speak in turns seamlessly.

'We talked about it for days after the newscast asking for volunteers,' Angeline explained.

'At first we thought we wouldn't be suitable because neither of us is particularly gifted, if you know what I mean?' Bella added.

'But I said let's just go for it and see what they say.'

'It turned out we were just what they were looking for.'

'Our DNA tests suggested Bella had the best chance of a long healthy life.'

'So that's how I ended up playing the part of the Host.'

'And me the Essential.'

'Best thing we have ever done,' they said in unison.

It was when David and Judith introduced themselves that Millie thought her mother was actually going to faint.

'I've never identified myself by my body,' Judith explained. 'It was perfectly functional and serviced me well for seventy-three years, but I was never particularly attached to it. When the psyche tests suggested I was a perfect match with David, I didn't need to think twice about accepting. It took me a few months to get out of the habit of sitting to take a pee.' She laughed. 'But all in all, it's gone very smoothly.'

'Hey, I just thought Judith had such an important career as a bio-food engineer that it would be a terrible waste if anything happened to her. And I get to live a great life doing basically what I want without any pressure on me to achieve anything else, and I know I'm doing my bit for future generations.'

As David's and Judith's images faded, Doctor Child reappeared.

'In this final segment of our broadcast, I will introduce to you a married couple who each is one half of a Dual partnership. I'm sure many of you will immediately recognise them from the Algerian hostage rescue we saw play out before our very eyes two short years ago.'

As he spoke the broadcast cut to the drone footage of Bailey rescuing Quinn from Basem. When it ended Child reappeared, and with him were Bailey and Quinn sitting hand in hand on a comfortable looking sofa.

'Quinn, Bailey, I'm sure everyone wants to know how you guys are after the terrible events in Algiers.' Child quizzed in the way only a politician who had perfected the art of faking sincerity could.

Bailey was the first to speak. 'Thank you, Doctor Child, as you can see we are both very well. The surgeons did a fantastic job on my shoulder, and I'm now enjoying my new role which I know is even more critical.'

'What about you, Quinn?'

'*Hola*. First of all, I want to thank everyone for the kind messages I have received from the many people around the world. As you can see, I am perfectly safe and well now.'

'You wanted to appear tonight to give a message to everyone. Is that right, guys?'

'Yes, Doctor Child, that's correct. Bailey and I want people to know why we have chosen to be part of the Duality Project and why we passionately believe our choice will become many more people's choice in the future. If you have seen my newscasts over the past ten years or more you will know the world is in crisis, but I often felt my voice was unheard. Bailey and I are now part of the Dual community. Just like the others who have spoken tonight, we are awake two weeks out of every four. Over the coming weeks we will introduce you to the Essential personalities who share our bodies. Tonight we are here simply to testify to the success of the Duality Project, and that we believe by committing to the ultimate act of sharing there is hope for everyone for the future.'

'Thank you, Quinn. Thank you, Bailey. And thank you to the other Duals for sharing their stories tonight. Before we end this broadcast, I want to introduce to you to Doctor Daniel Moccasin, who is the United States of America's Chief Scientific Advisor working with us on the Duality Project.'

Millie's eyes and ears did not register the rest of the broadcast. Seeing Moccasin's VR image in their living room had convinced her of what she had only suspected when she had met him at The Facility. He was the American in the cave declaring war on the People's Council. It was Moccasin planning to blow up The Facility. It made no sense, but she was convinced it was him.

Millie sat in silence, oblivious to her parents' chatterings, trying to work through the implications of what she knew.

'Millie, are you deaf or what?' shouted her father.

'Sorry, Dad, I was miles away. What did you say?'

'I asked you if you are planning on becoming one of these Duals, because if you are your mother and I will have something to say about it.'

Still preoccupied with her thoughts, Millie's reply lacked the filter she usually employed when asked something tricky by her parents.

'I think I'm too young, Dad. But maybe you and mum should seriously think about it?'

TWENTY-THREE

It's all in the Data

EN ROUTE TO The Facility, DI Simmons had time to reflect on the case and her predicament. She knew she had bet her career on being right about Karen Summers. If wrong, Macey would not hesitate in throwing her under the proverbial bus. She would do the same in her situation and wouldn't hold any grudge against Macey if things turned out for the worse.

Interestingly, just like being thrown to the wolves was no longer a real possibility in the UK, being thrown under a bus would be hopelessly ineffective for dispatching anyone. It had been at least twenty years since passenger vehicles were fully automated, and in that time not a single fatal accident had occurred. Being thrown under one of these buses would most likely only cause a minor case of whiplash to any passengers still onboard as sensors detected the obstacle and applied emergency brakes.

Unfortunately, she didn't have the same reason for throwing DS Brent under any sort of bus, to the wolves, or even to a vicious poodle. He was in the enviable position of being too stupid for anyone to think he was a threat, that is, as long as he was at least two ranks below their own. How he'd got to be a DS was something Simmons put down to friends in low places, but he had undoubtedly peaked.

Simmons, on the other hand, knew she was an underachiever. Bright but not smart enough to have found someone's shirttails to hang onto. Police work was not a passion for her but a means to an end. It provided her with just enough perks to make her want to keep the job, but not enough to make her want to die for it.

She suspected she could have risen above Macey had she been focused or even remotely bothered to do so. Macey knew this. She had played her limited hand well, so good luck to her. Simmons chose to play just enough to stay in the game. She knew this made her unpredictable and, therefore, a threat to

Macey. Yes, if she managed to crack the mystery of the landfill raids Macey would claim the credit. But everyone in the chain of command that mattered would know that it was her, DI Simmons, who had done the leg work and even outsmarted the all-knowing AI and those who programmed it. So far she had secured enough collars to warrant her continuing position as a DI, but the last one was over a year ago. She needed this one.

Simmons knew something was brewing. She could smell it. Twenty years ago, she would have thought drugs. Now the use of recreational drugs is picked up immediately on a person's bio-stats. The non-domestic narcotics supply has been virtually eradicated. If anyone were stupid enough to try mixing their own cocktail, they and their family would face months of psyche rehabilitation plus public shaming even for a first offence. It was virtually impossible to form a habit.

No, this was something else.

Even though the food situation was still precarious, people had for the most part accepted the reality of rationing and had adapted.

Even so, Macey's threat of assigning her and DS Brent to food patrol was not to be taken lightly. Illicit food was now the drug of choice for many, and a thriving black market existed for all types of food and drink.

Private security firms with police and military assistance made it too dangerous for anyone to contemplate turning over any of the central food distribution warehouses. Being assigned to patrol one of these was in effect being thrown under a bus, and Simmons knew she would die inside if that were to be her fate.

Stealing food was now almost exclusively done at the smaller stores and supermarkets that couldn't afford to hire an army to protect them. They naturally relied entirely on culprits being dissuaded by the certain prospect of being caught on the location database and put under the scrutiny of the lie-detecting scanners. Perversely knowing they would be caught meant any would-be food scoundrel could command a decent payout from the racketeers who quickly offloaded their booty. Under sixteen, first-time offenders rarely got anything more than psyche rehabilitation for themselves, a price many thought worth paying if just for the rush.

No, this didn't smell like that either. It smelled completely different. It smelled subversive.

To successfully pull off these landfill raids without detection suggested a level of organisation and sophistication that she thought no longer existed amongst the criminal classes. She needed the geeks at The Facility to tell her how Summers did it.

'See here,' commenced the geek, a young data analyst, assigned to help her. They were staring at a close-up satellite map of the town Summers lived in and the surrounding area that included the landfill site. A blue zigzagging line showed the routes she took back and forth with the times overlaid.

'Yes, I know what the system is showing, but we both know some clever sod has built jammers that interfere with the signals.'

Exhaling a deep sigh, the geek looked at her in a way that Simmons recognised as something along the lines of 'I'll take this very slowly so you can follow'.

She felt her hackles rising.

'We are aware of these jammers and are close to having a way of alerting us when one is activated.' Switching to what Simmons assumed was the actual data logs for Summers, the geek pointed at the image. 'See this here, it's a double count.' He fell silent, smirking, clearly waiting for her to ask the next dumb question.

The little shit was enjoying his moment of knowing something she didn't and was dragging it out to magnify her ignorance and his importance. If this were anywhere else, she would have got DS Young to give him a good slapping for wasting police time. But she was here and on her own. Looking closely at where his still pointing finger rested, she casually said, 'Oh yes, I see. The same records repeated. Is that when the jammer is switched on?'

Deflated by her unexpected response, the geek replied, 'We think so. It isn't a glitch in the software. I know for sure because I developed this bit.'

'And you didn't take this into account when testing the system?' She knew she was pushing her luck here having no real clue about IT but repeating something she'd heard her brother once say.

'Not even the AI could think of everything,' he replied defensively.

Gotcha you smart arse.

'Anyway, we now believe the jammer is just one part of the kit they are using. The other piece must record their own implants data and retransmit it when they activate the jammer. It is intelligent enough to change the original dataset date and time but not smart enough to synchronise correctly with the jammer. That's why sometimes you get these double counts, overlapping data.'

Now she couldn't stop him talking.

Speaking very slowly, she asked, 'Now, this question is really important. Would this affect our scanner's ability to pick up lies under questioning?'

The geek's face dropped further.

'Possible, but I cannot see how unless…'

'Unless what?'

'Well, if the suspect somehow hid both the jammer and this other device while you were questioning them, then the brain waves being picked up would have been recorded and so show no reaction to your questioning. But I don't see how you could miss the jammer. It would have to be on the person, close to or more likely on their head. You couldn't possibly miss it.'

You bloody little bitch. I'm coming for you, lady. Simmons was already feeling the pleasure of exacting her revenge on Karen Summers.

'Thank you. That has been most useful. Now tell me, what are you going to do about it?'

Seeing the geek cheer up when she thanked him, she paused to let him save face. She knew he knew he had missed something in their precious AI system. What's more, he now knew she was no mug. He needed to come up with something or she would go to his superiors and demand to know why their system allowed all and sundry to roam the countryside undetected. He would be toast.

'As I said earlier, we were already working on the problem of the jammer. We hadn't considered the implications for the lie detectors, but with that extra information I can update the systems to recognise when anyone is using one of these devices and raise the alarm bells.'

'Excellent! How long will that take and do I need to speak to anyone to get it prioritised?'

'A few days, max,' the geek replied willingly. 'I'll work night and day on it.'

'Thank you. Given what you now know, would you be able to get me a list of people using these devices?'

'Yes, no problem. I can look for these double counts. It might take days to run the report, though, given how much data we have to sift through.'

'Look, it's taken me over a week to get a pass into this place. I need this before the weekend. For now, I'm only interested in the last two weeks. Will that help?'

'That will cut down the run time considerably. I can get it to you tomorrow.'

***

A young woman already inside smiled at her as she entered the lift that would take her to the basement car park. Exiting moments later, they took different routes.

God help us, she thought. *Are they all straight out of nappies in this place?*

TWENTY-FOUR

Robert Confronts his Past

STARING AT THE report on his PDA, Robert Collins debated his course of action. Four hundred and forty-two names listed in alphabetic order. First on the list was Millie Adams.

His role as Director of Operations covered all the projects that were running out of The Facility. The Citizen Implant program was into its twenty-first year, and although his attention was now on the Duality Project, he still had overall responsibility for both. Whether working in the labs or IT, all staff knew that he signed off everything before it left the building.

Today proved why that long-standing instruction was the most important he had ever given, but even so it would only buy him limited time to act. The knock on the door signalled the arrival of the young Ms Adams.

'Good morning, Millie, I thought we could take a walk outside for a little fresh air.'

They walked in silence along the balustraded terrace that separated the building from a large lawn. In his younger days, when The Facility was a grand country hotel, he had stayed here with his late wife, and they had played croquet on this very lawn. He still missed his Millie terribly, but in a cliched fashion had thrown himself into his work. He would sit out here to remember that old life and converse with her spirit from time to time. He thought she would approve of him taking this new Millie under his wing.

Millie broke his reverie. 'I'm glad you've asked to see me, Robert. I've been thinking about the problem of the assembly lab and how to scale up the process. I need more time, and I really need to speak with Heather, but I think I know how–'

Interrupting her mid-flow, he turned to face her. 'Millie, please, I didn't ask you in to discuss your work. I need to show you something.' Handing her his PDA, she scrolled through the details of her location records that he had extracted from the main report.

The realisation shown on her face was as immediate as he had expected from someone with an IQ of 325. She looked crestfallen. Tears welled up in her eyes. He gave her the time she needed to compose herself.

'I know I've been stupid, Robert. I was going to come to you sooner. I knew I would get caught. It was her the other day, wasn't it? I knew when she got into the lift with her visitor's badge on, her grey trouser suit with sturdy black shoes. She had a smug look on her face. I was just hoping it would be…' she didn't complete her sentence.

'Millie, this is a deadly serious situation. I'm sure you know what will happen when the police get this. Your position here would be untenable.'

'They are going to blow up The Facility.'

'Who is, Millie? What on earth are you talking about?'

'There are lots of angry people out there, Robert. They don't like what we are doing here. I know you have no reason to believe me, but I needed to find out what they were planning. That's why I used a jammer to go to their meetings.'

'Who, Millie? Who?'

'I can't prove it but Daniel Moccasin is behind it. He used AR to make it look like he was at the meeting. Only the Americans have that sort of technology. He must have had someone there to get it to work in the cave, but I know it's him.'

Allowing her to tell her story of the meeting in the cave, he realised he had taken his eye off the ball. He had been too busy with his own plans for Millie.

'Millie, stop right now. Stop. Now listen here, Millie, you cannot go throwing accusations like that around. Why would Daniel want to do anything to threaten the project? The Americans are desperate for us to give them the technology. Do you honestly think they would destroy the very thing they need more than us?'

'I know it doesn't make sense, but it was him, I'm sure.'

'Millie, I need you to stop this. Regardless of what you saw or thought you saw, you are going to get yourself locked up for who knows what charges they will bring against you and everyone else on this list.'

He knew he was just as trapped as she was, but even if he couldn't save himself, he could save her.

'Millie, I'm going to do something that I would never consider for anyone else. I hope I do not regret it. I'm going to remove your records from this report before sending it to the police, and I will get the data deleted from the location database so it cannot be reproduced.'

'Why would you risk that for me, Robert, if you don't believe what I've told you?'

'We need you on this project. Heather will struggle on her own. She needs someone with your intellect to challenge her,' he replied, choosing a half-lie, 'but you have to promise me never to use a jammer again. The police have asked they get notified immediately anyone uses one. If you don't do as I ask I will not be able to protect you a second time. Do you understand?'

'Yes,' came a forlorn reply. 'What about my friend, Karen?'

'I'm afraid anyone who has used a jammer will be getting a visit from the police very soon. I cannot help them, Millie, they knew the risks they were taking. You mustn't tell anyone about this, especially not your friend, or we will both be visiting the South Atlantic.'

'I wish you would believe me about Daniel Moccasin.'

'Millie, you've seen the security around here. There's no way anyone could get past the front gates. If Moccasin were to try anything he would be picked up on our surveillance cameras. I'm sure what you heard was just hot air. Nevertheless, I will make my own inquiries discreetly. Does that satisfy you, Millie?'

'Thank you, Robert. I didn't know what to do. I promise I will work twice as hard to repay you for trusting me.'

'Right, you just carry on as normal. I will sort this report out. Oh yes, you need to get rid of the jammer and mimic device you were using. Just in case you get a visit as well. Clear?'

'Yes.'

'Good, now Heather will be waking tomorrow. I suggest you concentrate fully on your ideas and we can discuss them with her next week. Let's get back inside.'

Back in his office he went over to the metal filing cabinet. Inside he kept old research documents he had authored from long gone projects. None of these paper tomes were of any practical use now, of course. Still, they did serve as a reminder that he was actually rather good at what he did in his day. But this was before he had succumbed to becoming the glorified admin assistant he was today, before he had become like the subject in his favourite song, 'Comfortably numb'.

He took out the battered box file at the back of the bottom drawer. Inside was the prototype jammer and mimic he had made all those years back.

He remembered very well the early days of the Citizen Implant program and the heated arguments he had had with the then Spencer Child before he had decided to aggrandise himself to be known as Doctor Child.

'You cannot treat people like farmyard animals,' he had reasoned. But reason, just like fresh food, had been in short supply for some time.

Child and the zealots in the People's Council had an easy job convincing the population that the world outside of UK borders was to be feared. Child's peculiar charisma had beguiled the easily fooled and those desperate for the good old days of plenty into believing the UK was at imminent risk of invasion by a European Army, desperately seeking fertile land to feed their own citizens.

In the end he had queued like the rest of the sheep to be chipped. But unlike everyone else he knew how the implants worked and he knew their weakness.

At first he had convinced himself that making the prototype jammer out of old junk tech was part of his job, that he was probing for deficiencies in the design of the implants. Of course, he never mentioned his success to anyone else. Ensuring others in the project team failed to create a similar device using only components available to the general public, the implant was signed off.

He had rarely used his jammer, but just knowing he had it let him pretend he was still a free person. Unfortunately, his ego had led him to share his device's design with a colleague, a trusted friend at that time.

Pulling up the report once more on his PDA, he saw that Doctor James Kingsley had used a jammer on the same day and at the same time as Millie Adams.

It was time to visit his old friend.

TWENTY-FIVE

Handover Preparations

TRYING TO SOUND more upbeat than he felt, he recorded his handover message for Grey.

'Hi, Grey, welcome back. The body is in great shape. Your physio helped tremendously. He suggests we keep up with the treatments until we have no more discomfort. I've taken the liberty of booking you in for a session at noon tomorrow.

'It was great to see our bio-stats confirm our overall health is excellent. I appreciate you digging them out for me. As you know, I don't really trust shrinks, I reckon they just mess with your head.

'You may want to catch up on the newscast that Quinn and I did, as it looks like Duality is going global. The Americans are now on board. Quinn has been giving their top man Daniel Moccasin the grand tour. Just to warn you, Heather may not be in the best of moods when she hears about the role he has been given. He's definitely one to watch.

'Take care, buddy.'

He went back into the lounge where Quinn had just finished her handover message for Heather. Mellow classical piano music filled the room.

As usual, on handover evening, they made sure the apartment was spick and span. They ate a light meal and only drank water. They knew how much they appreciated Grey and Heather following the same routine as it made the awakening less of a trauma.

After taking a shower they liked to listen to music together. Unlike his choice of pre-programmed wake-up song, Quinn got to pick the wind-down tracks. He was unfamiliar with the composer, but Quinn had chosen well. She huddled up close, and they listened in silence.

As the clock counted down to the witching hour they retired to their bedroom. One final goodnight kiss.

'See you in two weeks, darling,' she whispered.

'You bet.'

***

'What's the point of being so bloody brilliant if I keep screwing up?' Millie asked herself. But being smart, she also knew that whatever answer she came up with was by definition flawed. Being objective about yourself was not as easy as the self-help gurus claimed. In fact, she decided, they had no fucking clue what they were talking about.

Two weeks into the career she had sacrificed so much to obtain and she had already received her first verbal warning. It was no point making excuses about having done what she did to save the world. How could she ever hope to save the world if she was locked up?

On the upside she was still employed at The Facility in a vital role. Despite his rebuke, Robert clearly had confidence in her. No one else had ever risked their liberty for her, so that had to count for something. She was still in the game.

Another positive was she had come up with ideas, lots of ideas on how to scale up Duality Band assembly. Why Heather had chosen the particular method she did was strange, perverse even, almost as if she wanted to come back later and say, 'Hey, everyone, I've had a brilliant idea on how to speed things up.'

Shit, now I'm being judgemental about my new boss and mentor before I've even spoken with her. Carry on like this, young lady, and you won't last the month.

'Incoming call, Karen Summers,' her PDA announced rather too loudly.

'Hey, Kaz, how's it going?'

'I've been trying to get hold of you all week, Millie Adams. Where have you been lately? It's happening tomorrow. We need you there with the rest of us making a statement against those bastards at the freak factory.'

Annoyed at herself for taking the call, she knew there was no way on earth that she could go to any demonstration. What had Robert said to her only a few hours ago? What had she said to herself only seconds ago?

'Wow, Kaz, amazing. What time?' What the hell was she

saying?

'Starts at midday. I've got some placards for both of us. We'll meet up there, yes?'

'Sure, wouldn't miss it for anything.'

'There's bound to be police, Mill, so you'll need to get ready to leg it when I say so.'

'I'm younger and fitter than you, Kaz, so I promise they'll catch you before me,' she laughed.

Ending the call, she put her heads on and played Slipknot at full blast. Part pleasure. Part punishment. She was not sure which she preferred.

***

Anticipating the big event tomorrow, he sipped what they lamentably called coffee in the guest quarters in the best of moods. *The Brits had been the perfect Hosts and are sure to become so in the future,* this thought eliciting enough laughter to cause him to spill his drink.

His elevation to Chief Scientific Advisor was the perfect steppingstone to his ultimate goal of taking over the project's running. From there he and his friends would reign supreme in the coming new world order.

'Play "American Marches" by Sousa,' he ordered the house assistant. As horns of 'The Washington Post' filled the room, his head and shoulders moved to the drumbeat.

An unscheduled call coming to his PDA from Kingsley abruptly changed his *joie de vivre*. *This had better be pretty damn good, Kingsley,* he fumed to himself.

Taking the call in the relative quiet of the bathroom, he hissed down the microphone, 'What the fuck do you think you're doing calling me here?'

'I had no choice. Robert Collins has asked to see me tomorrow. We haven't spoken since I got turned down. I can't imagine what he wants, but it can't be a coincidence.'

'Is that it? Is that why you risked this conversation? You are not thinking straight. If he knew anything you would already be arrested and me too.'

'You're probably right. I'm just a bit jumpy.'

'What time are you seeing him?'
'Midday in my consulting room.'
'That's even better as you'll have the perfect alibi for when things kick off here.'
He ended the call just as the pyrotechnic drum and bugle of 'The Thunderer' were in full explosive flow.
'Now that's what I call music to my ears.'

TWENTY-SIX

Deception

'THANK GOD. MY thumping head must mean I'm still alive. It worked,' Grey mumbled to himself, struggling to get his jaw to work.

Not waiting for Heather to awake, he got up from their bed.

His head spun, his eyes stung from the dim morning light, and his stomach felt as though it were about to explode. However, this was no Bailey hangover, but the reaction to not giving the body the time it needed to adjust to him being in control once more.

No one had yet managed to explain to him why, given his consciousness resided in the Duality Band, he still had to suffer from headaches at all. Heather had tried to explain that the pain was feedback from the Host brain to which they were attached.

'Without pain you're not going to stop doing the thing that's damaging your body, are you?' she had lectured to him.

'Okay, but maybe an off switch would be nice once I'd got the message,' he had argued without success.

Regardless of how he felt, he needed to know if his gamble had paid off. He headed into the lounge. 'Mute wake-up music and play my messages.' The parrots of the rainforest fell silent as Bailey's image appeared in front of him.

Moccasin and Kingsley, not Heather, he thought to himself after listening to the communication. The possibility he could have been wrong about his wife gave him hope. He hated going behind her back. But then why had she left the potential to hack the mind clock in her design? But then again, why Kingsley? He had been his counsellor for a year now. He had trusted him totally with his secrets. In his rush to change his mind clock, he had forgotten to cancel the appointment with Kingsley. *Did Bailey go? Oh my God, he must have gone and learnt everything about me. Kingsley must have known it was Bailey all along. But if he did know and said nothing, did nothing – oh shit, Bailey.*

But that still doesn't mean Heather was not involved. Unless Heather's final signed off design minus the mind switch never made it to the labs. What if Kingsley had somehow intercepted it?

Heather had despised Moccasin for as long as he could remember. He had got to the point where he just switched off whenever she started ranting about him. Had he confused Heather's genuine concerns for the arrogance she was famous for?

Returning to the bedroom, Heather was sitting up, her PDA in hand.

'You have got to be bloody joking. Grey, you won't believe what that traitorous Child has done. He's only gone and given that imbecile Moccasin a senior advisory role on the project. How dare they do this without consulting me? I am going to call Child now to give him a piece of my mind.'

'Heather, we need to talk.'

'Can't it wait? I need to call him now while my blood is still boiling.'

'No, it cannot.'

Fifteen minutes later, having filled Heather in on the events of the past few weeks, he paused. Her silence bothered him more than if she had erupted into one of her now-famous rants. It was so unlike her, but maybe it was the guilt. He wanted her, no, he needed her to come clean.

Finally, she spoke.

'I don't get it, Grey. After all these years, how could you think I had anything to do with altering the mind clocks? I would never do anything that jeopardised my life's work.'

'That's just it, Heather, *your* life's work. That's what you care about, not the lives of the people involved in your experiments. We're lab rats for your research.'

'Grey, you can't mean that.'

'I can and I do. I knew what I was getting myself into. At least I thought I did, but I don't know if I'll ever get used to waking up in this white man's body.'

'I thought you were coming to terms with it. It's YOU I fell in love with, not your body.'

'I know, and that's the same way I feel about you, but I'm

struggling, Heather. Besides, that's not why I didn't trust you. Were you ever going to tell me about Quinn, and more importantly, were you ever going to tell her?'

He could see his question had hit home. Her eyes widened with a look of fear. The fear of someone found out for doing something unforgivable.

'I swear I did not know at first. Quinn and Bailey were desperate to volunteer, and your algorithm had matched our psyches.'

'Don't you try and put this on me, Heather. My algorithm would have also highlighted the DNA match. You chose to ignore it. You chose not to tell her you are her biological mother.'

She sank back against the headboard. The look of fear now replaced by something else. Was it regret?

'I was young and stupid,' she started. 'It was just a holiday fling, a Spanish guy. You may not believe this now, Grey, but I am pro-life. Why do you think I am so passionate about Duality? But I knew I couldn't care for a child. I would have been a terrible mother. He didn't want to know. I organised an adoption before she was born. I only held her once before she was taken from me.'

'You should have told her, Heather, she had a right to know.'

'I know.' Her voice started to falter. 'I can't excuse my actions. I thought this was my chance to care for her.'

Not knowing what to say to her, he fell silent.

After a good fifteen minutes, she spoke again.

'I'm sorry. I've been selfish. I can see that. I can't undo what I've done, but I will tell Quinn. You have to believe me, Grey, I had nothing to do with messing with the mind clocks.'

'I believe you, Heather. Look, we have to put our own issues aside for now and work out what is going on between Kingsley and Moccasin.'

'Kingsley seems to have fallen under Moccasin's spell. I don't know how he forged my authorisation to get the prototype bands produced, but I have to take responsibility for not double checking. I thought I had learnt my lesson years back with the memory prosthetics.'

Before he could answer the home assistant interrupted.

'Appointment reminder for Grey Bernard. You have a diagnostics session at The Facility midday today. A shuttle will pick you up outside the administration suite at 11:45.'

'Damn, I could do without that right now,' he said.

'You go, Grey. I'd be interested to know what the diagnostics pick up about your unscheduled sleep. Meanwhile, I will pay a visit to Kingsley. We can talk more later.' With that, she squeezed his hand tight and looked him full in the face. 'I'm sorry I've let you down, Grey. I've let Quinn down and I've let myself down. I'll do my best to make amends.'

That's all he needed to hear. Taking Heather in his arms, he declared, 'We'll get past this, but it's going to take time.'

***

Laying on her bed, Millie was trying to understand why she was being so reckless. Her logical brain was sure it was a bad idea to attend the planned demo Karen and her friends had organised, but the appeal of some excitement was strangely overwhelming. *All work and no play make Millie a dull girl* was her compelling thought.

At eighteen she felt she should be out with her mates having fun, but her mission demanded relentless study. Every hour already spent getting to where she was would require ten more to make possible her plan to save the world.

She had started to doubt whether she had the stamina or the single-mindedness of purpose necessary to pull it off. In Heather Bernard, she saw one of the qualities she believed she would need to emulate; a ruthless determination that did not allow for the possibility of being wrong. 'The question then is would I become what I intend to destroy?' she asked herself. This question was enough for her to realise why she needed to go to today's demonstration.

Robert was right, there's no way Moccasin could or would blow anything up. First of all, he'd need to plant a device undetected in a high-security area. Second, he'd have to avoid getting caught up in the blast. Thirdly, he'd be putting the whole project, including US interests, at risk. Fourthly, he'd be the number one suspect. In any case, Robert had said he would check him out.

Before leaving her house she put on her leathers and picked up her cycle helmet removing the jammer, and as she walked to the shuttle bus stand discarded it with the mimic down the drain.

As the bus approached The Facility, Millie began to wonder if the whole thing had been called off. *Where is everyone?* she thought. It was 11:50 and no one in sight. But as she stepped onto the road five very old person operated lorries appeared in convoy from around the bend. Out of the back of each lorry jumped at least twenty helmeted figures.

Many were holding placards that declared 'My Body Is Not For Sharing', 'People's Council You Won't Steal My Body', 'Freedom From Duality'.

Amongst the group she picked out Karen.

'Hey, Millie, over here,' Karen waved frantically, 'get yourself a placard and start making some noise.'

Now that she was here it seemed even more of a bad idea. The guards at the security gates had come out to see what was going on and undoubtedly alerting others. Drones were flying overhead, watching their every move.

'What's the plan, Kaz? Those guards over there don't look too happy.'

'Just a bit of distraction, Mill. All I know is we need to hang around until twelve while someone inside blows up one of the labs. Then we get out of here, and no one will be any the wiser to who we are.'

Millie began to get a horrible feeling in her stomach. She knew this was a sure sign her brain had figured something out, but it hadn't hit her consciousness yet.

***

The call came in at 11:15.

'We have the names, Ma'am. You're not going to like it,' DS Young intoned.

'About bloody time. Now let me guess, the Truly Deserving Ms Summers likes to go walkabout?' she asked.

'Yes, Ma'am, along with over four hundred others apparently.'

'Christ all bloody mighty. Let me see.'

Eyeing up and down the list, she knew this could be her big break. She had to be careful about handling it though. The last thing she needed was a promotion and become a clear threat to those desperate wannabes on the career ladder.

No, what she wanted was just enough kudos to keep her ticking along quietly with Macey off her back for a year or two. Get those involved in the landfill raid, give Macey the big swoop and go back to being anonymous.

'Right, let's pay Ms Summers another visit, shall we?'

Twenty minutes later, standing outside her flat and with no answer from within, it was clear that 'going walkabout' was quite a thing for Karen Summers.

'Ma'am, do you think we should call this in? She could be up to no good again. It wouldn't look good if we had the chance to stop her and didn't ask for backup.'

They can't use their jamming devices all the time, she thought. Using her own PDA, she called up a list of anyone shown to be in the exact location as Summers for more than thirty minutes, possibly indicating a friend or co-conspirator. Cross-reference to the list of names and *voila.*

'Well, looky here. We have a Doctor James Kingsley who works for The Facility who also likes to go walkies, and Millie Adams who likes to hang out with our Ms Summers, also employed by The Facility. Let's take a trip out there and see if these three ramblers are having a picnic, shall we?'

Five minutes from reaching The Facility, they received an urgent communication from HQ.

'Reports of a large unauthorised demonstration outside The Facility. Drone footage confirms approximately one hundred persons. We cannot, repeat cannot, ID the demonstrators. The location database shows only five security cleared employees.'

'DI Simmons and DS Young, five minutes from the scene,' she called in, 'send me the names of those five employees.'

'Will do. We are advised troops stationed at The Village are also en route.'

As they approached the crowd blocking the road, Simmons

could see many of the helmet wearing demonstrators drop their placards and make a run for it into the trees. Their lorries drove off at speed.

'It seems they weren't expecting us to be here so quick,' DS Young remarked.

'Clearly not,' she agreed. 'Now we know who they are we can pick them up later, but the question is, what the fuck is all this about?'

Coming to a halt, they left their vehicle and crossed over to the security gates where four uniformed guards stood holding onto a leather-clad young woman holding a helmet.

'She was one of the demonstrators,' a guard exclaimed.

'My name is Millie Adams. I work here at The Facility. Here is my ID. We have to hurry back to The Village now. I got it all wrong.'

***

'Well, well, if it isn't my good friend Robert Collins come to pay me a visit and ten minutes early. To what do I owe this rare honour? It must be important.'

'I had a visit from CID yesterday. They seem to think there are people using jamming devices to avoid detection by the location database.'

'Really, and what has that got to do with me?'

'You need me to spell it out, James? I stupidly gave you my designs for the jammer, and for some reason you have decided to share them with local villains.'

'How dare you accuse me! You are not the only one who could have come up with a way of jamming the signals.'

'Possibly, James, but you see the signatures match.'

'What are you talking about, you old fool? What signatures?'

'Only a mimic device built to my spec would carry the unique code, my signature if you will, embedded in the dataset that is transmitted.'

'Okay, big deal, so I helped a few people out who wanted some time to themselves. How was I to know they would end up in the hands of criminals?'

'You're lying, James. I don't know why, but I know you are. You see, CID now has a list of everyone who has used a jammer in the past two weeks and guess what? Your name is on it. And so are many others who all went out for a similar walk at the same time.'

'Why are you telling me this? Why didn't you wait until the police just picked me up?'

'Because I need to know what you and Daniel Moccasin are planning. It's not too late for me to help you, but I need to know now.'

Kingsley's wide-eyed expression confirmed his guilt, but of what exactly he was still unsure.

'How heroic of you, Robert, but I think maybe you are more concerned about yourself. About everyone finding out about your little protege.'

He winced at being confronted by Kingsley's truth.

'I see I have touched a nerve, Robert. You do remember how you begged me to instil in her "Her mission" during anger management psyche sessions as a kid.'

'She is special, Kingsley, you must see that.'

'Oh yes, I saw her at the cave, no doubt convinced she was following her own will and not yours. Really, Robert, I played along with your game at the time because it amused me planting those little trinkets in her subconscious, but if you think she can save this fucked-up world, even if she were the second coming is just laughable.'

The truth spewing from Kingsley's lips hit home hard. Millie's psych profile was unique. He knew because he saw everyone else's in the UK. There she was, a genuine genius who simply wanted to rid the world of predators. She just needed a little push to make it her mission. He still believed he was right to provide that push.

'Just suppose you are right, James. That does not change the situation. I help you; you help me.'

Kingsley seemed to be grappling with his limited options but eventually shrugged his shoulders.

'It's simple. With the lab destroyed and with demonstrations outside The Facility, the Americans will demand the project to be taken over by them, by Moccasin.'

'And what do you get?'

'My choice of Host of course. You and that bitch Bernard stopped me once. I deserved my place. You might not care about dying, Robert, but I certainly do.'

He watched as Kingsley went over to a cabinet and pulled out a silver box about thirty centimetres tall and wide with three touch buttons on the top surface. Kingsley placed it on his desk.

'A gift from Moccasin. This is a portable augmented reality transmitter. The Americans use it for games. Can you believe that? It's just a toy to them but it is also a brilliant holographic communications device. You can project yourself anywhere in the world with near perfect clarity. This should be enough to prove Moccasin's involvement. Now, how exactly are you going to protect me, Robert?'

Robert was only aware of the intense light and shockwave emanating from the 'toy' on Kingsley's desk for a second or two before he and Kingsley dropped to the ground, dead.

***

'Please hurry,' Millie pleaded. But a hundred yards from the entrance to The Village the car came to a sudden halt.

'What the fuck? What's happened to the electrics?'

They got out of the disabled vehicle and ran the remaining distance. As they turned to approach the security gates, Millie knew she was too late.

'Dear God,' cried the female officer at the unfolding scene of residents in The Village stumbling around with their hands to their ears while others were lying on the ground where they fell.

'Urgent medical assistance to The Village. Multiple casualties, bring hazmats,' DI Simmons shouted at her non-functioning PDA.

'I don't think it's chemical,' Millie offered. 'We would be affected by now.'

'Okay, Ms Adams, you may be correct, but I'm not risking it. Let's get back to the road.'

Instead, Millie ran straight into what resembled a war zone.

Close to a small shuttle bus, she counted twelve dead. Each had blood oozing from their ears. Further away from the bus, people were still standing. Some were just confused; others were being violently sick. All had their hands on their heads.

She tried to get the doors to the bus to open as those inside desperately tried to get out. Finally, someone spotted the manual emergency lever and the doors opened.

As the passengers piled out, they seemed shaken but mostly unaffected.

One of the male passengers rushed to where a woman was lying near the building's doors.

'Heather, Heather, oh my God. Someone help, please. She's still breathing. Someone help.'

Drones hovered overhead and ambulances and other military vehicles appeared. Residents started to emerge from the apartments to help as best they could but were told to return inside. Medics attended to the living and blankets were draped over the dead.

The heavily armed military entered the building nearest the bus where Heather, still lying on the ground, was being watched over by who she knew must be her husband, Grey. A medic scanned her head to assess her bio-stats.

Millie stood frozen, unable to move a muscle. Shock was setting in as it dawned on her that she had been fooled into believing The Facility was the target. She and Karen and the others were a distraction, but not in the way they had thought.

People were dead because of her stupidity and recklessness. Heather may still die because of her. But they were also dead because of one man. Daniel Moccasin was behind this somehow, but she no longer cared about proving it.

TWENTY-SEVEN

Crime and Punishment

'ALL I CAN tell you is that Robert Collins had impressed upon me the importance of my work. He needed me to find ways of scaling up the production of Duality Bands.' She knew this stalling would not save her for long.

Staring vacantly at a damp patch on DI Simmons' office wall, and trying to hold back her tears, Millie still felt numb by what she had witnessed just three hours ago. People are dead because of her stupidity. Heather may yet die because of her stupidity. To top it all off, she was facing questioning that would surely reveal her part in the events. Fooling the scanner held by her interrogator for any length of time was not possible.

'Oh, we know where you work and your security clearance, Millie. Your outfit that day, you wore cycle leathers and had a helmet, and yet you took the bus. Can you explain why?'

'I was going to go out with my friend later on that day. We were going to go for a ride in the Peaks.' *Still true*, she thought to herself.

'Yes, your friend Karen Summers who is now in custody for her part in the demonstration and for using illegal jamming devices.'

'That's terrible, but what has that got to do with me?' *No lie yet. The next question will expose me. Keep stalling.*

'I've known Karen for several years. You could say she is my best friend, but that doesn't mean I know everything about her or what she gets up to when I'm not with her.'

'Look, we know you weren't one of those using these devices, but your friendship with Ms Summers and your position at The Facility makes it necessary for us to ask these questions.'

Here it comes, a direct question I cannot avoid. She felt her heart pounding.

'When we stopped at The Facility, you pleaded with us to go to The Village. What did you mean when you said, "I got it all wrong"?'

'You don't have to answer that question, Millie,' Doctor Child said as he entered the room, looking agitated and sweaty.

'Who the heck…' DC Simmons started before realisation of who it was that had just stormed in. '…we are trying to establish…'

'This is a matter of national security. Ms Adams will come with me right now.'

She was probably more surprised than anyone at the intervention. There was no reason to be hopeful though, as it was a certainty she would soon find herself being interrogated by those less friendly than DI Simmons.

They travelled in silence back to The Facility, where dozens of armed soldiers were patrolling the grounds. Being given a military escort was a new experience, and under different circumstances her father would have been very proud. Only when the door to Robert's office was closed behind them did Child speak.

'Before we get to your part in this disaster, I need you to hear what happened back at The Village. Fifteen Duals dead, five soldiers dead, Robert Collins and Doctor Kingsley, both dead. Eighteen Duals, including Heather Bernard, well, let's just say we don't know if they are dead or not.'

Hearing that Robert had been killed was too much for her. She started to sob uncontrollably. 'He told me to…'

'Silence!' Child ordered. 'You need to listen to me and not interrupt. It did not take us long to get your "best friend" to explain your part in all of this. For now, I do not care what your motive was. We will address that later, be very sure of that.

'We have found Robert's technical drawings that prove beyond doubt that he not only designed the jamming devices used by the demonstrators, but also that he and Kingsley supplied jamming devices to those who took part in the demonstration.'

'But…'

'Shut the bloody fuck up. If I didn't need you, Millie, you would be on a plane to the South Atlantic right now, never to be seen again. So please be quiet until I ask you to speak.'

'What was left of the EMP device that caused so much destruction was found next to Kingsley and Robert's bodies. It appears they were about to place this device where it would cause the most damage when they accidentally activated it. I take it you know what an EMP is? Now, you can speak.'

'It's an electromagnetic pulse. It will fry any electronic component that the pulse reaches.'

'Those closest to it when it went off died immediately as their Citizen Implant exploded inside their skull. Further from the centre, the effects were random. Some avoided injury altogether, while others, like Heather, are in some sort of comatose state. She is here with the others hooked up to an array of machines. They are all being watched over by clinicians and technicians. They tell me it is unlikely she or the others will recover, something to do with the Duality Band and the mind clock. Heather must not be allowed to die. That is the only reason why you are sitting here right now and not on a plane out.'

An involuntary laugh left her body at the suggestion she could do anything to help Heather and the others. 'I have been employed here for just two weeks. I have only just started reading Heather's detailed research notes. What can I possibly do that those who have been working here for years cannot?'

'Heather must have seen something in you to hire you ahead of all these others. Whatever it is you've got that they haven't, I suggest you find it quickly.'

'You know, don't you? You know it wasn't Robert. You know it was Daniel Moccasin.'

'You still don't get it to, do you? Without Heather, Moccasin is the only other scientist who is vaguely qualified to complete the Duality Project's rollout. Unless you can find a way to bring back Heather, I don't care if it was Moccasin or not. Save Heather, save yourself. Get it?'

'Oh yes, I get it,' she replied.

And while I'm busy saving Heather and myself, I swear to God I'll find a way to eliminate Moccasin and every other motherfucker on this planet.

TWENTY-EIGHT

Inside the Abyss

BLACKNESS DOES NOT get close to describing the nothingness, but that was the only word Heather knew that went some way to explaining what she did not see. There were no random flashing sparks that manifested themselves like when in a sealed room with no windows or other source of light. The depth of this void was beyond her senses, but infinity seemed an appropriate approximation.

Total silence. No matter how hard she tried to hear, there was nothing, not even the sound of her breath or rhythmic throbbing of the pulse that often invaded her inner ear when lying down for too long on a soft pillow.

There was no pain. That was good. At least she felt it was, if indeed 'felt' was the right word to use, as she actually felt nothing when scanning for the slightest external pressure. No tingling, no warmth, no cold either. If the body was damaged, it did not register.

The lack of any discernible odour now made her acutely aware of how little attention she had paid to this particular sense. Smells, good or bad, were just that, 'smells', and now she found it hard to recall what a real smell was. This seemed equally true when she searched for any sense of taste and found none. Trying desperately to remember her favourite chocolate dessert, she could picture it in her mind, but could not conjure up the complex flavours.

How long have I been like this? she thought to herself. Without any external stimuli, there was no way of knowing how much time had passed. It was like travelling through endless space without any stars or planets to act as reference points. There was no way of knowing how far she had travelled.

However, what she did have was a perfect clarity of thought and full access to her memories without any distractions. This meant the Duality Band itself was intact and functioning. With this realisation she set about diagnosing the problem.

She dismissed the idea she was merely asleep, and Quinn awake. The most apparent difference to the normal process of being asleep as in between cycles was that she was now fully conscious. She was never aware of anything when Quinn was awake. The Duality Bands were designed to prevent any accidental crossover that could cause both minds to attempt to work the body simultaneously. Her Duality Band behaved the same as when Quinn, in her comatose organic brain, was unaware of anything when Heather was awake.

Was she still inside Quinn's skull? Her last memory was of seeing people collapse around her – hands to head. *That's right, I felt an explosion in my head. Sabotage!*

Oh God, was Quinn okay? There was no way of knowing, but if Quinn's brain were dead that would explain why she was now in total blackout. If only she had some way to know how much time was passing. Her Duality Band would die after a few hours of being attached to a dead brain. They would have to save her by removing the band and placing it back in one of the assembly lab tanks. *Is that why I feel like I'm floating?*

Being a hard-nosed bitch when you have a functioning body and all your senses working was one thing, but Heather started to panic as it dawned on her that without the stimulus of the outside world and given the speed of her thoughts in her ultra-efficient neural network, then only a few nanoseconds could have passed since the incident.

How could she prevent herself from going insane while she waited what would be for her a lifetime for a relatively quick death, if Quinn was already dead or the truly frightening prospect of enduring an eternity to be saved?

2056

TWENTY-NINE

Bailey Seeks Wise Counsel

AFTER TWO MONTHS of doing nothing he simply couldn't sit around any longer. Quinn was lying in the clinic and there was nothing he could do to help her. That was down to others. All he could do was trust that she would eventually wake up, and meanwhile he got back to work as they had agreed.

Now, each day as he went to work, he stopped briefly at the memorial holo-garden for those who lost their lives in the attack. The funeral services for the victims of the blast had been subject to a total news blackout. The fact that all UK citizens were vulnerable to any crazy with access to good tech was something the People's Council did not want to be made public. However, Child did agree to the surviving Duals' demands for a permanent monument to those who had died.

As he tripped the sensors along the path, holographic images of the dead appeared, ghostly but paradoxically seemingly full of life in the coolness of the late winter sun. When an exuberant Mike-Russell stood before him, standing in two inches of snow that had fallen overnight, Bailey repeated his promise to uncover all those involved in their death. He didn't buy the story about Robert for one minute, so he was pleased when Child approached him and suggested he resume his role in Military Intelligence.

'We are entering uncharted waters, Bailey, we need to keep our eyes and ears open. I need you to focus on looking out for specific threats to our Duality program here in the UK. Especially from our friends in the US.'

If he saw anything change in Bailey's face at using the word 'friends', he chose to ignore it.

Back at his desk in Block D's basement, he soon realised that trying to spy on the Americans directly was futile; their tech was literally decades ahead of the UK. Still, after weeks of listening to all the chitter-chatter elsewhere and studying satellite images, a grim picture soon emerged.

Conflict hotspots had increased in number and ferocity as the slow but inexorable global warming impacts began to take hold. Displacement due to rising coastal waters and encroaching desert was intensifying on all continents.

In Central and South America, hundreds of thousands of refugees were steadily moving inland and north. In the USA he could see troop deployments predictably moving south to the border with Mexico. Surprisingly, more troops had moved north to the Canadian border, followed by dozens of naval vessels.

Meanwhile, an armada of European naval vessels was moving up the west coast of Greenland.

Calling Child on his personal channel, he confronted him. 'You know already, don't you, Child? You must have had numerous reports on your desk from our intelligence agencies. The US is gearing up to invade Canada.'

'No one is using that word, but yes, that about sums it up. Canada was never going to be able to defend itself against a desperate but still powerful USA,' Child replied, 'but as annexations go, it will thankfully be bloodless. The Canadian Premier will be making a simultaneous broadcast with the US President next week announcing a new strategic alliance in the battle against climate change and the formation of the North American Green Zone Joint Administrative Region.'

'So why get me to waste my time if you knew this already?'

'You needed something to do, and I needed you to see this for yourself, Bailey. There are no friends out there in the real world, and it is starting to get very ugly. We are still decades away from the worst of it. The slimmest chance we have in the UK of avoiding a similar fate to Canada rests on the Duality Project and our ability to hang on to it.'

'And why should the Americans even care about Duality now they have acquired this prime real estate?'

'Just because Canada is in the green zone doesn't mean it will escape all the fallout from warming. Even with the new megacities and advanced food production technologies, we estimate that a population of about two hundred and fifty million will be the top end of comfortable sustainability, a shortfall of two hundred million for the USA alone.'

'But that's nowhere near the figures they were talking about originally. What about Central and Southern America?'

'That is why they are also moving to secure the southern border. Seven hundred million in Latin America will be locked out. They'll have to settle in the Southern Green Zone.'

'And Greenland?' Bailey asked.

'The Americans had their greedy eyes on that as well but were eventually dissuaded by the Europeans threatening to align with Russia if they so much as put one foot on the island. Like I said, it's getting ugly.

'So the answer to your question, Bailey, is "yes", the Americans do still care about Duality and, incidentally, so do the Europeans, who I believe will be making their own announcements on the subject very soon.

'The mega-wealthy will undoubtedly find comfortable refuge somewhere, but as for the rest, well, what are the real choices apart from to stay where they are and slowly die from starvation or lack of water? Some think building underground cities is an option, and admittedly there will be plenty of solar energy. I dare say some subterranean shelters will get built, maybe hundreds even, but if it comes to a choice between living like a mole or living as a Dual I won't bet against the latter being the preferred option. I'm convinced that come the time, there will be people queueing to become a Dual which logic dictates will be a minimum entry requirement to any green zone.'

'Quinn and I had come to a similar set of conclusions, but what about the rest of the world?'

'That, as they say, is the sixty-four-million-dollar question, Bailey. Will they blow themselves to smithereens in a fight for land or do something they have consistently failed to do for centuries and work together for the common good?'

***

On his own, Bailey had plenty of time to reflect on Child's predictions and his own recent experience. He was only too aware that technology, on its own, was never going to solve the problem of the greed that had infected people and had brought the world to its current state. Duality in the wrong hands would just be another form of oppression, and it would take more than a nicely worded Protocol to protect humanity from its darker side.

Besides Quinn there was only one other person who he could trust implicitly and who would have sound advice to give. Unfortunately, there was no way to contact his former mentor who seemed to have gone entirely off-grid.

Uncle Vince's cottage was tucked away in the Hope Valley, away from any other home. The nearest village was a good three miles distant. As a teenager it had come as a shock to discover anyone could live without mains electricity. Uncle Vince had relied on a series of solar panels to provide warm, but never hot, water and a wind turbine that charged a battery bank for power. The only heating was a large prehistoric-looking and very illegal wood-burning range oven. He was an expert in preventing the telltale smoke from emitting into the atmosphere, and on the odd occasion it did escape there was never anyone around to care.

A dish receiver in the back garden allowed Uncle Vince to 'check in on the world' as he called it. However, with none of his messages answered, Bailey found himself knocking on his door at 06:00 hoping to find him at home.

'Goddammit, Bailey, you're a sight for sore eyes. Come in. Come in.'

On entering the cottage that he had not been in for so many years, he was immediately transported back in time. It was exactly how he remembered it, the low internal doorways a hazard to anyone like himself over one hundred and seventy-eight centimetres. The main living room was sparsely furnished with two armchairs and a side table but was dominated by a huge bookcase that covered the entire wall and filled with books of all descriptions, history books, encyclopaedias, novels and even old newspapers.

Uncle Vince, now in his eighties, looked thinner and somehow shorter than he remembered. Clean-shaven and dressed in a crisply pressed shirt and trousers, he nevertheless looked tired, as if he had trouble sleeping. His eyes, though, were still full of life as they searched him up and down for what seemed a hundred times.

'Goddammit, Bailey, what on earth were you thinking?'

'You've seen the newscasts, Uncle Vince?'

'Couldn't believe what I was watching. Whatever possessed you, son? Is this other chap listening to us, by the way?'

'It doesn't work like that, Uncle Vince.'

He spent the next two hours pouring out everything while Uncle Vince just sat and listened, with only the occasional request to repeat or explain something.

'There you have it, Uncle Vince. I don't know who to trust or what to do next.'

'How about we go out for a run?' came the reply. 'I've got your old kit here.'

And so they ran together, their old route to Mam Tor. He had to slow his pace considerably to let Uncle Vince keep up, a further sign of his ageing, but he refused to give in, and they made it to the top where they sat on a limestone outcrop to eat bacon butties and drink coffee, both fake, of course, these days but fantastic all the same.

'There have always been shites, Bailey,' Uncle Vince declared, 'the world's full of them. You seem to have found yourself in a nest of them at the moment, and that seems to be blinding you to the obvious.'

'I don't understand,' Bailey said.

'You're looking in the wrong place, son. Forget the shites, you need to find yourself an angel.'

'A what?' he said, thinking he had misheard the old man.

'Now, don't start thinking I'm turning religious or anything, but the one thing I've learnt in life is that for every ten shites out there, there is at least one angel. You've been focusing so hard on working out who the shites are that you've not even tried to find the angels.'

Bailey's immediate thought was to dismiss what his mentor had said. *Angels, oh boy, the old man has finally lost it. I shouldn't have come.* But given how Quinn had to point out how wrong he had been about Moccasin, he stopped himself from responding to let his lungs fill with the glorious air of the Peaks. As his lungs filled his brain suddenly kicked into action, and he could see that he was only dismissing Uncle Vince's advice because it was so blindingly obvious that he felt stupid for not considering it himself. What's more, he knew precisely who the angel was. She had, after all, already been caring for his wife for the past five months.

Three weeks later Bailey received a call from Uncle Vince's solicitors letting him know that he had passed away peacefully at his home. It seems he was only hanging on to see Bailey once more. They couldn't explain how he had managed to run with him that day, except to say it was the sheer force of his will and possibly aided by some illicit drugs.

Uncle Vince had left him his cottage in his will and a note that read:

My Dearest Bailey,

Sorry for keeping this from you, but I didn't want to take you away from your mission. I would have torn down the satellite dish a long time back if it wasn't for you and wanting to see how you were getting on.

Maybe if I had not been such a cantankerous old bastard, and I'd let them put a chip in my head like everyone else, they would have spotted the tumour. I'm glad you grew up smart enough to not follow all of my advice.

I have to say I couldn't do what you have done, but becoming this Dual person proves you're one of the angels, Bailey. You take care of that wife of yours, you hit the jackpot there.

I'm immensely proud of you, Son.

Uncle Vince

For the first time in a very long time Bailey cried himself to sleep that night.

THIRTY

Canary in a Gilded Cage

'*HOLA*, MY DEAR friends, it gives me real pleasure to report on the continuing success of the global rollout of Duality.' Quinn's smiling face beaming with vitality filled the bedroom of Millie's 'cell' at The Facility.

'I can report that in the UK we have officially passed the ten thousand Duals milestone. Twenty thousand UK citizens have now made the ethical choice to protect themselves and future generations from the impacts of climate change and reduced resources. But as you see, their lives are so much richer now.'

As she spoke, footage high above one of the newly completed purpose-built Villages showed carefree Duals walking along a river. Others were eating in a cafe-bar from a generous buffet, and finally to others working in a tech hub boasting the latest AR equipment.

'This is the first of many such Villages currently being constructed by an army of drones and bots to house the Truly Deserving Duals. Phase two will see our older towns and cities rebuilt to house our smaller, more affluent population.'

The scene changed smoothly to show Quinn standing on the Lower Manhattan sea wall with her back to the New York skyline. The sea defences that were constructed only twenty-five years ago to protect the financial district were nevertheless now thought to be vulnerable to the ever-rising sea levels, a potent symbol of what lay ahead.

'Here in the USA, the first Duality clinics will be coming on stream within weeks and hundreds more planned in Europe, Africa, China and India as the world embraces this last chance historic human evolution.'

Millie turned the broadcast off, picked up her PDA, and left what she had decided to refer to as her five-star cell.

As prisons go it was not bad at all; one bedroom with en-suite, a living area and a study room. The kitchenette with an intelligent fridge cooker was more than enough for her needs, preferring, as she did, to bring in most meals from the canteen.

Her freedom extended to the labs and the wards where the unresponsive Duals were being cared for. It was to the latter that she now headed. It was the same lab ward where all the volunteers had come nearly two years ago to have the Duality Bands implanted.

As was her habit now, she stopped briefly to read the engraved words that each volunteer must have seen as they entered the ward for the last time as a single person entity.

DUALITY PROTOCOL
First Precept

Each personality, having provided their informed consent, willingly agrees to share a single physical body in perpetuity until the eventual death of that body, and does so in the full knowledge and acceptance that neither can lay sole claim to the physical body. Similarly, each personality agrees to protect the physical body they share.

Second Precept

Each personality agrees without precondition to respect the other personality's cognitive liberty and right to take physical action to support that liberty. This right to be established by the immutable alternating equal cycles of conscious awakened time.

Third Precept

Each personality retains all legal rights and privileges as other 'Persons' save that each personality waivers those rights enshrined in national or international law relating to 'The Self' or 'The Person' that cannot be reasonably applied without breaching the First or Second Precept.

'Good afternoon, Ms Adams,' said Jeff, one of several armed security guards that now patrolled inside and outside The Facility.

'Hey, Jeff, how's it going?'

'No complaints from the patients,' he said, which was the alternative to his other well-trodden quip of 'I could complain, but no one's listening.'

Jeff may have been correct on both counts for the first six

months after the EMP had struck them down, but scans now confirmed activity in the auditory cortex of the temporal lobes of all eighteen Duals.

'Just be careful what you say, Jeff,' Millie cautioned. 'I'm sure they are listening, and they will be able to recite everything you whisper word for word once we've got them fully awake.' She doubted that was true but still enjoyed seeing the horrified look on his face.

Quinn-Heather lay motionless, wired up to monitors and being fed intravenously. They lay on and inside a fully automated 'LeanBody' workout bed, supplied by the Americans. The beds provided all the cardio and weight-bearing exercises required to keep the body well-toned without the mental discipline that traditional gym exercises needed. Adored by the wealthy lazy in the States, they were perfect for the comatose Duals.

Stopping at the first bed she spoke to the women lying there. 'Hi, Lucinda, you'll be glad to know they are talking about adopting the Protocol worldwide, but I know they are going to need your help in setting up effective oversight. Hi, Stephanie, don't you worry about things. I'm here to protect you guys now. We need to get Quinn and Heather up first, but then you guys will follow on soon after.'

Moving from bed to bed and speaking to each in turn, she then came to the last patients.

'Hi, Heather. Hi, Quinn. You guys sure look good. I'm a bit envious of your flat stomach. I've been eating like there's no tomorrow since you've both been asleep. I wonder if Doctor Child will let me borrow one of these beds once I wake you up?' Taking their hand, she smiled for the cameras she knew were watching her every move.

'Heather, your research notes have been a fantastic help. I've been able to adapt some of your assembly processes to work intracranially to repair the damage. Isn't that cool? The burnt-out neural filaments look to have been fixed. Tomorrow you will have the new US manufactured EMP-proof and totally unchipped mind clock installed, and hey presto, we should be able to wake Quinn up and then you in two weeks. You'll both be free to roam wherever you want without being tracked and telling massive lies will be fun again. It looks like Child will use the Citizen Implant's removal as an inducement to encourage Duality's take up.

'Quinn, I hope you'll understand why we had to keep you in a coma all this time. It was too much of a risk to bring you out while we were still fixing Heather. Anyway, your digital self is a big hit worldwide. You're in New York right now would you believe, soon to be attending the opening ceremony of the first Duality clinic. You definitely get out and about more than I do.'

Leaving Quinn-Heather, she went to each bed in turn, speaking to each of the Duals, Host and Essential, letting them know it wouldn't be much longer now.

Well, Dad, it looks like you've got your wish after all. Look at me, a regular Florence Nightingale.

Having summoned her father into her mind's eye, her mother also made an appearance. Child had told them that their daughter was doing important work for the 'future of our country and the world' and would be away for some time. What he didn't mention was that she was under house arrest.

Child seemed to take great pleasure in telling her about the fate of Karen and the other demonstrators who had been convicted of domestic terrorism charges in a closed court and deported to the Falklands to serve their ten-year sentences.

She knew he told her this to let her know he held this same power over her. 'You play ball with me, Millie, and I'll get your friend back. Mess up, and you'll be joining them.'

Naturally, Child suppressed all news of these so-called terrorists and the deadly attack on The Village. Digi-Quinn only reported good news about the Duality Project, the words in her synthetic voice scripted no doubt by Child himself and Bailey having no choice but to let him do it while her real body lay here. *Boy, are these two going to be pissed when they awake!*

'Play some workout music,' she called out halfway through her round. As the high tempo beat filled the room she did some star jumps, squats, and a little dance jig. The guards were used to her being a bit 'odd' and now ignored her improvised exercise routine amongst the comatose patients. When one of the guards had suggested she should show some respect, she laughed and said the music was therapy for the patients and helped her keep her as fit as them.

More importantly, the exercise also was to mask her raised heartbeat as she checked on the fluorescence levels present in the cocktail of chemicals surrounding the patients' Duality Bands. Her excitement was nobody's business but hers and hopefully Heather's.

'Time please,' she commanded.

'The time, Millie, is 11:59 and 20 seconds,' came the fake-friendly reply of her AI watcher.

Forty seconds, she thought to herself, counting down in her head: *Three, two, one.*

The door to the ward opened and Bailey-Grey entered the room like they have done every day at the same time for the past nine months. Today it would be Grey who would hold Quinn-Heather's hand.

'Hi, Grey,' shouted Millie, greeting him with genuine affection. As the only married Dual with a partner lying here, she had come to admire Bailey-Grey for their devotion to their wives. Bailey and Grey were like chalk and cheese, yet both spoke highly of the other and were clearly besotted by their partners. *Quinn-Heather were lucky to have them,* she thought wistfully.

'Hello, Millie, are you all ready for the big day tomorrow?'

'As ready as we'll ever be, Grey. Look, I know how you and Bailey have got your hopes up, but like many things around here this will be a first. I'm sure we'll be fine, but best to keep grounded.'

'I understand, Millie. I just hope Heather and Quinn appreciate why we've chosen to offset our cycles by one day. Bailey and I have learnt that you really need to speak directly with the other couple from time to time. This new arrangement will mean I'll get one day with Quinn and Heather will get one day with Bailey.'

'It sounds like you and Bailey have talked it through. The ladies will be fine, I'm sure,' Millie replied, while privately thinking, *Rather you than me trying to explain that one to these two, the mood they will be in when they discover what's happened during their absence.*

'Tomorrow's procedure will start at 10 am. The surgical AI

has been programmed for the new mind clock, and there will be a bunch of technicians and a real surgical consultant on hand.'

'Child has briefed me already. It looks like none of this would have been possible without you. I hear the Americans thought the damage was too extensive. I just want to thank you for sticking with it no matter what happens tomorrow.'

'If you want you can watch the procedure with me in the observation room while the surgical team does their work.'

'Thanks, Millie, I'd like that. Look, I just want you to know that I disapprove of Child's methods. He had no right to lock you up here.'

'Don't worry, Grey, it's fine, but it's nice to have someone on my side.'

From his pocket Grey produced a small package. 'I hear you're a bit of an amphibian nerd.' Handing it to her, he continued, 'I thought you might find this an interesting read in your spare time.'

Later that evening on the terrace where she had had her last conversation with Robert, and that now was her only permitted access to an outside space, she opened Grey's gift. It was an actual colour illustrated book, *The World Book of Frogs*. She smiled as she looked through the pages of colourful and often deadly species. A piece of paper fell out and written on it was a message from Grey.

'Beware your bio-stats indicate a growing tendency towards violence. Child is watching.'

Staring at Grey's message, she reflected on her present situation.

Years of meditation and chanting 'I am that I am' had helped her accept the challenges she would inevitably face. It had also kept the teenage psyche counselling visits to a minimum as she learnt to squeeze her bio-stats into the acceptable range.

She knew her training was starting to fail her as she struggled to calm the steadily rising anger that coursed through every vein, every cell, every ounce of her being. The window of opportunity was drawing closer, and she needed to remain focused.

She needed her revenge on Robert's killer and all others like

him. Only then she would find peace, so her inner voice recited her new mantra.
I am that I am so that they no longer will be.

THIRTY-ONE

Moccasin and the Astronaut

FREE TO USE the fully encrypted private communications channels in the comfort of his own home, the mark he believed of genuine free-market-economy democracies, Moccasin awaited the call he had prepared for.

His time in the UK was far more successful than he had dared dream possible, and with all loose ends tied up to boot.

It was a pity about Kingsley, who had been useful as his eyes and ears, but he had become a liability. Robert taking the fall was an unexpected bonus, not in the original plan but immensely gratifying. And dear old Heather, even if they do bring her back to life, she is irrelevant now. He will insist that the US team only works with the socially awkward Adams woman who seems eager to show off how clever she is. Everything was in place. He just needed to convince his 'friends'.

He adopted his preferred power pose of sitting behind his large oak bureau with crossed hands resting on top. He was ready.

Twenty-five minutes later, and just as he thought he'd been let down, the call arrived.

'Incoming communication from an undeclared caller. Should I accept?'

'Yes, full visual.'

He remembered not to smile as his full 3D image was being scanned and transmitted to God knows where, but to remain professional and calm.

To his surprise the image of a fully suited astronaut appeared in his lounge. Inside the domed helmet he could make out the face of a young man. He waited, trying to remain expressionless.

'What do you see, Daniel?' asked the astronaut.

Not wishing to state the obvious, he nevertheless did just that. 'You're wearing what looks like the Mars expedition spacesuit.'

'Indeed, and manufactured by AI robots at a fraction of the cost of those used in the Apollo missions.'

The image changed. Now a child eerily with the same face as the astronaut, but somewhat contorted. With wide, bloodshot, vacant eyes, a series of spasms randomly moved his limbs and mouth. 'Safe, cheap zombie drugs have been around for decades, the illicit narcotics market has been decimated.'

The image changed yet again; he was now confronted by an anatomically correct multi-gender sex automaton. They smiled lasciviously. 'Even the oldest business of all is in decline as the distinction between real skin and synthetic is imperceptible to the average punter. Are you getting my point yet?'

'It looks like a lot of people are being priced out of business.'

'That's one way of looking at it, Daniel,' a young woman said, now standing in her lounge wearing a regular suit and sipping on what looked like whisky. 'The other way of looking at is that we humans have always used our ingenuity to find better ways to satisfy our desires.

'Yet despite all our technological advancements, there hasn't really been a new idea, a single new thought, or a new desire, new vice or even new virtue ever since mankind dragged itself out of the swamp. Think about it.'

'I'm afraid I'm not much of a philosopher,' he replied, not knowing where this strange conversation was heading.

'Very well, Daniel. I will spare you any more of my musings. The only desire that has so far eluded even the wealthiest or most powerful is that of immortality. The ancient Egyptians believed they had the answer with their gods and pyramid tombs. They were conned by their priests and priestesses who were more than happy to live off the wealth conferred onto them by the pharaohs. Some of these charlatans did pay the price in the end though, by being entombed alongside their masters.

'Nowadays, of course, we have scientists like yourself instead of priests. My friends and I like to keep abreast of the latest anti-ageing technologies, but the sad truth is if you are already living in an old body, there is nothing to turn the clock back. Gene therapy will not come to our rescue. Who wants to live another hundred years in a ninety-year-old body?' As she spoke, her image changed once more, her face ageing rapidly, her body shrinking and bending.

'Cloning offers us no comfort. We have no desire for a bright young lookalike to take our place living off our hard-earned ill-gotten gains. And despite those advances in sex dolls, moving into an entirely synthetic body is still in the realms of science fiction.

'But now we have this British technology and a glimmer of hope. Maybe this could be a bridge to the future. The pent-up desire of those of us that can afford to live a thousand lifetimes is stirring.

'So, Daniel, please tell me more.'

Jesus, he thought to himself, *I guess you can be as wacko as you like when you've got real money.*

'That glimmer of hope you speak of is now more like a beacon. The British technology is now in our hands,' he replied confidently.

'So you say, but it would be very disappointing to me personally and to my very particular friends and clientele if the full access you are promising turns out to be a part-time arrangement.'

'No, I absolutely guarantee full access from day one as long as we use only those clinics I will control. There are going to be hundreds of regular clinics opening up all over the globe, but only those under my supervision can offer this unique service.'

'We like your idea, Daniel, we really do, but so far as we can see, it is just that, an idea.'

'What more can I do to prove my credentials? I'm the Chief US Scientific Advisor. I have full control over the specifications for both the selection process and the access technology.'

'What concerns us is that we have seen the UK newscasts, and this Duality Protocol goes against what you say you can offer. This is why we need more than just your "guarantee". You see, it appears to us that just like the pharaohs, we would be the ones taking all the risk, whereas you would like to only have to sit back and take our commission.'

Showing his frustration, he replied, 'I'm not a wealthy man. Otherwise, I would not need your services. I don't know what more I can do to convince you.'

'You may not yet be a wealthy man, Daniel, but we would nevertheless like you to stake something other than just your reputation. To be blunt, and to use a cliched yet entirely appropriate phrase, you need to demonstrate you really do have skin in the game.'

'You mean–'

'Exactly, Daniel, if the product is all you claim, I would have thought you would already be first in line for a new skin.'

THIRTY-TWO

Quinn Awakes

HER AWAKENING WAS very different this time.

For a start, there had been no nightmare; in fact, no dream at all that she could remember. No music either. Instead, a slow, steady 'beep beep' invaded her head. She tried to open her eyes, but her eyelids felt glued in place so that all she could see was a peachy blur with dancing lights of yellow, green, and blue.

Something or someone was holding her down; she attempted to raise her arm but could not do so. Her legs felt as though made of lead and her feet were so cold. Panic started to set in and she shuffled her body as best she could to remove whatever was restraining her.

But then a voice penetrated through the fog and she could feel someone's hand take her own hand.

'Slowly, Quinn, slowly. Take your time. You are safe. You are in the clinical ward at The Facility. I'm here,' said the consultant soothingly.

'Bailey,' she thought she said, but no sound escaped her parched lips.

More scrambled voices.

'It will take an hour or so for her to regain full consciousness,' said one voice. 'This is perfectly normal as she comes out of the coma. Her vitals are looking good. ECG is approaching normal.'

'I'll wait,' she thought she heard Bailey say as she drifted in and out of the woken world.

Then her eyes opened, and she smiled as Bailey looked back at her. He showed her a glass of water and she was able to sip from it as he held it.

'It will take a little while to get you up and about, Quinn. Bailey will be here tomorrow.'

'Bailey?'

'No, it's Grey. Sorry to add to your confusion, but Bailey will be able to explain better when he wakes tomorrow.'

Her head began to clear, but still nothing made any sense.

'What happened?' she asked, still struggling to make her mouth and jaw work.

'We almost lost you both, but you'll be fine now,' Grey replied.

'You need to let her rest and recover slowly. It will take her brain and body a while to be able to process the additional sensory stimulation.' She could see someone take Bailey... Grey by his arm and lead him out of the room.

The lure of sleep was too hard to resist.

***

Sitting up on her bed, Quinn faced Bailey. 'Please, Bailey, you have to get me out of here. They say they want me to stay in for another forty-eight hours, but you tell me I've been lying here for nine months already. I think I've had enough bed rest, don't you?'

'They are just being careful, Quinn, and they've got to consider Heather as well. Her Duality Band was badly damaged.'

'I know, Bailey, but that's two weeks away. Now that my head has cleared I feel amazing. I feel supercharged. Just look at this muscle tone.'

'You do look amazing, but even so–'

'They can't expect me to stay in here the entire cycle,' she pleaded, interrupting him. But then she saw in his eyes there was something else, something more than her health that was bothering him.

'Bailey, what aren't you telling me?'

She could see him struggling to answer, but she remained silent until, eventually, he spoke.

'Grey had wanted to be the one to show you Heather's message. That's one of the reasons we decided to stagger our wake-up cycles.'

'What are you talking about, Bailey? What message?'

'It seems so unfair to show you this now, but you have the right to see it.' *Why was he avoiding eye contact?*

He took a PDA out of his jacket pocket and handed it to her.

'She recorded this the day it happened.'

He watched her with a look of dread on his face as she played the message, and Heather's voice stumbled at what she needed to say.

'...I know I should have told you before the procedure. What I've done is unforgivable. I promise I will find a way to switch with someone else. It may take a while, but you have my word.'

The colour drained from her face as salty tears streamed down her cheeks unchecked and into her mouth.

After five minutes Quinn could see Bailey was about to speak, but she silenced him by putting her index finger to his lips.

'When I was a child living with my father in Spain, I used to ask him about Momma. He told me she was an important doctor and that she died in an accident in England when I was still a baby. He showed me pictures of a beautiful young woman. He never said anything other than nice things about her. Although he raised me on his own, I never felt as though I missed out on being loved.

'You know, Bailey, I could choose to be angry, furious even. Maybe I should be, but somehow, if I'm honest with myself, I think I already knew the truth. I told you I couldn't explain why I felt safe with her being here,' pointing to her head as she spoke. 'I realise now she was trying to be a mother. No, Bailey, I refuse to feel angry or betrayed or be a victim. There is too much at stake. Instead, I choose to feel grateful for fate bringing us back together. She once gave life to me; I now give life to her. What could be more appropriate? This is my choice now, Bailey, and from what we both know of this world I think many others will have to face the same choice. Now, please let's get out of here and finish what we started.'

'Alright, Quinn. I think it's time we thanked the person who saved you and so many others. I'm not sure if she is an angel or not, but she may be the nearest thing we have right now.'

THIRTY-THREE

Millie Amazes

HEATHER WATCHED ENTRANCED as Child paced back and forth the length of the conference suite. The regained use of her five senses had left her feeling more alive than at any time in her life, even more so than after the original procedure when taking control of Quinn's body for the first time had been such an exhilarating rush. Every movement Child made seemed like a slow dance; every word he spoke reverberated with a church choir's tonal quality. The multi-layered aromas and tastes of the synth coffee that she had so detested before were now exquisite while the warm, textured feel of her clothes caressed her body.

The experience of an eternity of pure thought, and of being forced to relive her own flawed existence countless times, had not receded exactly, but had at least now been tempered by the sheer awesomeness of being fully alive. With this new awakening, she had no choice but to face up to the truth about Quinn. That it had been her decision to abandon her newborn child despite the pleas from Quinn's father. There was no adoption, as she had told Grey. She had simply run away. All she could do now was to try and atone for her past selfishness.

This almost religious conversion made it difficult for Heather to maintain the level of anger she knew intellectually was appropriate after being briefed on what had transpired in the past nine months. Still, she was determined to try her best to fake it.

Sitting next to her was the young Millie Adams to whom she owed her this new life. She had never felt so indebted to anyone; it was not something she was entirely comfortable with or knew how to respond to, but she was indeed happy that her choice for assistant had proved to be such an astute one.

'We could build more assembly labs, but the chemicals we need are not available in the quantities required to scale up the process substantially,' said one of the dozen or so technician scientists that had worked for her on the prototype Duality

Bands.

'Is that all you can come up with after nine months?' asked an exasperated Child. 'I need you all to leave the room. I cannot let the US Vice President hear what you have just said.'

When the door closed he stopped pacing to take a seat at the head of the table. 'Ten thousand in nine months is simply unacceptable. At that rate, it would take seventy-five years to create one million Duals. What on earth am I supposed to tell the US Vice President? I promised we would have a scalable process for their new clinics. He's going to call in ten minutes for an update.'

'Has not your good friend Daniel Moccasin solved the problem?' Heather asked, a rather bit too sarcastically.

'I'm sorry, Heather. I don't have time to massage your ego today. Either you know how to scale the process up, or you don't. Which is it?'

'Massage my ego, is that it? You chose to hand over our work to the Americans when you must have known Moccasin was the only one with access to EMP technology? I always thought there was some tension between you and Robert. I know he hated the People's Council and your wretched Citizen Implant, but he was no terrorist. He was a decent, honest man worth ten of you, or me for that matter.'

'Do not overplay your hand, Heather. On this one occasion I will overlook your remarks. I can see you are upset and disorientated from your experience.'

'You condescending prick. I bet you knew about Moccasin's experiments on altering the mind clocks as well. Admit it.' Heather watched with unhealthy pleasure as Child squirmed under the full force of her wrath, clenching his fists so tight the knuckles went white.

'You would not be alive if it were not for me,' Child countered. 'I had no choice but to work with the Americans. There was no guarantee you would have recovered.'

'Actually, Heather, Doctor Child did ensure I had all the resources I needed to bring you and the others back.'

'Thank you, Millie,' Child replied, looking genuinely surprised but grateful for her intervention.

'I'm not sure why you're defending him, Millie, after he's

locked you up for nearly a year.'

'I am not defending him, Heather, just stating a fact. As for locking me up, I would not have wanted to be anywhere else than here. By working on reviving you and the others, I can now say that I know exactly how to scale the process up. Give me two volunteers and I can create a Dual in a week. Not exactly the couple of hours that Robert challenged me to achieve, but not bad from the present three months lead time.'

Heather looked at Millie quizzically but, knowing what this young woman had achieved already, decided not to dispute her claims in front of Child. She would speak with Millie later.

'Why, for the love of God, then have you not spoken up sooner? Why waste everyone's time here this morning if you already have the answer?' demanded Child.

'Because, Doctor Child, I have no intention of sharing this information unless my terms have been met.'

'My God, finally someone with more spunk than me,' Heather laughed.

'I'm not sure what game you think you are playing, Millie,' sneered Child, 'but you must know that everything you did in the labs was being recorded. Anything you requisitioned has been logged, every procedure you undertook is reproducible.'

'I don't think so, Doctor. I could not be sure until just now, listening to the others failing to give you any answers to your questions. It seems they were not paying much attention to my work, or maybe they just don't understand what I was doing. You told me yourself that only Heather and perhaps Moccasin were capable of completing the project, yet Moccasin clearly has not come up with anything or you would not be so desperate now.'

'And now Heather is back. She will resume her role, review what you did, and you can go back to being the hired help once more, that is once you've satisfied our psyche counsellors you're not a danger to anyone.'

Sensing that this was a pivotal moment for her life's work and indeed for her soul, Heather quickly chose her side, knowing that it would be the end for her career if she got it wrong, but now it was more important that her soul remains intact.

'Just because you spent some money on reviving me do not assume you own me, Child. Even if I decided to help you, it would take me time to study what Millie had done without any guarantee that I could develop the same ideas. If you haven't worked it out already I believe Millie has got you by the balls, and as surprising as that is to you and me both she is seemingly unafraid of applying the necessary pressure to make you squeal.'

His eyes told her that what she had said hit home.

'Very well, Millie, what is it you want?'

'Thank you, Doctor Child. You must understand that all I want is for this project to succeed, but this requires the right team to run it. First and foremost, Heather has to be reinstated as the Chief Scientist for the global rollout. I will be her deputy. Bailey, Grey and Quinn will become part of the lead project team. I'm sure Quinn will much prefer to speak her own words out of her own mouth. Bailey's Military Intelligence background and Grey's IT skills will be vital as we engage with the rest of the world.'

'But the Americans have already insisted that Daniel Moccasin must be in charge now.'

'We let them manage the North America rollout, I'm sure that's what they really want, and since they designed the new mind clock let Moccasin be in charge of ensuring production and global distribution, a vital but rather tedious task that will keep him off our backs.'

Heather threw Millie a look that she hoped conveyed her astonishment at such a suggestion, but saw in Millie's eyes a woman who knew what she was about, so again resisted her instinct to speak out.

'You are insane,' Child said, looking more and more ill as Millie spoke, 'your bios don't lie.'

'Maybe I am, but not in this respect, and if you want to be sure the Americans don't go back on their word and leave the UK unprotected, you tell them we will maintain worldwide rights to the production of Duality Bands.'

'Have you quite finished?'

'Not yet. Lucinda Stiles must be allowed to continue with her work as Chief Advocate on the Protocol, getting it incorporated into international law.'

'Why on earth would the US agree to all this?'

'Oh, sorry, I didn't tell you, did I? You see, there is something we have right here in Derbyshire that exists nowhere else in the world. It is a vital ingredient in the new Duality Bands' assembly – our unique selling point.'

Heather saw Child looking with something akin to bewilderment on his face as Millie paused, undoubtedly for dramatic effect.

'Blue John, a rare type of fluorite with unique properties and soon to become the most important mineral on the planet.'

***

An hour later, a visibly relieved looking Child took large gulps of water from the glass he had been nursing throughout the call with McNeil and Moccasin.

'I'm not sure what happened just then, but it seems, Millie, you have miraculously squared the proverbial circle. I had expected a lot more noise from Moccasin.'

'Yes, he did take it very well, didn't he?' remarked Heather. She was desperate to get Millie on her own to explain her thinking. *Moccasin in charge of the mind clocks. What is she up to?*

'He had no choice. Once McNeil had bought into it, he seemed to accept the situation. Now, hopefully, we can go our separate ways.'

'However, you have pushed me into a tight corner, Millie. If we fail to deliver the goods there will be hell to pay, and if I go down because of this, rest assured you'll be going down with me.'

'I am keen to resume work, Doctor Child,' replied Millie, ignoring Child's threats. 'Now that Heather is back with us, I believe we will make rapid progress. I take it I am no longer under house arrest. I need to see my parents,' and pointing at her head, she continued, 'after all, you can still check up on my whereabouts.'

'I agree with Millie. We have spent enough time talking. I need to catch up on Millie's work as a priority.'

'Very well, Heather, you heard McNeil. We've got five weeks before they send over their volunteers. That means you've only got three weeks with Millie.'

'Then that will have to be enough. Go see your parents, Millie, but we'll still be watching you very closely. Understood?'

'Absolutely, Doctor Child.'

***

Back in the labs Heather went through Millie's research notes, questioning every deviation from the current assembly process.

'Most of what I have done was already in your original papers, Heather. To be honest, I was confused as to why you didn't follow through with your ideas.'

'Then you must have seen the problems I had with degradation of the neural network caused by the breakdown of the photosensitive coenzymes.'

'But look what happens when we add micro-particles of Blue John to the mix.'

'That's amazing, the degradation is no longer present.'

'Yes, the wavelength of the thermoluminescence in the Blue John counteracts the effects of the virus-generated green light that is emitted when using the high coenzyme loads required to speed up the neural transfer through the band's interfacing filaments. Once the Duality Band is in day-to-day use, it absorbs the residual light and safely emits it through the Host brain when the Duality Band is in sleep mode.'

'How did you know to use Blue John?'

'I was thinking about a visit I made to a cave last year. That's what landed me in so much trouble. But then it hit me out of the blue, you might say.'

At this, Heather laughed out loud. 'Well, I really don't know what to say, except that is pure genius. I'm feeling a bit cooped up, Millie, how about we go for a stroll outside? I think we've earned a break, don't you?'

As they walked in the bright summer sun, they made small talk until well out of earshot of any surveillance device.

'Any fluorite will work, won't it, Millie, not just Blue John?'

The expression on Millie's face seemed to suggest she was engaged in an internal struggle.

'Quite probably, with some minor adjustments for the differing wavelengths, but that can be our little secret, can't it, Heather?'

'And I'm right in thinking if anyone were so foolish as to attempt to mess with the mind clock, they would live to regret it. Oh my, my, I really wouldn't want to get in your bad books, Millie, you're quite the artist, aren't you?'

Still working through the implications of what Millie had revealed so far, Heather could see there was more to come.

'This is not easy for me, Heather,' Millie said. 'You see, I was not sure whether I could fully trust you or not.'

'You had no reason to, Millie. We hadn't met in person until you woke me up. Who fully trusts anyone, anyway? Certainly not me.'

'I should have trusted Robert. I wish I had confided in him, but I didn't, and now I deeply regret that. I know now that I need to trust you for this to work.'

As she waited for her to continue, Heather could see the internal struggle Millie was dealing with. Despite her remarkable brain, she was probably as messed up as anyone, more so maybe.

'The thing is, Heather, I did think that I might end up killing you.'

Stunned by what Millie had just said, Heather instinctively moved apart as though Millie was about to produce a knife and do her in.

'Inadvertently that is,' Millie quickly added.

'If you hadn't just literally saved my life, I would be calling security right now. I think you need to explain yourself.'

What Millie had to tell her about her lifelong quest to fulfil her mission and how she was planning to do it was jaw-dropping in its audacity. She wanted to stop her from talking about such lunacy but found she couldn't. She wanted to tell her that she was mad, stark raving bonkers – a would-be mass-murdering psychopath. But instead, something inside herself was captivated by the possibility that Millie was actually right.

'And you thought I might be one of those you plan on killing.'

'Technically, you would be killing yourself, even if you didn't realise it, but I guess you wouldn't try it, what with Quinn and everything.'

'You know something, Millie, just because I can be a first-class bitch doesn't mean I would steal my daughter's body or anyone else's for that matter.'

'That's why I gave up with my first plan to remove anyone who had a psyche profile, indicating a lack of EQ. I finally figured you shouldn't condemn someone just because they're a prick. No offence, Heather. No, it's much better this way, a sort of natural selection.'

'My God, Millie, what gives us the right?'

'Who else is going to do it, Heather? I wish I could trust Bailey, Quinn, Grey and the others, but the problem with having a high EQ is they would probably try to stop us. Unlike you and me, they're just too nice to do what needs to be done. If you want to stop what is already in motion then I will not deny anything, and you can find an alternative solution to the production of the bands. The ball is in your court now, Heather.'

THIRTY-FOUR

US Volunteers

MILLIE TOOK HER usual seat in the conference room next to Heather. The last five weeks had been the happiest of her life. She would never have imagined how exhilarating working as part of a team of Duals could be. Despite the pressures they were all under, they still worked in a genuinely collaborative way, discussing issues and agreeing on a way forward without any drama.

She had come to regard each of the Duals as a friend. Bailey and Quinn talked so passionately about turning the tide on warming. She listened as they spoke of fewer people consuming less, and how as part of a Dual learning to live with another person in the same body had reinforced their belief that we could all learn to share the planet's resources, without destroying everything.

Dear Quinn had even told her that the world would one day look back and recognise her and Heather as the architects of modern humanity.

'I do hope so, Quinn, I really do,' she had replied at the time. 'Let's hope that we succeed in building a world on better foundations this time,' while thinking to herself, *Yes, but without the arseholes we have in charge now.*

Whenever she felt a bit low she would call Stephanie over to share a pizza. That girl really knew how to lift her mood with her risque tales of getting two guys for the price of one in The Village. Cross-cycle dating, as she called it, was a big thing with the singles, but had nothing to do with going out on a bike to get fresh air.

Lucinda was far more sensible, driven by the idea the law should protect the vulnerable. She was precisely the right person to champion the Protocol but was not nearly as much fun as Stephanie.

It was so unlike the years of studying on her own and her childhood memories of bullying teachers and pupils, but she would not let this new set of friends stop her from finishing what she had started.

Unsurprisingly, Heather had pieced things together, but could she trust her? Was her experience and hatred of Moccasin enough for her to remain silent? On balance, she thought so.

'I just need to point out that the volunteers would not pass the selection process we have adopted in the UK. The algorithm we use makes selections based on matching psyches. These American volunteers do not fit that profile.'

'Does it really matter though, Grey?' Child asked, 'we cannot dictate to the Americans or any other country for that matter how they decide to pair up individuals.'

'Okay, I know, but I just wanted to put it out there that all the Duals did have their psyches matched for compatibility here in the UK. Heather, Millie, this has to be your call, why the heck have we bothered otherwise?'

Before either could answer, Lucinda jumped in. 'Grey, there is nothing in the Protocol that requires the parties to match on psyche tests, only that they have given informed consent.' She brought up the bios of the volunteers onto the display. 'Twenty-five volunteer Hosts, all currently waiting on death row and twenty-five terminally ill individuals of various backgrounds. I must say pairing murderers and rapists with former teachers, doctors, and lawyers does feel like a recipe for disaster.'

'Isn't that for the Americans to manage?' Child suggested.

'It raises a ton of questions, that's what it does, Child,' said Lucinda. 'Have they each read and agreed to the Protocol without any form of coercion?'

'McNeil has appointed a lawyer to make sure all is done by the book,' Child replied. 'Look, I know it's not how we would do it, but we have to be realistic. Besides, the one thing they all have in common is imminent death if we do nothing.'

Finally, Heather spoke. 'To answer your question, Grey, this is why we adopted our stringent pairing process. The incompatibilities are apparent to see. Having said that, the process itself will work. I have no doubt about that.'

'We should still run our own psyche tests,' Millie suggested, 'not that I don't believe the US data, but we have all heard of people getting convicted for crimes they did not commit, and I would like a chance to study the results.'

'Good, it looks we have consensus,' Child said, not waiting for more objections. 'They arrive tomorrow.'

***

Daniel Moccasin smiled to himself as he stood in his spacious fifteenth-floor suite in the brand-new state-of-the-art New York Duality Clinic. The three-sixty-degree panoramic view of the New York's Financial District and harbour overlooking the sea wall was simply stunning. Not even the AR generated panorama he had at his old home could match the ultra high definition detail of simple, full-length glass walls.

Moving outside onto the wraparound balcony, he could hear the hustle and bustle of city life below. It was not the noise of vehicle traffic that had long since been silenced by newer technologies, but the sounds of tens of thousands of people going about their daily lives, shouting, laughing and cussing.

The harbourside seafood restaurants' heady smells rose to confront him, urging him to pay them another visit. Previously he had not been a big fan of shellfish, but his new body seemed to have an affinity for anything the ocean could deliver.

It irked him that despite now having the appearance and trappings of wealth, he was still only a state employee. This apartment was his while he remained in his post, to recognise his position on the Duality program and his selflessness in becoming one of the first Duals out of the clinic.

It was not enough, but all that was about to change.

McNeil's strategy to get everyone used to the idea of Duality was on track. Canada's annexation to form the Green Zone States had seen the President's personal ratings jump to a record high. He knew that nothing beats flexing the USA's considerable military muscle to get the crowd onside, and even though scientists still confirmed the full impact of warming was several decades away, it was considered a smart move.

Piggybacking off the outpouring of this patriotic pride, the Duality promotional campaigns were also now in full swing. Against the background of relentless news of dust bowls, coastal flooding, fire storms, the ever-shrinking wheat harvests and predictions of worse to come, people were ready to listen to anyone who could show them a route to better times. Recent polling had shown the older demographic was definitely bought into Duality's selling points. At over thirty per cent of the population their support was not guaranteed, but when the President confirmed no inheritance tax liability would arise when anyone relinquished their old body to form a Dual, there was a massive upswing in applications.

Sure, there would always be those who hated progress and make a nuisance of themselves, crawling out from the woodwork when anything new comes along, but they were being silenced as quickly as they appeared. Just like the Brits had figured out, the correct messaging with the proper series of inducements and penalties worked every time.

More surprisingly, at least to him, was how many under thirties saw Duality as a once in a generation way to save the planet and that they owed it to their children to volunteer. *How fucking noble and how fucking naïve*, he thought.

Others, like Brett, saw being a Host as a way of having an easy life at someone else's expense. Brett was a handsome but unambitious surfer who spent all his energies 'getting barrelled' as he called it. His application to become a Dual stated he was prepared to give up half his life for guaranteed funds to do nothing but ride the supercharged waves resulting from warming. To Moccasin, what made him the perfect Host was an absence of close family and no long-term relationships.

'Well, Brett, I can promise we'll have a great time. I was a half-decent surfer myself as a kid,' he laughed to himself.

At first, he had hated the British term 'Essential' to describe the Dual's non-Host personality. He thought it was pure British exceptionalism to describe their so-called elite with this word, but now felt it correctly represented the symbiotic relationship's true nature. Without the Essential, the Host was just another walking, talking resource-hungry body. The world had too many of those. But insert the mind of someone of great talent, someone who knew how to navigate this messed up planet and come out on top, and you indeed had something worth preserving. It was natural selection in all its glory.

He now understood the inherent flaw in the Protocol, the Essential being awake for only fifty per cent of the time was plainly unjust and did not consider individual circumstances. Why, for example, should those murdering sons of bitches that came back from the UK see the light of day at all? Where's the justice? Isn't one day a month more than they deserve? Still, he knew how to address the balance and today was the last anyone would hear from these particular Hosts. No one will be any the wiser as the relatives will simply learn their executions had been brought forward. McNeil himself had suggested it after he was reminded by their mutual friends it was payback time for them getting him elected.

'Doctor Moccasin, you have an incoming communication from an undeclared caller. Should I accept?'

'Yes, full visual.' His life was about to change forever.

A familiar image of the young businesswoman appeared, but without any of the theatrics of their previous call.

'Daniel, I cannot tell you how marvellous you look.'

'Thank you, not bad, is he?'

'Not bad at all. I believe you have now proved your commitment to our joint venture.'

'I will need to play the part of this Host until such time I am out of the public eye, but that will not impact our working together.'

'Glad to hear that, Daniel. Now, I believe you are ready to give us the final proof from our selected volunteers in the British trials?'

'Yes, as you know they have been in our clinic since returning from the UK. All Hosts and Essentials have survived and are in excellent health. The process took just one week.'

'Excellent news.'

'As you know the mind clocks are designed to give both Host and Essential two weeks of awake time. The Hosts were due to wake up this morning, but yesterday I changed their clocks so that now the Hosts will never wake up. They are free to leave the clinic.'

'That is simply brilliant, Daniel. I will arrange for someone to pick them up. There are many of my friends eager to see them and dispel any remaining doubts they may have.'

'I must say I was surprised at your choice of volunteers. Hosts from death row and terminally ill Essentials from middle-class America.'

At this the young woman smiled at him. 'My apologies, Daniel, but you see, we weren't entirely honest with you.'

'I don't understand.'

'We weren't sure of your commitment at that point. The truth is you have it the wrong way around. The Essentials are not the terminally ill but those who had been incarcerated on death row for far too long. McNeil pulled some strings on our behalf, made it look like it was for national security.'

'But then what about the Hosts?' spluttered Moccasin. 'Surely they can't be terminally ill, that would be insane!'

'Yes, in a way, they were. They owed us. We made clear the only way to pay their debt was to volunteer or see their families killed, or worse, one by one. Look at it this way, Daniel, it's hardly murder, is it? No one dies, do they? They just take a long sleep.'

Staring at a reflection of himself in the glass walls, Daniel Moccasin no longer recognised who he saw.

2058

THIRTY-FIVE

Millie's Trial

IT WAS NOT a typical courtroom, or at least not like what she had seen in movies. The judges from the USA, Russia, China, India, France, Germany and the UK sitting behind a long desk were not wearing any gowns or wigs, nor were the lawyers sitting at their own desks on either side of her.

Lucinda had explained that the trial was to be held 'in camera', an odd legal term that strangely meant nobody from the public would see the proceedings. Actually, Millie could see several cameras were recording every movement in court.

Lucinda had also explained that in cases of genocide, guilt is determined by the judges, not by a jury. Three very young-looking judges were Duals; the others were middle-aged Solos. Lucinda had objected to there being a majority of Solo judges, arguing that only Duals should adjudicate on the Protocol's breaches. This argument was dismissed on the grounds that Solos were still the majority of the human population, and that Duality is a surgical procedure undertaken on Solos, and that the Protocol is merely an adjunct to international law.

One of the prosecution lawyers stood to question her. Millie knew her bio-stats would be scanned for any lies by the palm reader attached to her hand.

'Ms Adams, you say you do not deny designing the Duality Band in such a way that it could permanently lock out the Essential personality.'

'Yes, sir, that is true.'

'And you do not deny hiding this design feature from your colleagues, falsifying data in an attempt to ensure this never came to light. You were so successful in your deceit that you even fooled the renowned Doctor Heather Bernard.'

'Yes, I falsified data that would have raised concerns. I did not want my colleagues jeopardising the rollout.'

'And so you cannot deny your actions may have led to the

death of hundreds of thousands of people. An act of genocide by any definition, do you not agree?'

Lucinda stood before Millie could answer the question. 'Your honour, it has already been established that no one has died. There is not one dead body anywhere in the world caused by my client's actions. No one has any idea of how many Duals have been affected. Can the prosecution provide even one dead body as evidence of manslaughter, let alone this preposterous accusation of genocide? To accuse Ms Adams of an act of genocide is simply a political stunt brought about by certain well-connected Solos who fear they may not now get the chance to buy a Host body for their exclusive use.'

'Ms Stiles, please sit down. We have heard your arguments, but the fact remains these Essentials have been denied life.'

Refusing to be seated, Lucinda continued. 'Oh yes, mobsters, military dictators, people traffickers, billionaire oil magnates who seem hell-bent on destroying the planet, so very *Essential* to the planet right now, wouldn't you agree, your honour.'

'They are not on trial here, Ms Stiles. They have been deprived of a voice with which to defend themselves from any such accusations. Again, please sit down and let us get on with proceedings.'

But Lucinda continued. 'Not one Dual has come forward to testify against Ms Adams.'

'That's enough, Ms Stiles. Your client will answer the question.'

'Thank you, your honour,' replied the prosecution lawyer. 'Ms Adams, I repeat my question, did you knowingly design the Duality Band with the intent to kill millions of innocent people? People who were simply following their respective government's calls to reduce population numbers in preparation for living in one of the designated green zones?'

Millie took her time before replying. 'While Heather and the other Duals were in a coma caused by the EMP blast, I redesigned the Duality Bands with a failsafe feature that would prevent the build-up of dangerous radiation that would eventually destroy the Host's organic brain. This same feature would prevent any Essential from gaining exclusive long-term access to the Host's body. The interfacing filaments that allow control of the body have to discharge built-up luminescence during the sleep cycle, otherwise they degenerate as in these Essentials.'

'You are not answering the question, Ms Adams. Is this because the bio-scanner will reveal you to be the mass murderer you deny being?'

'These Essentials are not dead. I'm sure your scans have already confirmed they are, in fact, busy whirring around.'

'But they may as well be dead. We know from Doctor Bernard's testimony of her own experience that their fate is infinitely worse than death.'

'Yet no harm has come to Doctor Bernard,' argued Lucinda.

'Your honour, I present the defendants' psyche reports.'

Rising to her feet to object, Lucinda was instantly told to sit down once more.

'Please continue.'

'Ms Adams, your childhood psyche reports confirm you were "an angry child", apparently angry at the existence of predatory animals such as snakes and that you wished God would make such creatures extinct. Is that what this is all about, Ms Adams? Did you want to play at being God so that you could make what you deem to be human predators extinct?'

Finally, she thought, *someone asking the right question.*

'Yes.'

'You admit it?'

'It is pointless to deny it,' Millie replied.

'You admit you wanted to kill as many as you possibly could?'

'By my estimations and based upon the very low EQ brainwave signatures recorded at the time of their Duality procedure, there are now over two million fewer predators walking around,' Millie replied.

'And how does that make you feel, Ms Adams?' The lawyer, knowing he had won, now went in for the kill.

'It gives me a warm feeling inside.'

'You have no remorse?'

'I only wish the Duality rollout had not been stopped because I'm sure there are millions more out there we could have caught. Still, I think I must have got some important ones, or I wouldn't be here. Don't you agree? If you want to reactivate them that's entirely possible, but you'll do it without my help.'

THIRTY-SIX

Gibraltar Clinic

LIFE IS SO strange and seemingly random, and yet there is a mysterious symmetry that seeks to impose itself on all of us. That was the thought that came to her mind as they arrived back at the same hospital in Gibraltar, where Bailey's damaged shoulder had been treated five years ago.

It was to be shut down but had been given a new lease of life as the UK's only European Duality clinic funded by a wealthy benefactor who wanted to remain anonymous, but who had insisted that the clinic was to be used for those fleeing Africa.

Child had been more than happy with this proposal as it was good PR for the campaign and showed the world how the UK was playing its part in helping refugees reach the North European Green Zone. Eighty thousand Duals had emerged from its labs and were now resettled in New Longyearbyen, on Svalbard in the Arctic, the fastest warming place on Earth.

Since Millie's arrest and conviction, the clinic's future and all others around the world were in doubt. Quinn knew her mother must have known what Millie was planning, yet Millie had somehow protected Heather from the fallout.

As they entered the building, a tall and rather striking young woman greeted them.

'Ms Diaz, Bailey, it is so good to meet you both in the flesh at last and… oh my,' she paused and stared at Quinn's large bump. 'Ms Diaz, I hadn't realised you were expecting. What wonderful news!'

'Thank you, and please, call me Quinn.'

'Well, many congratulations, Quinn, you must all be thrilled.'

'We are. My mother is over the moon.'

'Grey and I are equally excited,' Bailey joined in, his face beaming with pride. 'Slightly nervous, but we know between the four of us we will be fine.'

'The others will be thrilled when I go back to America and

give them the news.'

'Anyway, thank you for coming, Ms Garcia,' said Bailey. 'It is Garcia, isn't it? You aren't exactly the easiest person to track down. I wasn't even sure my message had reached you.'

'My apologies, but I'm sure you'll understand why in a moment. Come, we will find somewhere comfortable to talk.'

Sitting around an ornate marble table, a mean-looking heavy-set male served them coffee.

'Thank you, Adam, we'll be fine now.'

Without any reply, Adam left.

'Right, let's try to sort out the confusion. Bailey, as you probably have guessed, I am not Maria Garcia. Yes, the scanners would show that I am her right now, but I am, in truth, Caroline Kirk, Host to Maria Garcia. Officially I am still a Dual and Maria is currently awake, but you'll have to take my word for the fact she is not. She has not been awake for over a year, and I pray to God it stays that way.'

As they both listened, Quinn could see that what Caroline told them fitted the same pattern as all the other reports of unexplained acts of benevolence Bailey had told her about from his intelligence briefings.

The first report that made the news was that of a wealthy Dual couple who had suddenly decided to pledge vast sums of money to climate research and the refugee crisis. It made the news only because in their old bodies, they had once been prosecuted under anti-slavery laws in India for paying their employees below minimum wage.

Then came the story of the big-time climate change denier who made his fortune from oil. He announced that since becoming a Dual it had opened his eyes, and he now wanted to spend his new lease of life restoring the balance with nature.

Then came another and another, all Duals, all Essentials with mean reputations, many infamous and rightly feared. However, most cases involved what everyone thought of as 'ordinary folk' having a complete 'change of heart' on what matters some months after becoming a Dual. Bailey said about ten per cent of Essentials had exhibited such a change.

'At first, I thought there had been a mistake,' said Caroline. 'It certainly didn't feel as though I had been asleep for months on end. But when all the house assistants kept referring to me as "her" and I saw the date, I knew it was true. She had stolen my body.'

'I am so sorry, Caroline,' Quinn said.

'When I got over the shock, I discovered I had access to all of her accounts and details of all her contacts. I can tell you both, I recognised many of the names, and they were not nice people. I had expected they would find out I was not her and they would come after me, but it never happened. Do you know why?'

'I think I can guess, but you tell us,' replied Bailey.

'Well, I did a bit of digging on the net, and it seems a lot of her friends have ended up like her, like me, that is. Isn't that a thing! Anyways, to cut a long story short, I made a whole bunch of new friends, very wealthy Host friends, and we discussed what we should do.'

'You decided to give all the money away?' Quinn asked.

'Sort of. We decided this money probably came from a whole lot of misery. Nothing we could do about that, but we could use it to try to change things for the better. Tip the balance in the other direction, if you know what I mean.'

'That's why you decided to fund this clinic?'

'Exactly, but as you now know, Maria Garcia is funding this clinic, not Caroline Kirk. When I got Bailey's message for Maria, asking to meet here in person, I was unsure what to do. I've wanted to meet you both for some time, your passion and commitment to changing this messed up world come through so powerfully on your newscasts. But before I could agree to meet up, I had to be sure it was Bailey and not some of Maria's henchmen. Not all of her friends became Duals, and those that didn't are not amused at Maria's sudden retirement, which has left them without any network to ply their grubby trade. So, we have to be very careful. Adam, for example, is a much better bodyguard than a waiter.'

'Understood,' nodded Bailey.

'And it wasn't just Maria Garcia and her gangsters that Daniel Moccasin sold Hosts to but whoever would pay his fee,'

Caroline continued.

Quinn and Bailey exchanged looks at the mention of Moccasin.

'If you are up for it, my friends and I would very much like you both to become patrons of our support group for Hosts affected by the body snatching scandal.'

'We would be honoured,' Quinn answered for both of them.

'I knew you would accept. Those assholes in our heads are going to make amends whether they like it or not.'

'We just wish we could help the one person who saved all of us,' said Quinn.

'Many of Maria's friends were not just wealthy but in positions of authority, not just in the USA but everywhere, and I mean everywhere, from local officials right up to presidents. Don't you fret yourself about Millie Adams, wheels are in motion as they say.'

THIRTY-SEVEN

Port Stanley Correctional Facility

AS THEY STEPPED onto the tarmac at Port Stanley airport, Millie looked around at her surroundings. It was not as bleak as the government newscasts had portrayed, but it wasn't your typical idea of a beach holiday island either.

Apart from herself and the recently promoted DCI Kerry Simmons, only a handful of passengers were on the flight from Buenos Aires. Simmons had barely spoken on their long flight. That suited Millie, who concluded the DCI was still sore at not being allowed to finish her interrogation five years back when she had the chance to stop Millie in her tracks.

Instead, Millie spent the flight catching up on the islands' history from the information Lucinda had given her after her trial.

She learnt that the Correctional Facility for the Criminal Undeserving had never held more than two hundred inmates. Even so, newscasts in the UK showing large working parties dig ditches in barren landscapes and help build coastal defences had proved very effective in deterring most of the disaffected from engaging in open dissent while simultaneously sating the desire for harsh punishment the more fervent People's Council supporters craved.

Until last week, hundreds of would-be Duals would have been on board the flight. At its busiest the clinic was turning out six thousand Duals a week, the vast majority resettling in the South Atlantic Green Zone's Patagonian sector. Now everything was on hold while the heads of governments figured out if it was safe to continue with the program.

As they entered the terminal building, it was evident the shutdown had not been fully completed as they were welcomed by Digi-Quinn hovering above the concourse.

'*Tenga listos sus acuerdos de protocolo firmados y la prueba de compatibilidad.*'

'Please have your signed Protocol agreements and proof of

compatibility ready.'

'Welcome to The Falklands, Chief Inspector,' said the human border guard. They were expected, and so a quick scan was all that was required before he escorted them to their waiting transport.

As they left the terminal, a waiting ambulance pulled up. The front door opened, and the driver emerged.

'Sorry we don't have anything more appropriate, but it's only a short ride to the clinic.'

'Thank you, this will be perfectly adequate,' responded Simmons.

'Are we going to the clinic first?' Millie asked, confused.

'It's en route,' Simmons replied bluntly. 'We are meeting someone first.'

***

Illuminated over the large entrance door to the clinic was the dual-faced image of Janus, the Roman god of beginnings, endings, and duality, resurrected after three millennia to witness a new birth of the world.

A small, rotund man leapt to his feet as they entered the reception area.

'Ha, ladies, welcome. I am Javier Mendoza, Clinic Administrator. You must be exhausted. Would you like to freshen up before you inspect our clinic?'

'Thank you, Mr Mendoza,' replied Simmons. 'If there is somewhere we can shower and change, that would be wonderful.'

She was in no hurry to get to her cell and her nose told her that a shower was a good idea right now, so she followed Mendoza and Simmons to a guest room on the ground floor.

'You go first, Millie. I need to make a call.' With that, Simmons left the room.

The hot water and fragrant soap worked their magic and she emerged from the shower refreshed. Grabbing a towel, she went back into the other room, where she had left her smelly clothes. They had gone, replaced by a fresh set of underwear, leggings, fleece top and cap.

Not the prison outfit I was expecting, she thought, *but passable.*

As she dropped her towel to get dressed, the door opened.

'Hey, Mill, how the hell have you been? I hear you've been a really bad girl. Great tat by the way, your dad would be so pissed at you, Mill.'

Dumbstruck, Millie just stood there butt-naked, proudly displaying the tattoo emblazoned across her midriff which she had hidden from view since she was sixteen. She knew for sure it would freak her parents out, so she had kept it hidden.

DCI Simmons came back into the room. 'Right, Millie, Javier will take you to the operating theatre.'

Karen must have seen the look of terror on her face. 'It's okay, Mill, you're going to get your chip removed. I've had mine done just before you got here,' she explained, showing her the bald patch on the top of her head.

'But what...' Millie started to ask.

'No time to chit chat, Millie. There's a boat that will pick you both up in forty-five minutes.'

'Why are you helping us?' Millie asked in amazement.

'You've removed more scum from the streets than I could ever manage in a dozen lifetimes. We all owe you one, but as for me personally and you pair, we are now quits.'

Javier opened the door to the room and beckoned for Millie to follow him.

'Go now, Millie, before I change my mind. One of you will have to whack me hard and tie me up and then bugger off.'

'I'll do it, Mill,' Karen offered. 'You couldn't swat a fly.'

'I thought you might jump at the opportunity,' sighed Simmons.

***

As she lay on the table staring at the ceiling, the robot arm moved slowly towards her head. No need for restraints. The birdcage device on her head glowed as it sedated her skull sufficiently for the probe to enter her cranium and remove the Citizen Implant that had been her lifelong companion.

The probe retreated, and as Millie shuffled about her new fleece top rode up above her midriff, revealing the tattoo of a smiling frog with a knife in one hand and the Bible in the other, standing on top of a partly skinned snake. Below in Gothic script were the words *The Meek Shall Inherit the Earth.*

THIRTY-EIGHT

Tidal Waves and Theta Waves

RIDING THE MONSTROUS breakers at Jaws in Maui, Hawaii, Brett was in a small minority of those who had fully embraced the opportunities rising sea levels afforded. Free to use his newfound wealth, he had purchased a luxurious Winnebago, which he now shipped all over the world in his quest for the ultimate rush.

Inside Brett's skull, nanosecond by nanosecond, Daniel Moccasin screamed a silent scream of someone damned to face eternity alone.

About the author

A successful career in software development has prepared new author Christopher B. Lane with the ammunition for an explosive debut novel.

Now living on the edge of the Peak District in Derbyshire, he made the switch from designing banking systems to fiction after choosing to take early retirement.

Christopher, who lists the likes of Isaac Asimov, Iain M. Banks and Douglas Adams among his favourite authors, has used all of his technical expertise to hatch a gripping plot with the world in full climate crisis.

Influenced by a growing concern over global warming and artificial intelligence, the walking enthusiast has set Duality Protocol some 30 years into the future – when mass migration from regions no longer habitable has led to the closing of borders in the remaining Green Zones.

The self-confessed 'late starter to writing' has created an absorbing narrative based on an accidental neuroscientific breakthrough, whereby an organic implant allows two personas to share the same body and so offering a potential solution for humanity to survive its self-inflected doomsday scenario.

Nightmarish prophecy or humanity's saviour?

matlocklane70@gmail.com